Book One
Stealing Steam Series

Lions & Lamps

K.M. Robinson

LIONS AND LAMPS: Book One of the Stealing Steam Series
Copyright © 2019 by K.M. Robinson.

Published by Crescent Sea Publishing.
www.crescentseapublishing.com

Cover designed by Reading Transforms.
Image copyright © K.M. Robinson Photography.

All wishes require a little sacrifice.
This is for those of you willing to make that sacrifice for your
big dreams. Never let giving something up get in the way of
reaching your goals.

And to Jessica, without whom this series never would have
existed.

Chapter 1
Aladdin

"You are *not* going to the Market like that." Mother's words are sharp, but then, they always are.

"Would you prefer I walk out of here with *nothing* on, Mother?" I challenge. I wouldn't be above leaving most of my wardrobe behind to prove a point.

"Aladdin! You will do no such thing! I—"

"I know," I cut her off, slicing a hand through the air to silence her. "You say the same thing every time. It's time you get some new material, Mother."

"If your father were here—"

"He's not." At my words, she reels back like I slapped her. I instantly regret it, but never one to back down, I push forward. "And I have to go make sure we get paid, so if you'll excuse me…"

The door creaks as I open it. The Market is far enough away that if I don't get out now, I won't make it in time, likely rendering me without a job for the day.

White smoke drifts up to the sky that's actually blue for a change. It's been raining so hard for the past two weeks, I don't remember what a nice day looks like. People fill the streets, clad in gears and leather. Chains sound behind me as a man stomps up to me, nearly catching the back of my heels.

"Watch it," he grumbles, pushing past me as I turn to confront him. Not everyone would find me so easily dismissed—I can be imposing when I want—but the man is massive. One leg is made entirely of metal, right down to the peg. Chains sway on his other hip and on his vest, creating the noise I should have noticed before darting into the street.

I don't have time to pick a fight this morning, so I let him go. If it had been earlier though, I likely would have shown up for work with a black eye and a good story. Instead, I duck down an alleyway and rush by a group of children on their way to classes.

Brass and copper tones fill the streets, lining every stone barrier, acting as railings, even creating walls along the edges of buildings. I glance up as something shifts above me—a series of intricate metal circles nested inside of each other, spinning with the wind off a balcony. Even in the slums, people like to be decorative.

The sun glints off the metal, blinding me every few steps as decorations move and catch the light. Lamps hang from the shop entrances, still glowing despite the rising sun. A few banners wave in the breeze the crowd is creating, announcing the type of shop it hangs outside of—the air is still aside from the rush of wind we're causing as we hurry.

In the distance, the train sounds and I wish it was close enough that I could catch it. The trains don't run to the rookeries though. Life was far simpler last year when I could spend all day on the rails if I liked.

As soon as I reach the entrance to the alley, I hustle around the school children, grumbling under my breath. I certainly never minded leaving school earlier than most of the others did, even in this part of town. I learned more out on the streets than I did anywhere else.

Steam shoots out from a side vent, burning my leg as I walk by a building. Clenching my fists at my side, I push forward, not a battle I want—or *can*—get involved in.

The closer I get to the market place, the louder the roar of rushing water becomes. Three large waterfalls pour into the stream that surrounds the Market. Not too far away, smoke from the exhaust of the steam-powered city drifts into the air.

Stepping onto the bridge, I begin to run—I can't be late. I refuse. I won't go groveling to Kacper again.

There's a bit of space between the dark, metallic tones

of the city and the bright, airy colors of the Market and Halls. To the left is a second bridge, this one much smaller, that leads to a staircase. The steps going up lead to the Main Hall where the officials hold their meetings and run Horallen. The lower level descends to the walkway beneath it, keeping our esteemed government from having to see the peasants unless they're making an announcement. Merchants mill in the garden island on the mid-level between the two platforms, selling their foods and wares to officials and workers alike.

I bypass it and take the straight path, ducking down to the lower level beneath the garden island. Tables are cranked up all around me, resting above the small boxes men and women use to carry the portable trade tables in. At the end of the day, all they have to do is crank the table back down into its box and carry it home, assuming they have something to transport their goods in as well. A few of the merchants who have made out better than the rest have tables that do the work for them, powered by steam or coal, that carry their goods for them when they leave each night.

Given the chance, I could probably create my own version of it, but I'd need access to the metal first. Horallen has a tendency to keep men like me away from materials outside of our day-to-day jobs.

A crowd already waits at the far end of the Market, looking for work as Horallen's upper class slowly fills in to find workers for the day. Minimum pay isn't good enough to survive on, but if you can't get that, you go hungry.

Loud stomping sounds next to me, mixed with the rattle of chains. I know who it is before I turn.

"Step back, *boy*," the man from earlier bellows in my ear.

I can't get into a fight. I can't get into a fight.

He puts his hand on my shoulder, wrenching me back so he can move closer to the front of the line.

I'm getting in a fight.

"You're a fool, Aladdin." Kacper's words are crisp and full of condemnation. "You have one simple job."

I fight to hold my tongue as Kacper applies a bandage to my temple, staunching the flow of blood. At least I avoided a black eye this time.

"I'm sorry, Uncle." I bow my head out of respect for my late father, *not* my uncle.

"Weren't you *just* in a fight last week?" Kacper's obvious disdain for me fills the room.

Books pile around us, littering the floor, tables, chairs —every inch of the room is covered in them. For someone who likes to study so much, I'd think he'd keep them in better order. Instead, some are on their side, others left open, and still some are perched precariously on top of each other, sliding open inch by inch until they collapse, bending the pages.

I'm sure he's kept a record of my transgressions somewhere in all this mess. Most of these are histories of Horallen, though many are on the boring technical developments of our ancestors. His fascination with the past and how it will affect our future isn't uncommon for the citizens of Horallen, but most don't horde knowledge like my father's younger brother does.

"You're lucky Byron found you when he did." Kacper flicks his wrist at his bodyguard, more machine than man. Byron nods from the corner, metal arm hissing with the movement as it adapts to its new position. While I can't know for sure, I'd guess perhaps his head and chest are the only thing still human about him. "Well don't just sit there, boy, thank him."

Kacper's angry words jolt me out of my thoughts.

"Thank you, Byron," I say automatically.

"Come now, how are you going to explain this to your mother?" Kacper asks as I slide off the table. He removes his pilot's hat and sets it on the round side table so that the black brim is pointed at me as if accusing me of messing up again. The medal on the front gleams in the muted light coming through the exceptionally tall windows.

Kacper glares at me, wrapped in the long dress coat

he wears over his shoulders. The brocade fabric of his suit jacket peeks out from behind it, open enough to show off his vest and tie. The thin mustache on his upper lip twitches as he waits for me to answer.

"Well?" My uncle shakes his head. I still haven't figured out how he could possibly be related to my father.

"I didn't start the fight," I confront him. "I—"

"You think that matters?" he cuts me off, angling across the room straight at me. He miraculously doesn't trip on any of the books crowding the floor. If the other officials could see this mess, they'd likely kick him out of his position in the Hall.

Byron steps forward, ready to back his master should his scrappy little nephew decide to take a swing at him. I focus on Byron's long, blond hair pulled back into a half-ponytail behind him. His metal appendages could put a serious dent in a person—the man who attempted to hit me only gets a few swings in before Byron backhanded him across the Market.

Kacper's hand goes up once Byron is close enough to make me worry. He backs down, holding his position. The man—or machine—watches Kacper closely.

"I'm coming with you to explain this to your mother before returning to the Hall," he announces. "Fetch my hat."

I hate it when he treats me like a lapdog. *Fetch this,* and *fetch that.*

Slipping to the side, I maneuver around him and his history collection and quickly move toward the table where he *just* set his cap. He mumbles to Byron, but I ignore him.

I will get my mother and myself away from this man if it kills me.

The walk is painfully long with Kacper and Byron by my side. I look like a dull copper next to them the way they shine. The merchants on side streets and corners glance over us before deciding if it's safe to approach an official while he is escorting a delinquent through the city. Most decide it's worth the risk and run to Kacper's side to try to pawn their wares off on him.

He ignores all but the food. He delights in ordering for himself and Byron and then waving it next to me until my empty stomach growls loud enough to produce a smirk on my uncle's face which he tries in vain to hide.

I've never understood the change in my uncle. I've never been close to him, but he was friendly enough when my father was alive. Now that he's gone, any compassion the man had seems to have been buried with his older brother the day my mother and I said goodbye.

Kacper cringes as soon as we cross over to my side of Horallen. My mother was a proud woman and refused to move into Kacper's care once we had to give up the house under my father's name. My mother still owned property in this area from before she married my father twenty years ago. He had died suddenly, and they didn't have time to transfer it to her name before his heart stopped beating, so it was taken from us a mere week after his death.

She packed up her eighteen-year-old son and moved us to this neighborhood, covered in shattered rugs hanging on ropes from one window to the next, lifeless lanterns swinging beside them close enough to cause a fire if people weren't careful. Debris fills the streets, but no one has time to clean it up—our lives consist of waking, working, and occasionally sleeping.

The smell of dust fills the air. I find it charming—perhaps even comforting—unlike the smell of my uncle's mansion. He, however, finds it as repulsive as having me for a nephew.

"Emmaline!" Kacper calls out the moment I open the door. I cringe accidentally as he yells in my ear. Byron squeaks behind me—perhaps Kacper should oil that gear.

After a moment of shuffling, Mother appears. Her eyes grow wide when she sees my uncle in the house, then quickly narrow at me when she realizes it's my fault.

"What did you do?"

Stripped, Mother, isn't that what we were talking about me doing before we left? I roll my eyes, unable to help it.

"He was fighting *again*," Kacper answers for me. "May we come in?

Mother motions for the men to join us, leading them to the kitchen. I won't be able to explain myself while Kacper is there, nor will I be able to talk myself out of whatever lies Kacper is going to spin this time, so instead of watching the airship collision while it's happening, I veer off, taking the stairs up to my room.

Once inside, I close the door and go straight to the window. Prying it open, I come away with crumbling pieces of dried, flaking paint on my hands. I brush them off on my pants, removing the clip of bullet casings from around my shoulder and dropping them on the small cot I call a bed.

The morning air feels cool against my skin now that I'm not rushing to get to the market place for work. Kacper will give Mother money once again, so I'm off the hook for the day's wages.

I duck outside, pulling my legs out behind me to sit on the fire escape. The metal rattles as I settle on it, but even as it sways, I feel safer here than anywhere else in the city. Mother might not like this part of town, and admittedly, I'm not a fan of the rats, but it feels like home here, even without Father. He always said he liked visiting the house when he was courting my mother.

Below, the streets are quiet. Papers and junk rattle when the wind sweeps through. The buildings create a wind tunnel and sometimes I wonder if we should be trying to harness the wind's power instead of always relying on steam and coal.

The windows must be open below because I can hear Kacper's annoying voice drift up to me. Byron, in all the years that I've known him, has maybe only said two dozen things to me—or anyone other than Kacper, leaving Kacper to talk my mother to death without his input.

Unable to stand it, I leap up and swing over the railing to the fire escape, landing on the floor below, halfway between the first and second story of my hovel. This time, I take the steps, not wanting to elicit attention from my relatives inside.

On the ground, I start to walk. It doesn't matter *which* direction, as long as it's away from my snake-of-an-uncle. He's been trying to flirt with my mother since a month after the funeral—I'm surprised he had the decency to wait that long out of respect. I don't *think* my mother is falling for it, but eventually, I can see it happening. I have to get her out of here before she decides it's a good idea to elevate us back up in society.

I find myself once again on the same route toward the Market, dashing through the streets quick enough to escape, but not to cause anyone to look at me with more than a passing glance and an eye roll.

I know better than to do anything that someone might remember me by.

I tug at one of my fingerless gloves, adjusting it so that it sits more comfortably on my wrist as I move down the streets of Horallen. The chain from my silver pocket watch swings slightly from my chest to my pocket, tapping softly against my black vest. Reaching up, I push my white dress sleeves up higher on my upper arms, but it's tight enough against my muscles that I can only push it up so far.

The town seems settled now. Everyone is at work or taking classes. The upper echelons are busy with their governmental work or researching our histories for any indication of what we should do next, while the lowlifes are rummaging the streets to steal what they need to survive.

I've had to do it a few times, too—steal. I always watch my targets though, ensuring I'm never taking from anyone who needs it as badly as I do. I go after people like my uncle who have an abundance of wealth but are unwilling to share. Well, except with my mother, that is.

My stomach growls again. I'm sure by now, Kacper has given part of the food he collected on our trip to Mother, leaving me on my own to find something to eat.

If I had been smart enough to bring my arm gear with

me, it would have been a lot easier to steal something to eat. Having left it in my tiny room, I have to resort to doing the work myself.

A few streets down, I find a line of vendors with cog-supported tables waiting near the bridge to the Market, hoping to sell to the officials on their lunch breaks in an hour. They yell to women walking by on their way to visit their friends, hoping to convince them to take a hostess gift with them.

The women sashays away in their long dresses and bustles, parasols on their shoulders. A few stop—usually those who married into an upper tier recently who haven't learned to ignore the siren-call of the merchants.

I wait, knowing the classes release earlier than the Hall does for break. Or rather, the advanced schools. They give the officials' children more time to wander and explore than they do for the kids from my side of town. Their breaks last only a few minutes, prohibiting them from wandering where they might be seen. Of course, there's nothing they can do about the orphans who don't bother going to classes at all—they run wild in the streets.

I bend, brushing the dirt off my cargo pants. Running my fingers through my hair to tame my locks enough to look presentable, I stride purposefully toward the vendors. Confidence is the key to successful self-preservation.

I turn my nose up at the first two vendors, even though the smell makes my mouth water. I pause at the third, examining the bread before I turn and stride away.

If I act like a snob, they'll assume I'm above my stature. My clothing suggests otherwise, but attitude is everything. If I carry myself with head held high and shoulders back, I'll at least be able to get close enough to swipe something and run off before they can catch me. They're all middle-aged men anyway; they can chase me all they'd like and still slow before I do.

Pursing my lips, I set my sights on a table at the far end and stride toward it, bypassing the others. The merchant is talking to a group of boys a few years younger than me, waving a sandwich in the air as he speaks animatedly.

"Can you believe it?" the merchant sings. "And here I thought they wouldn't bring that back this year after everything that happened last year."

His words pique my interest, but my mission comes first.

"Just because some girl won it—"

"That's enough, numbskull," a second boy cuts off his friend. "Don't talk about her like that."

"Like what?" the first boy challenges as I sidle up next to the table covered in food. If I play my hand right, I can pocket at least one of the half-sandwiches before the merchant realizes it's gone, and hopefully steal another one or two—I've got the pockets for it.

I lean my elbow against the table, pretending to be interested in the conversation. The boys ignore me, but the merchant glances at me, accepting me as a part of the group. *If he'd like to assume I'm one of the boys, who am I to correct him?*

"They're not going to ban girls from competing, idiot," the second boy redirects, obviously not wanting to comment on his respect for whoever the particular girl is.

"They can't let her be involved again, can they?" a third asks.

"Now, now, boys," the merchant interrupts. "The Governor will decide what he wants, but I'm sure he's not going to let his daughter play again. She'll be a showpiece for this year's event. Someone has to crown the winner, after all."

"He'll trot her out like the little girl she is," the first boy sneers. "You'll appreciate that, won't you, dummy?"

For children of the officials, these kids sure are bad with insults.

"She's older than we are, moron. Besides, it's the Proprietor running the event, not the Governor. He won't have any say in how this works."

The boys rib each other as they tease the one with the crush. The merchant eyes them warily, leaning over to pick up a sandwich to get them back on track. He waves it in front of them and as he turns his attention to the argument, I pocket the closest meal.

Another group of teens wanders over. I suppose it's true that people assume a place with a crowd is the place to be. Had these boys wandered to the vendor I had just left, the others likely would have gone there without hesitation. I doubt they would have even glanced at the others. The leader picks the lucky merchant and the others follow.

Dressed in everything from cargo pants and vests, to dresses with bustles and corsets, the students crowd into the row of vendors. Some of the wiser girls are intelligent enough not to follow the crowd and spread out to tables without lines.

A girl with goggles pushes through the crowd, fighting for first dibs on a sandwich. I snatch another, quickly, passing it to the hand that's not leaning on the table, and I stuff it in a pocket on the opposite leg.

Third time is a charm for some. It's a trap for me.

The merchant glares, lunging forward.

Chapter 2
Cyra

"Cyra!" The shout fills the hallway. "Cyra, come here this instant!"

The stiletto heels on my tall, black boots click down the hallway as I follow the echoes around the mansion. Surely he can hear the loud pings, but he calls again anyway.

"I'm here, sir," I answer as he shrieks one more time.

I drop my skirt, letting it settle straight. I always have a habit of lifting my skirts even when I don't need to. On occasion, I even try to do it when I'm wearing pants while racing around the city.

"Where have you been?" the Governor snaps.

"Downstairs, sir, in the arboretum."

He appraises me, looking me up and down before continuing. "We have work to do, Cyra."

"Yes, of course, sir." I look down, dropping my eyes to the floor. I hadn't been late—in fact, I'm still early for our lessons—but he finds fault in me all the same.

"I didn't bring you into this house to let you run wild, girl." He walks over, placing a hand on my shoulder in a fatherly way. "We have to do better."

"Yes, Governor, of course." I nod, still not meeting his eyes.

The Governor adopted me when I was a child. He picked a young girl with hair swept back over an aviator cap and goggles, wearing a black vest and tan blouse with billowy sleeves, and a long green skirt and thought, *yes, this is a girl I can train to steal airships.*

My dress catches in my peripheral vision as I look down and flashes black and white, a blur of the long stripes I wear. A slightly shorter layer sits over the long stripes in solid black, pulled up by straps over both knees. A third layer of stripes, this time running horizontal, is draped over that, also taken up in the straps in the same location, creating a beautiful sweeping effect. It's cinched in at the waist, laces hanging down the front over top of a black corset. A matching black and white striped parasol rests in one hand and I position it like a cane alongside me. With a hem of black ribbon and my ultra-high boots, it's a perfectly powerful outfit—just right for asserting my command over Levi.

"Levi is waiting on the conservation deck." He taps his cane and spins on his heels, the tails of his long, black coat trailing behind him as he walks forward at a clip slightly slower than I can tolerate.

I take in a deep breath, count to three, and then stride behind him, staying far enough back that should he look over his shoulder, I'll be there, but far enough away that I won't accidentally step on the back of his shoe when I forget I have to pace myself.

We take the short flight of stairs to a landing. It isn't a full floor above where we were, but since we were already on the third and highest floor, the conservation deck is considered an elevated extension on the floating mansion.

Levi stands with his back to us and turns when he hears the Governor's cane and my heels enter the space. His dreadlocks are tied back, mainly dark with bits of bright red embedded in it for a pop of color. Goggles rest around his neck, the lenses sitting over his collarbone. He looks as though he's been covered in dust, but instead of particles he could brush off, it's part of the fabric of every single piece he wears. He tugs on one long, black work glove and offers me a snarky smile, wire wrapped around his other arm. I'd love to send the Governor's cat after

Levi's coattails, but I know my protector wouldn't approve.

The mansion suddenly dips—we must have hit some turbulence. The building was constructed to float off the heat generated from coal furnaced below. The ground beneath where we're tethered is scorched from the heat we produce. We each balance ourselves quickly before falling. The Governor grumbles, mumbling something about leaving us to it.

I turn back to Levi. "I don't want to know why you have that," I say, nodding to the wire.

"No, you don't." Levi is smug enough to think he can outsmart and outperform me, but he also knows he's not there yet and needs to learn from me first. He believes he can outwit me in the end and take my place in the Governor's admiration. He wants the praise and accolades I receive publicly, and even though he's been with us for two months, he still doesn't realize it's not so appealing to live in the mansion.

I could shoot him right now and rid myself of the problem.

Of course, that also means I'd have to train someone new, and they likely wouldn't have as much promise as Levi, and I'd never fulfill the Governor's wishes of winning another airship, which would probably leave me out in the cold.

Would that be the worst thing?

I shake my head, clearing the thoughts. I have to get Levi ready; there's an airship and accolades at stake. I can't afford my fantasies of running off and stealing the airship on my own.

Or can you? A little voice in my head asks.

No, I certainly cannot. Besides, the Governor is as close to a parent as I have, and I'm as close to a daughter as he has. I'm going to support his wishes.

Flipping my parasol up, I pop it open and rest it on my shoulder. I nod that Levi should follow me as I stride forward.

The conservation deck is encased in a giant, glass dome, allowing us to look up into the sky. Metal rims hold it in place, giving a palatial look to it and a giant telescope sits in the middle for observers to use. Several tables are spread throughout the room, scattered with books.

"Put your wire down, Levi," I command over my shoulder. I've had some of the men clear one half of the sitting room just off of the conservation deck. It's a small, private room without any windows—perfect for working without any passing airships being able to take notice.

"Don't think it will be a fair fight if I use it to trip you and tie it up, Cyra?" he quips. The metal wire clinks as it slinks to the floor. When it settles, I respond.

"If you have that on you once training begins, I'll be using it against you faster than you can get a few kicks in, Levi," I remind him snobbily.

"You may have stolen the Empress last year, Cyra, but

the Stourbridge is an entirely different kind of airship. It requires finesse."

"You're still connecting with the wrong part of your boot when you kick, Levi." I point out his inadequacies. "The contest is in a month."

"Yes, and only one of us will be participating in it."

While the contest hasn't even officially been announced yet, the Governor is friends with the Proprietor—the man sponsoring this year's event—and he has advanced knowledge of the competition just like he did for the Empress. The rules say a winner can't participate under the same benefactor during two consecutive years. The Governor cannot reap the benefits of working with me again until next year—thus the need for Levi—and he certainly wouldn't loan me out to work with anyone else, which leaves me banished from the competition.

I force my hands to stay at my side even though all I want to do is rub my temples in frustration. After a moment of tension-filled silence, I wave the men over. Marching to the sofa, I lean against the armrest and nod for them to begin. Once Levi has warmed up and I've assessed where he needs work, I'll step in and snap at least one muscle painfully enough to prove a point.

The arboretum is warm once I find my way back down

to the lower deck where it's kept on a protruding floor, also encased in glass. I don't leave the mansion too much these days—my benefactor wants to keep me safe now that everyone knows who I am—but I appreciate the trees and greenery far more than I enjoy the metal-crusted city below.

Several flowers are starting to bloom and I take my time admiring them. I'll be forced out soon enough. If I could set up a cot here and bury myself under a pile of blankets, I'd be happy. Instead, I'm relegated to a giant room on the Oasis deck where we all live.

At least I have a veranda that isn't enclosed in glass. It allows me fresh air from time to time, as well as a route that is overlooked to escape while the Governor is at work and no one is watching me closely.

My fingers dance over the opened petals of several brightly-colored flowers as I turn to go. My room is calling my name, but not nearly as much as the city below is.

I stomp through the halls, ensuring my heels make noise. I want everyone to know where I'm going and that I have no desire to speak to them anytime soon. The staff knows enough to leave me be when I take the halls quickly like this, seemingly on a mission.

I crank the handle on my door to the right, followed by a quarter turn to the left, then back to the right. It unlocks and I enter, closing it behind me. The room is massive—even larger than the sitting room where I train Levi every day.

Tapestries cover the windows, giving me privacy when I want it. I draw them closed so no one can see inside as I change out of my dress, though there's rarely airships nearby to see inside. Walking to the vanity, I drop the long skirt and bodice over the back of my chair —I'll move it before I do my makeup tomorrow.

I slip into tight black pants and a matching black shirt. Adding a brown leather corset over it, I clip it shut, cinching in my waist again. Then I shrug into my matching leather shoulder guard, placing it over my left side. My utility belt wraps around my waist, grounding my outfit, and I quickly search for my cog-and-oval earrings.

Knowing I need to cover myself, I wrap a scarf around my head that fades down into a short cape that covers most of my back. I use the matching neck wrap to cover my face, leaving only my eyes visible through the breathable fabric.

I tuck a few weapons into my belt, add a tincture bottle on a strap for good measure, and attach a few additional straps for fashion's sake. Glancing in the mirror, I appraise what I've done to hide my identity—no one must know I've slipped out.

Typically, we leave the mansion through a system of pulleys attached to a covered platform that moves us away from the ground below the mansion's tethers to keep away from the intense heat. I don't have that luxury.

Instead, I slide down the metallic rope attaching our home to the ground, running the instant I get near the scorched earth to avoid coming in contact with the blazing heat that rolls toward passerbys in visible waves of rippling air. I feel like it singes every part of my body as I run, but I'd rather face the heat than be trapped. Returning is even harder, but I don't have to deal with that until later.

I move quickly away from the floating mansion, hoping no one is watching—but then, they never do.

Quietly, I make my way into the city. It gleams in the late afternoon sun, sparkling like diamonds. I lift my fingers to my brass necklace tucked under the fabric of my cape and hood, touching the butterfly like I do each time I enter the city in disguise.

"If you could enter the competition, what would you be doing right now?" I whisper to myself, formulating a plan for my time in the city. I may not be able to fight for the Stourbridge, but that doesn't mean I can't have a little fun while I'm free.

Once the competition opens up, the southern half of the city and the expansion beyond will be opened up to those who wish—and can afford—to engage in a blood-thirsty battle to win the newest airship the Proprietor has provided Horallen with. It's a vicious game and many lose limbs along the way, but the winner is given the honor of control over the ship, and those with the power of transport hold the key to everything. Whether they chose to keep it to themselves, open it as a resort, or turn it into a mode of transportation, they are the ultimate citizens in charge of Horallen until the following year, save for the officials.

Last year, I won.

Last year, I lost everything to win.

What if you could win again this year? My adrenaline won't stop talking, whispering foolish and dangerous ideas in my head. *What if you played for yourself?*

"I can't betray him," I whisper harshly to no one in particular.

Betraying my benefactor—the man who took me in, protected me, trained me, and gave me a comfortable life away from the orphanage and running on the streets with a pistol in her pocket—is unforgivable.

Win it for yourself, but gift it to him later.

Could that possibly work? Would it be seen as a slap in the face—*an insult*—to the Governor? He'd have what he wants, after all, but it would be my name and my glory instead of his.

Still, if I could win it, I could be on my own. I don't need a mansion. I could travel the world in my airship. I could sell rooms and suites on it and take tenants with me, which would supply an income for me. If I had people along with me, I wouldn't have to do all of the work.

It's a possibility.

But the Governor's wrath and disappointment would be hard to deal with.

It's a stupid idea…*right?*

The waterfalls sound in the background and I veer to the right, hurrying down the cog-covered streets. I've always admired the architecture in this part of town. I duck into side alleys when I hear people coming, refusing to be seen unless I have to be.

When a small group of women wanders toward me, I run, kicking off the side of a building as I stretch up to catch the bottom of a retracted fire escape. It sways under my weight but I quickly shift to the fixed part of the platform away from the steps that lower when stepped on from above.

I pull myself up before the women reach me. I know better than to be seen by the gossipy busybodies who stroll the streets while their husbands are working in the Hall. Unlike men who notice you for a moment, decide your value, and then forget about you once you've passed, women observe you with a keen eye and tuck every last bit of information away for another day, right down to the laces on your boots.

I don't need anyone remembering me here.

Once they pass, I scramble all the way onto the platform, no longer holding my body up by my forearms as my feet dangle from the underside of the landing. Using the stairs, I allow them to sink down to the ground and I walk down like the victor I am.

Hurriedly, I make my way to the broken-down part of town. The streets are familiar from my childhood, though I rarely get back. When I do, it's with money I smuggled out of the mansion or with food I picked up along the way.

My fingers stretch up to my necklace once more and I pull it out from where it slipped under the fabric, exposing it to the world. Clock hands form a point, graced by a mechanical butterfly in brassy tones. I let it settle over my collarbone and chest.

I lived on the streets once. Most of the children who are there now I only know from my trips back—the children that were here when I was young have since grown. Many of them find work wherever they can. Some don't. A few of the girls have escaped into marriages, making themselves presentable enough for one of the boys in town to fall madly in love with before realizing she came from nothing.

A small gasp sounds from behind a pile of what can only be described as rubble as I walk near it. Turning to the right, I investigate, discovering a small girl peering back at me.

"It's Cyra." A girl about seven or eight rushes to the

small girl's side from the burned-out inside of a crumbled building. "It's okay."

The tiny girl looks to be about four or five. She's old enough to really understand the world she lives in, but not old enough to even begin to fathom how to survive it. Her friend takes her hand, patting it as she pulls the girl out.

I step back, appraising the scene. A building burned—recently enough that if I lean in, I can still smell the smoke. I wouldn't be surprised if embers still glowed somewhere in the heart of the mess, posing a threat should they grow.

"Amany, what are you doing here?" I ask the older of the two girls. "I thought they took you in."

"They did," she confesses. "We still have to work though."

The orphanage holds as many children as possible, but it's not feasible to care for them all, leaving the children to scavenge and beg during the days. The headmistress doesn't ask questions when one of the orphans returns with food—she knows it's likely stolen, but if they've returned with all of their body parts intact, it means they got away with it and at least a few of the children will have food that night.

"You look awfully dirty for having a bed and a place to shower," I point out.

"If you want to rummage through a burned-out

walkup, be my guest, Cyra." For seven, she's awfully cynical. I suppose I was like that, too, once.

The small girl tugs on Amany's hand. I bend down, getting on eye level with the girl. I tug the scarf away from my face so she can see me, extending a hand for her to shake.

"Hi. I'm Cyra."

"She's the one who brings us things," Amany reminds the girl.

"See this?" I lift my necklace up. "This is how you'll know it's me if it's hard to tell sometimes. No one in the world has a necklace like this."

I let the girl examine it, feeling the different pieces that make up my jewelry. When she pulls away, I continue. "Sometimes I have to come in disguise so no one knows I'm here. I have to hide my face and my hair so they don't know it's me. I always pull my necklace out though—that way you'll know it's safe."

I smile, pulling back a bit. Reaching into one of the small pockets on the front of my corset, I snap it open and let my fingers linger inside.

"I have a present for you today." Slowly, I pull out a coin—a high-level copper. "I couldn't stop for food today but give this to the headmistress and tell her to use it for bread and meat."

Amany nods solemnly.

"I'm going to let Amany hold this one, but I have

something for you too, little friend." I take a small copper out of my bag—one that won't be devastating to lose should she misplace it—and hand it to her. "Keep that safe and give it to the headmistress when you return."

She looks at me in awe, taking the copper from me.

"Now hurry back," I instruct the two, rising up off my knee.

"Thanks, Cyra," Amany calls over her shoulder, tugging the small girl along.

My trip was faster than I intended, but I don't need to stick around and get caught. I kick at the rubble, knocking bits of broken building skittering across the ground.

There's nothing more I can do here, so I turn, slinking down a side street or two for kicks before making my way back into the main part of the city that's brimming with newer life.

I slam myself against building walls and dart into alleyways whenever I hear someone coming. Most people in this part of town will turn a blind eye to me anyway, but I'd still prefer not to be noticed.

A woman steps out of her home, leaving the door open behind her. She glances left and right before bending down with a wrench in her hand as she tries to fix a broken lever mounted in front of the house. I could probably help her, but I'm not spending my time making friends and fixing things here in the rat trap.

I envy her short pigtails, held in place with goggles on her head—my long hair would never cooperate like that. I can loop it up, though, letting it sit in two sweeping, loose buns with the ends hanging down. I might wear it like that tomorrow for a change.

When she looks up, I move on, thankful I had tucked my scarf back into place once I sent the girls off. The sun is warm on my back as I step out of the shadows and hurry down another street, this time giving me a clear path where no one will see me.

The following street, however, I wish I had avoided it. At the end of the alley, a man enters at the same time I do. We stare at each other for a moment and he reaches for something on his belt—I assume a weapon.

I turn my shoulder away from him, putting my back to the inside of the alley, attempting to show him I don't want a fight. Keeping my hands where he can see them, I start toward him, still at an angle.

The man pauses, watching me for a moment. When I get close, I notice his eyes—they're practically glowing a vibrant blue. His face is covered in a shadow of scruff and his lips have a hard line to them as I approach. He lets his hand fall slightly away from his hip to show he won't try anything if I don't either.

Slowly, he takes a few steps forward, watching me. We face off as we pass each other, ensuring the other isn't going to pull anything. Once past, we turn, walking backward while facing each other. A few more steps back and I nod. He nods back.

We turn at the same time, having agreed to keep going. I walk to the end of the alley quickly, and I hear him walk away behind me. Once I reach the opening to the next street, I turn and discover him pulling himself up onto a fire escape much like I had earlier in the afternoon. I watch him climb for just a moment, quick and nimble. I leave before he notices me watching.

I step out onto the main street, turning at the next adjoining road. I haven't been down these streets since I was little and I'm not even sure if I traversed these particular roads then. This is what I get for taking a different path home.

The sun glints off the metal covering a pole hanging off of a makeshift shop in the middle of the block. I walk toward it to see who has set up a business there. I regret it, seeing what it is.

Ducking my head, I hurry down the rest of the block, knowing I want nothing to do with the area.

If I could get the children out of here, I would take them in a heartbeat.

If I could.

I pause. *What if I can?*

If I enter the competition and win the Stourbridge, I could give the orphans a home. I could take them on my airship and transport them wherever I'd need to. I could give them all jobs and we could run the ship like a resort or use it to transport people in order to earn money.

I'd have to be careful, of course, to protect the children and ensure their safety if I was to bring outsiders onto the airship, but it's a logical, sound idea for getting them out of this horrid place.

I could win the airship for them...and *that* is worth betraying the Governor for. Surely he can't fault me for doing the same thing that he did for me.

Chapter 3
Aladdin

"HE THINKS I SHOULD KICK YOU OUT SO YOU DON'T BRING shame on the family name," Mother says, fretting about the small kitchen.

"I work hard, just like everyone else out there," I protest weakly. She won't kick me out. "That guy tried to force me out of line so he could get a job before they ran out, that's all. I didn't even swing at him, I just blocked his punch and then Byron showed up."

"You're lucky he did, Aladdin. What would have happened if he hadn't?"

I would have pulverized him.

"Yeah, good thing…" I trail off.

"Your uncle wants to see you today after the announcement," she informs me, brushing her long bangs back with the backside of her wrist. The kitchen is warm with the oven on.

"What is this announcement again?"

"For the competition, Aladdin. Surely, you must have heard *something* about it."

I hadn't. I know there's some type of competition going on, and that they held it last year, but we were in mourning. I was busy trying to find the man who murdered my father and take care of my inconsolable mother. I hadn't even heard anything had happened last year until a week ago when the topic of the competition's revival had come up.

"I'm sure I'll learn about it at the announcement today—they're doing it before work hours near the Market."

I can't imagine wasting my time being involved in a competition. From what I've heard, you have to give up work for the duration of the contest and only one person wins riches and fame or whatever ridiculous thing they're spinning to get the people of Horallen to provide a little entertainment in the lives of the officials.

It's hardly worth it. I'll let the fools participate and I'll take all their jobs while they're gone and make some *real* money for myself and Mother. Maybe I can even secure a permanent job with one of the employers and I can work our way out of here.

"You'll go see Kacper today," she repeats. "Be sure that you find him."

"I have to go to work, Mother," I protest. "I don't have time to—"

"*You will find Kacper.*" Her words are sharp and pointed, leaving no room for discussion. I rake my hands through my hair, pushing it out of my eyes.

"Yes, Mother, of course."

One day I won't have to answer to that man.

The crowd shifts restlessly, swaying back and forth as they transfer their weight from one leg to the other. It's noisy as I stand on the outskirts of the crowd, not overly thrilled to be kept so long waiting for the announcement.

I arrived early and stood off to the left, close to the bridge leading to the Market in hopes that as soon as it's over, I can run over and get chosen first for work today. Keeping a sharp eye out for Kacper, I try to locate him so I can handle whatever he wants to talk about before the announcement starts, but he hasn't made an appearance yet.

Suddenly, the Hall doors open and the officials walk out, lining the platform outside the building. They take their places and wait for the announcement as well.

I attempt to make eye contact with my uncle, but he only raises an eyebrow at me—guess I can't get away with a run-by conversation once this is over. I just hope I can still procure a job today if he holds me back. I barely escaped the merchant I stole from yesterday and I'd prefer not to do a repeat performance today just to get a little food to eat.

The doors to the hall open again and a man walks out on what appears to be extended legs. His boots are strapped into stilts that bounce on the end, giving him a much longer, faster gait. For a moment I let myself think of how much easier it would be to scale buildings in those things if I could spring off walls.

He carries a large walking cane in his hand to stabilize himself—it's bigger than Byron is when he stands at his full height. His long overcoat reaches to his feet and would easily trip him if he wore it without the leg extensions. A holster is strapped over his vest, and his collar peeks out just enough to be seen. I admire his fashion sense.

When he stops walking, he reaches up to adjust the goggles on his head before addressing us. "Hello! I am Issac Von Hinten."

The crowd begins to rumble but I can't make out their words. Everyone seems to lean in.

"Last year, I created the Empress airship and sold her to Horallen as part of an elite competition to serve the country. This year, I am pleased to tell you that I have taken those funds and created a new ship—the Stourbridge—and will be hosting a *new* competition this year!"

He shouts his words, his enthusiasm rippling through the people. Many clap and cheer.

"Before I go any further, though, I'd like to remind you what is at stake!" He turns, motioning to the door he just vacated. It swings open and several people walk out, taking a place at his side. They look dwarfed next to him.

An older man with white hair down to his shoulders in a sharp, black suit with coattails and a cane stares out into the crowd, looking as icy as the silver adornments on his brocade vest and the intricate lapel designs on his jacket. After a moment, he smiles, softening his gaze, giving him a grandfatherly appearance. He's not quite old enough to be grandfather to the girl to the left, though. Perhaps he had children later in life.

The girl gazes out into the crowd harshly, but unlike the man next to her, she doesn't soften. She's draped in a skin-tight black dress that bells out on the bottom from her knees down. It's quite unlike what most of the females of Horallen wear. The majority of it is a dark black fabric but it's embroidered with gold and bronze colored metallic swirls in the shape of cogs and gears around the bodice part and from her knees down, save for one chain that wraps up and around her hip, connecting the two sections visually. It's the most stunning thing I've ever seen, and the crowd agrees as men catcall her.

I'm too far away to see the face she makes, but I'm

positive she made one. Her hair is long, drifting down her back. It sways as she turns to face the men.

"Last year, the Empress was won in a fierce competition that many of you *lost*," Issac reminds the crowd. "You're all familiar with Cyra, last year's winner. She fought against all of you for her benefactor, Governor Alias.

"The Empress has since been put to good use, earning the Governor the equivalent of one million coppers." The crowd gasps. No wonder everyone is so bent on competing. *I'm* even tempted myself, but I have to stick to my plan instead of some unrealistic pipe dream.

The girl puts her hand on her hip, turning to the crowd smugly. She has a right to lord it over them; she defeated them all in whatever gameplay she was forced to participate in.

"But this year is different!" Issac says, shocking even the people on stage. He grins wildly. The Governor turns to look at him, as does the girl. "The *only* good news for you is that none of you will have to compete against the lovely and charming Cyra, as she can't participate two years in a row for the same benefactor."

"I'll take her!" someone in the crowd shouts.

"I'll be her benefactor!" another cries.

The officials on the stage all look like they want to snatch her up too, though no one makes a move to steal her from the Governor.

"But the Governor has a new sponsored player, so you'll have to be quick to steal the Stourbridge out from under the gentleman, and I hear this year's competitor is even better than last years!" The girl cringes at his words. "This year's competition will be even more challenging!"

The crowd takes a collective step forward, accidentally moving at the same time, all wanting to hear the details of the competition to win the Stourbridge.

"This year's prize is even bigger than the airship that was won last year. It can accommodate more people, go farther lengths without stopping, and provides more luxury than ever before. Based on how the Governor did this year, the Stourbridge is expected to bring in double the value and the winner can anticipate a windfall of nearly triple what Governor Alias earned this year."

The group of people cheers, raising their fists into the air in celebration. One person will be set for life should they win this machine.

"Are you ready to hear what this competition will cost you?"

The crowd roars. The competition's new proprietor and sponsor pauses a moment, waiting for them to die down before continuing. He's clearly impressed with himself for taking the competition away from Horallen and making it privatized—he says as much.

"Like last year, you'll all be competing to not only find the airship where I've hidden it somewhere inside or outside of Horallen's city limits, but you'll also have to break in and steal it, moving the ship to a new location without breaking it. Should you cause any damage you cannot fix yourself to the ship, you'll have to pay for it in full."

That's a sobering thought—even if you find it, you have to steal it without causing damage while others are also doing the same. How on earth did that girl get it away last year without destroying it?

Must be nice to have a benefactor willing to pay for it should you destroy something.

"This year, there are some new provisions, however." The crowd goes still. On stage, the officials all turn in unison, eyeing the man warily. The Governor and his daughter look curiously at the man as his energy switches—I can already see a manic turn before he opens his mouth. "You can play the game like you did last year, friends, but I've hidden resources along the way that will help you."

Something isn't right. The hair on the back of my neck stands up, prickling against my skin.

A light switches on, projecting an image of the Stourbridge against the wall of the Hall building. We watch as it floats through the air, showing off the shape of the airship. A giant lion is painted on the side, mixed with the shapes of a thousand cogs and gears that appear to be real and working, spinning as the airship moves.

"Along the way, I've hidden resources to help you break into the Stourbridge. It won't be easy to find them, though it will certainly give you a tremendous edge to win the game." He looks out over the audience, grinning wildly. "I won't tell you *what,* but I *will* tell you *where.*"

He pauses for dramatic effect and everyone on the stage plays into it, leaning toward him—all but the girl on stage who rocks back on her heels and crosses her arms. *What does she care?* She can't compete anyway.

"I've hidden several key pieces to successfully breaking into the Stourbridge inside *the Collection Cave.*"

In response, the crowd steps back. The Collection Cave is where Horallen's junk is thrown. The cleaners toss scrap metal, broken objects and furniture, even things that have been procured from dubious places into a giant pit inside a cavern on the outskirts of the city. No one is to enter aside from workers because of the dangers of collapsing mounds of metallic trash, and even of those workers, half don't make it out alive when they're sent to create new paths through the massive stacks of things that have been thrown out.

"Once you enter, you'll be given as much time as you'd like to sift through the stacks and find one item that can help you later in the competition. Should you choose to skip the Collection Cave, you may still be able to break into the Stourbridge, but you'll be forced to wait there an hour. Any person that approaches the ship within that hour that *has* survived the Collection Cave and emerged to compete has the right to take the ship from you, immediately setting off on their flight to move the Stourbridge back to or out of the city limits, depending on where it's hidden at the time. You cannot stop them from taking your victory should you choose to avoid the Cave."

No one responds. He clearly expects a response.

Frowning, he stretches an arm out wide, still holding his walking stick with the other hand. "And because I like a good show, the competition begins *in ten minutes.*"

Everyone gasps, wide-eyed. Not only has the man changed the rules, coerced everyone to make a life-risking decision, and forced them into danger, he's also taken away the ability to think it through. By removing the time between the announcement and the competition, people can't talk themselves out of it. They can't think it through rationally. They either do it—and likely fail—or they walk away and regret it, leading to other stupid decisions.

"Make wise choices, my friends. Not everyone can get into the Cave at once, and you might spend the next two days waiting there, but rest assured, entering the Collection Cave is your best bet at winning the Stourbridge.

"One final piece of advice," he shouts. "*Only the lion can win!* Good luck to all!"

He spins on the edges of the curved stilts he's wearing

and bounces toward the Hall. Someone flings open the doors and the man disappears behind it.

"Wait!" someone shouts. "The competition! What do we have to do?"

More take up the cry, leaving the Governor to answer as the officials wringing their hands, looking like they want to run to the crowd to find someone to sponsor so they can win the airship now that their time to find a potential victor has been taken from them.

"You'll figure it out. Go to the Cave! Just like last year, there will be signs and signals along the way, and those smart enough to figure out what they mean will have a chance at winning the airship." He too turns, following Issac Von Hinten into the Hall, the girl on his heels, wide-eyed.

As soon as they're gone, the officials break their line, rushing forward toward the crowd. They hold up their hands, shouting propositions to the men and women who have yet to move. They offer money, glory, new homes—anything they can think of to try to find someone adequate enough to win.

Some even manage to take on several people, hedging their bets, knowing many won't survive the Cave, and those that *do* emerge, might not come out unscathed.

A hand clamps down on my shoulder. Byron hisses in my ear, pulling me back. Knowing there's no way to avoid him, I step backward, following his movements.

Kacper stands on the platform, trying to secure men who will accept him as a benefactor. He's calmer than most of the officials on the stage, but I can see the sweat starting to form on his brow as Byron drags me up the steps to the platform. Leaving Kacper to his business, Byron forces me inside.

The building is light inside, covered in dark pipes that turn into light sources. Outside of the main hall, the offices of the men in charge lay waiting for their occupants to return, either successfully or still in want of more people to pay to risk their lives for the chance at an airship worth millions.

Kacper's office is dark brown with black accents, much like the pipes outside in the hallway. Cog-covered lamps sit on his pristine desk. A round table rests alongside it, holding trinkets in bronze and gold colors. Along one wall, an octopus rests in a tank, glowing blue in the pale light shining down on it.

I stand in the middle of the room, facing his desk, Byron to my back. After a few moments, Kacper comes in, setting his coat on a hook off the coatrack in the corner. He places his gloves on the round table next to his desk and takes a seat.

"Well, Aladdin," he addresses me. "Looks like you and I will be working together."

"Excuse me?" Ordinarily, he might have slapped me, but he doesn't even flinch.

"The competition, boy." He watches me carefully. "I'm going to be your benefactor."

"I'm not competing," I say flatly. "I have work."

"You have a chance to win the most expensive airship in this country," he points out. "I know what you're capable of, boy. Don't think I haven't had you watched. I know your magnificently talented at stealing from others —you're lucky I haven't told your mother."

Apparently, I haven't been as careful as I thought.

"I know you want out of that hovel you live in with your mother, so if you do this for me, I'll get your old home back for you. Or, if you'd like, I'll give you an upgrade from that place your father bought when we were young men."

"So, your offer is risk my life for my old house back? You want me to go poking around in the Collection Cave and likely lose a foot or a hand, or die of some disease from slicing my skin open on a twisted piece of metal, or get lost in there forever and die surrounded by whatever rats run around that dump for *a house?* You've got to be joking."

"A house and enough money to never have to work in your lifetime again. Enough that any horrid little children you pop out one day won't have to work either. You and your mother will be provided for your entire lives, and not by me. It will be money *you* earned. You can't do that off day-to-day wages at the Market auctions, can you, Aladdin?"

The prospect of having money of my own and being in control of my own destiny is enticing, but he's only offering that *if* I win.

"And what if I die? What then? Who will provide for my mother? She won't take money from you, *Uncle. I'm* the one taking care of her."

"Win or die, Aladdin, Emmaline will be taken care of. Should you perish inside the Cave, or should you die along the competition route, she will be given a stipend large enough to live comfortably for the rest of her life. I'll tell her it was the money you earned for competing for me. Even if you fail, it moves her out of those rat-infested streets and back to a comfortable life where she doesn't have to worry about growing thin from hunger or being stabbed while walking down the street."

Even if I fail, she survives.

"Make your choice, Aladdin. I don't have all day."

"Did you find other people to sponsor?" I question, wanting to know how many people he has working for him that could potentially stab me in the back should I get close to winning. It would be an easy way for him to dispose of me.

"Two. You are the third, and though they have more muscle than you, I believe you to be my victor."

"Why are you doing this? Why would you give me the chance to elevate myself?"

"Your father would have wanted it this way," he replies, leaning back in his chair. "I'm willing to help you because of him.

"And," he adds, "because I'm willing to give you an edge here, I also have information for you. But you must make your choice first. I can help you win, Aladdin, if you play for me, but this offer will be rescinded in the next ten seconds because if you pass, I need to bring the other men in here to tell them what I know."

Pressure tightens around my throat. If I agree, my mother will be safe. But if I agree, I may die in the next two days once I enter the Cave. Even if I survive that, I could still die during the competition. But my mother will be safe. If I win, I could thrive in Horallen.

"What happens if I survive but don't win?" I ask. He raises an eyebrow. "Surely you don't mean for me to compete for nothing."

"What else will motivate you?" he challenges.

"I have no motivation if it's win or nothing. Offer me something for competing—it doesn't have to be the entire purse you've offered, but it needs to be something of value." I try buying myself time to think.

He raises a hand to his chin, stroking the fine hairs outlining his jaw. "Compete and I'll get your house back. Win and I'll give you the money as well. You'll have the money and two percent of the profits from the first year of running the Stourbridge. Is that fair enough?"

I nod. It seems fair enough, assuming he holds up his word.

"Your choice?" he demands.

I nod. "My house back for competing, and money to survive should I win—though it needs to be ten percent of the profits for the first year. I'll accept no less. And should I die, you'll protect Mother."

"Five," he counters.

"Ten." I hold strong. "Father would not bargain."

It seems to strike a chord with him and he relents. "Ten."

"You have a deal, Uncle."

"Good." He leans forward, placing his elbows on his desk. "Now, it's time to tell you about a little inside-information I acquired about how to win this competition."

Chapter 4
Cyra

"*The Collection Cave?*" Levi shouts, stomping around the room. "I didn't sign up for this—"

"You most certainly did!" the Governor argues. "Cyra taught you well—you can still win this."

The two argue as I pace the room, dress clinging to my legs, forcing me to take smaller steps. It's stunning but is barely functional.

If I plan to win the Stourbridge by myself, I now have to be willing to face the Cave. I can't just sneak out without being noticed, especially if I disappear. I'll have to talk to the Governor about my plan. Perhaps I can strike a deal with him. If I win the Stourbridge as an independent entity, I could trade with him, taking the

Empress for myself and the children and leave him with the airship triple the value.

The Governor has always been kind to me. He knew this original competition would happen many years before the others knew and he took me under his care to train me, but he's also played benefactor to others before, usually more quietly. I'm the only one he's taken into his home, but he's built homes before—like the updated orphanage where Amany and her friends live. He might understand my desire to do this and allow me to compete on my own.

Levi looks like he wants to toss a table over but holds himself back. The Governor watches him reproachfully. Eventually, he calms Levi's fears and the two devise a plan for surviving the Caves. I add my input where necessary.

Once Levi returns to his room, the Governor looks to me. His face is tired, showing the lines of his many years as he sinks into a high-backed chair.

"Sit," he motions to me, softening. His years show as he leans back tiredly. "You looked lovely today, Cyra. The ladies did an excellent job sewing that dress for you."

I settle into the matching chair, facing him. "Thank you."

"Today was quite the show, wasn't it, my girl?"

"Indeed, sir."

"Aren't you glad you don't have to compete this year?"

He smiles softly. "I don't know what Issac was thinking throwing the Collection Cave into the mix. I'm beginning to think his delusions of grandeur are starting to get the better of him."

"I think he just wants to see more blood," I mutter.

"I'll have to have a talk with that young man once this is all over. I'm sure he won't be reachable until after it's all over."

"I thought you were keeping your friendship quiet, Governor."

"Our friendship was many years ago, Cyra, you know that. He and I haven't been close in two decades, but I still believe the root of that old friendship is enough to be able to have a conversation with him when warranted."

It's strong enough that the Governor knew about the competition with enough years to take me in and train me. Of course, it took Issac years to build the Empress, and even longer to convince the officials to do the competition at all.

"Sir, I wanted to discuss something with you."

"Do you?" The Governor absentmindedly taps his fingers on the arm of the chair.

"Yes." I pause. "I have an idea."

"Oh? Go on." He nods graciously toward me. Over the years, he truly has become like an adoptive father to me, listening when I need to talk and lecturing when I need to learn.

"I have a proposal for you, sir." I'm nervous and he can tell. He shifts in his seat, leaning forward. "I would like to enter the competition as a private entity and then trade the Stourbridge for the Empress when I win. I want to use it to give the orphans a home and place to work."

I rush to continue, words spilling out. "You'd get the expensive airship and you'd reap all of the benefits from it. You can even have part of the profits from the Empress as well! I just want to give the kids a safe place off the streets to grow up and teach them skills to survive in this world. They'd each work for their room and board, and could earn a small living working on the airship—"

"Cyra," he says quietly. Pausing, he chuckles. "I love your enthusiasm, my girl, and I appreciate your ingenuity, but to compete, you'd have to risk yourself inside the Cave. I can't let you go in there, Cyra."

"But—"

"No," he says, words persistent but kind. He leans forward and pats my hand, narrowly missing the hard edges of the lion's face bracelet he gave me last year after winning the Empress. The snaps on the underside of my wrist bite into my flesh as they're pinched between the leather band and my arm. "I can't let you get hurt. It was one thing to compete last year—you risked enough—but I'm not willing to lose you to that ridiculous Cave. This year is different, Cyra. I know I brought you here as a sponsor, but I've grown quite fond of you, Cyra."

He locks eyes with me, and everything seems heavy and thick in the air.

"I love you, my girl, and as much as I want this because *you* want this, I'm forbidding it. I can't lose you."

Long before I came into his life, the Governor lost his family. It's why he chooses to live in a mansion in the sky on the outskirts of Horallen. I can understand where he's coming from.

"We'll find another way, my girl." He leans forward and pats my knee.

I know he will try, but for as vast as the Governor's resources are, he's never going to be able to accomplish what I could with the Empress or Stourbridge under my control. There's no explaining that to him though.

I sigh, long and desperate, looking to the floor. The deep red and tan hues of the carpet swirl in an intricate pattern.

"Come," he says, looking at his watch. "We have to see Levi off. Tomorrow, you and I will sit down and work on a plan to help the orphans."

He stands, waiting for me to join him, hand held out to me. "You know I would accept your terms if I could, Cyra. You're like a daughter to me and I want you to be happy. But I can't risk you for this. We'll find another way."

I take his hand and let him guide me up the staircase that swirls around the edge of the room to the second level where we'll leave the giant globe three times our size, hanging golden planets, orbs, and moons, and shelves of books behind and take the outer stairs down to where we'll be seeing Levi off to the competition.

I hope he's ready.

Wearing his dust-covered jacket and light brocade vest, Levi stands by the door, a new appreciation for the changes to the game evident as he leers at me playfully.

"Be careful," I whisper as I hug him. "Don't lose a hand."

"Aww, it's like you care about me, Cyra." He sways me backward in his arms enough to jolt me slightly. Levi grins at me. "I'm ready. You've trained me well. I'll win the Stourbridge and you can congratulate me with a kiss later."

"As if," I laugh. Levi and I might have our differences, but we're friendly enough to joke around.

"Enough," the Governor announces, breaking us apart. "It's time to go. I'll escort you as far as the Cave, Levi, but I can do no more."

Levi nods, slipping out the door onto the platform.

Before I can speak, the Governor interrupts. "I won't

leave until he's out safely," he assures me, hand up to stop me from speaking over him. He places his pilot cap over his head, making him look extra important. He nods once before slipping out onto the platform.

I don't wait for the mechanical whir to sound before turning. Standing around to watch them leave will just be a waste of my time. Instead, I take the familiar path back to my room. Turning the wheel, I open the door and enter, firmly closing and locking it behind me.

In an impulsive move, I launch myself toward the closet. I hang the dress up, pulling down my outfit from yesterday.

If I'm going to do this, now is my only chance.

Walking to the Collection Cave takes much longer than I anticipated. It's late afternoon when I arrive. Spectators mill around, watching for people to survive the cavern and its unknown dangers.

I watch for a while, hoping to find some insight. Young men and women exit one at a time, many struggling to get out while clinging to a piece of scrap metal, an old blade from the front of a plane, or a vial bound in leather. Some drag a foot behind them, dripping in blood. Some emerge without fingers. The entire sight is ghastly.

Occasionally, one exits without injury. Those people give me hope.

I wait for Levi to emerge. The Governor looks completely relieved when he spots his charge, shoulders dropping several inches. He has to hold himself back from rushing toward the boy holding some kind of tool. Instead, he nods, and turns to leave, knowing he can't remain there any longer—it's up to Levi now.

Soon, the Governor will return to the mansion. Within a few hours, he will realize I'm missing. It means now is my only chance.

I slip into the line waiting to be released into the Cave. Most who dare to enter decide to mill in the crowd before stepping up, making the line only a few people long at any given time. Two people stand in front of me— a girl I doubt will make it very far before turning back based on the way she's shaking, and a guy I'm positive will lose a limb because he is being reckless even while standing in line.

I pay the excessive entrance fee that will keep the lower-level people out unless they have a benefactor—or cost them several month's wages—and wait. The smell of people surrounding me is oppressive, reminding me that not everyone has the privilege of washing daily. It's grotesque.

After the girl disappears, the boy ahead of me stands fidgeting in line. The men operating the entrance finally signal him to step up. He approaches them, then turns on his heels and faces the camera on a tripod. It flashes with a puff of smoke, capturing his face they will later use to confirm he entered the cave should he reach the Stourbridge.

"Veil off," the camera operator commands once I'm signaled forward. If I'm going to turn back, now is my only chance.

I tug it down so it only blocks my lips. He raises an eyebrow at me and I mirror him.

"Move it on three, *Identity*." He holds three fingers next to the apparatus, signaling me when to reveal myself. The moment it flashes, I yank the scarf back up around my face so no one sees me. "Happy?"

I turn without responding. At least he helped me out a little, and none of the workers seem to be examining the photographs so perhaps I'll go unnoticed, at least for a while.

Another man puts his hand up, signaling me to wait outside the Cave. The entire thing is built into a giant rock. It's like layers of circles have been placed on top of each other, forming a hole in the side of a mountain. The center leads inside the cave, taking a sharp left or right to walk into the glowing rock. It shines blue from the lights inside. Orbs of metal strips form an industrialized-look, making it look more modern than the wasteland it is.

"If you don't come back out within thirty minutes,

you won't make it back out," the guard informs me. He's not being cruel, just giving me the facts. "Choose wisely. If you pick stuff off a stack, it can fall on you. If you get trapped, we can't help you.

"The Proprietor of the competition has stated that he's been throwing helpful items in here for several years in preparation for this, which means it could be anywhere. He marked them but hasn't said how. Good luck."

My skin glows blue as I'm released to walk inside. Faced with the decision of right or left, I realize I should have pondered my direction while waiting in line—I need to get my head in the game. This isn't how I won last year.

Right. I go right.

At the end of the tunnel is a room the size of the Governor's library. Branching off is another series of tunnels, each, I assume, that lead to another set.

If people have come before me, chances are that I'll have to go farther to find something of value. Going too far will cost me. I have to remember how to get back.

Picking up a piece of metal, I scrape it along the cave walls. It doesn't matter to me that they're marked with numbers—if I run out of time and panic later, I might not be able to remember the sequence or directions I've turned in. I draw a disgusting line along the wall, scraping unevenly against it with the metal. Then I pick a tunnel and dash through it.

The corridor is long but thankfully illuminated by the same blue glow that welcomed me at the entrance, giving me enough light to see by. At the end of it, I find another room, with more tunnels.

I don't know much about Issac Von Hinten, but from the stories the Governor has told, he's eccentric. He created the Empress, giving control of it to Horallen's elite. I'm positive he used it as a test run for the Stourbridge, letting them take the financial responsibility. I haven't spent much time with him, but I could tell from the meeting this morning that he's been planning this for a long time—longer than the Governor knew about it.

I pass by a girl frantically looking around the room, searching for anything that could help her. She looks ready to cry. I don't have time for emotions.

A guy across the room tugs on something at the bottom of a pile of metal, sharp-looking pieces sticking out at odd angles. He shouldn't do that. The top is already teetering, but he's positive he's found something and refuses to relinquish it. A man yells at him to stop, running toward him, but it's too late.

I turn, knowing I don't want to see what happens. I scrape my metal along the wall, knowing the wreckage of the pile won't reach me on this side of the room. The girl gives up, running out of the Cave as the metal pile slides...

If Issac has been planning this all along and if he's been putting junk in here for "years," then I need to go back. I study the words on the doors as the man screams, trying to reach the foolish boy who sliced himself in half.

I noticed a few people running in and out without bothering to check the signs. Most are bent on searching the mountains of metal in hopes of finding something the others missed. Many check their pocket watches frequently, obviously taking the warning at the gate seriously.

The halls are big enough for machines to come through to move the scraps. Everything smells like burned coal, an obvious sign of the steam-powered equipment the men use here. Amidst the chaos around me, I watch for footprints in the dirt and rubble. When I find a section with less traffic, I take it, marking my trail behind me.

The farther I walk, the more settled I become. I shift back into the girl I was last year when I hunted down the Empress. Every move is calculated.

When I finally reach the room I've determined is the end of my journey, I examine the piles, looking for a sign from Issac. I don't believe he hasn't slipped inside to hide things inside the Collection Cave. He's not dumb enough to think we'd actually find things he sent to be piled in here years ago.

The Collection Cave is highly regulated. No one gets

in or out, but if anyone were going to, it would be Issac. I have no idea how he managed to get the officials to allow people in here for the sake of a competition…perhaps he didn't tell them.

A key catches my eye first. It's barely wedged in between an old clock piece and a metal box that's been dented in with age. I work it out, ensuring nothing moves. Examining it, it looks like it could do something useful, so I hang on to it in case I don't find anything else I like.

Walking around the pile, I continue to look. Everything looks dark, the dull and corroding metal refusing to reflect the lights from the room. The blue flickers, suggesting the lights in this area haven't been looked at since they abandoned the room at least a year ago based on the dust covering everything.

Before stepping on it, I test the path covered in sheets of bendable metal. It supports my weight, but each sheet bends around my foot, leaving a strange impression behind me. I gently move around, searching for anything to help me.

The boy tugging on the metal in the other room flashes in my mind. The sickening sound of metal colliding with flesh makes me cringe even though it's just a memory. The incident will haunt me and I whisper a prayer that I don't run into any more scenes like that along the way.

"Come on!" a voice calls near the entrance.

Metal crashes.

"Nice aim!" a second voice replies.

A strangled cry sounds, making the two laugh.

"Don't!" The second boy's laughter suddenly cuts off as a female voice interrupts him.

"I suggest you turn around, little girl," the second voice adds. "He'll be gone by the time you reach him. This is the only chance you'll get to leave."

She—*whoever she is*—makes a frightened noise and turns, scuffling away. The male voices laugh and begin to walk closer to the entrance.

Last year, the competition had been dangerous. It had become cutthroat—I have the scars to prove it. The chaos is starting early this year, I see.

I scoot around a pile of metal. I'm trapped inside the room filled with so many mountains of materials that could kill me, and if they find me, they could treat me like that boy out there or worse. I consider attempting to topple a pile of garbage on them, sparing countless other lives, but there's no guarantee that it would stop them, nor can I ensure my own safety in the process. It wouldn't do very well to kill myself before I even spent a full hour in the competition.

Each of their footsteps is announced by the crunching of metal. One of them tries to climb the stable collection of junk on the left side of the room, actually scrambling to the top. Old coins, cogs, and creations crumble off of their resting place, clinking down to the metal-lain ground.

As they move, so do I. I watch their every step, judging their proximity by sound when I can't see them. Slowly, I make my way to the door as they move deeper into the room.

Before I can leave, an oddly-shaped wrench makes me snap to attention. I've never seen anything like it before—it has to mean something. Engraved on the handle are strange marks—several curved lines that could almost form the shape of a lion's face. The Governor always said he was one for symbolism, and it had certainly come into play last year when I stole the Empress.

It has to be part of the competition.

"Well, well. Look here."

I freeze. I got distracted by the wrench and didn't notice one of the boys sneaking up on me, his partner stomping away in the background to distract me.

Turning, I face him. He's tall with dark hair; much taller up close than I expected him to be.

"What did you find, little girl?" He takes a menacing step closer. His tone grows darker, face clouding over. "Show me."

I have one chance of escaping. I'll also need to use a distraction if I have any hope of getting out of here without them taking me out.

"I found it—it's mine," I inform him, holding my hands at my sides. I bat my eyelashes, hoping to distract him as I position the key in my palm so I can make it look like I'm picking it up out of the rubble.

"Show me what you found, girl." His friend stalks over to us, ready to back the boy up.

"I found the key and I'm taking it with me. Go look somewhere else."

"Listen up." He looks at me with disgust. "My brother and I are going to win this airship. We want what you found. Give it to us and we'll let you go. Otherwise, we'll kill you and take it. Your choice."

I let out an airy growl. Clenching my lips, I keep my eyes focused on the tall one while I lean to the side, feigning picking up the key. I'm now certain it isn't connected to the Stourbridge because it doesn't have the marking. As I straighten, I transfer it to my right hand, moving to give it to him.

He reaches for it and I quickly drop down, grabbing the wrench and yank it from the pile. I swing, connecting it with the tall boy's temple.

Run. The word pounds over and over in my head, knowing they're behind me. *Run.*

Faster. Don't stop. Don't stop for the piles of trash, don't stop for the people, don't stop for what could potentially be an avalanche ahead of me. Persist. Survive. Run.

The boys call to me, screaming threats as they chase me. Going around the piles of trash and scrap metal is taking too long. The boys have weapons, firing off a few shots as I round a corner.

Is it better to cut myself open while escaping or to be shot because I'm too slow?

Is it better to lose a finger or to die?

I'll opt for the mechanical hand the Governor will certainly buy me if I need it over bleeding out on the floor of a trash-cave because I didn't escape in time. My arms pump, feet flying over the ground.

I slip, slamming into the debris-littered path. I think I feel blood, but I'm not sure. It's superficial at most though, so I pick myself up and keep going.

The pounding of my blood in my ears is drowned out by the footsteps of the angry men chasing me. They topple piles behind them, push people out of the way, and scream for others to stop me, though none of them do.

I don't stop to look as another shot rings out. Someone collapses against a wall and I know it's my fault. I dart down another hallway, following the marks I left myself, desperate to escape.

Slipping again, I crash down. I slide backward, down a pile of metal. My corset protects my mid-section as I scrape against the trash people have disposed of. Sheets of metal, boxes, and old, broken tools skitter down around me. One slams into my forearm as I raise a hand to protect my face.

The loud, lurching sound of an entire mountain of metal falling apart fills the tunnel behind me, echoing off the walls. Machinery scrapes against other scrap metal in a sickening orchestra. If I didn't know better, I'd think the entire mountain was collapsing in on me. I turn to discover the boys have toppled the pile of metal I knew enough to avoid.

They've sealed the entire tunnel. No one will be able to get in or out. No one will bother to save the people trapped inside.

At least they were smart enough to regulate the number of people allowed in at a time—it's not the entire population of Horallen trapped inside now. But people will die in there tonight…or a few days from now, depending on how long they can hold on.

I look at the key still in my hand. I can only take one piece out with me.

Raising a hand, I throw the key as hard as I can toward the collapsed pile of metal.

"Take it," I call to them before turning to walk to the tunnel leading to the main entrance of the cave.

Chapter 5
Aladdin

"SHE ALREADY KNOWS," KACPER HISSES. "WHY DO YOU think she sent you to me this morning?"

"She didn't tell me why you wanted to see me." I adjust the goggles on my head and smooth my vest to make sure it laid correctly.

"To give you a job, of course!" He rolls his eyes like I'm being a petulant child.

"She knew you would be sending me into the competition?"

"Of course." I doubt that. "You don't need to go see her before you enter the Cave; it's fine. You won't have time to see her after either—you'll need to be on your way with the race, but she already understands that. She'll be waiting for you once you've won."

"But—"

"We're already here, Aladdin," he huffs. "I've had enough of this. Get in line and stop speaking!"

Byron's proximity is an ever-present reminder that I can't do anything outside of my uncle's will, and the blond man shoves a hand against my back.

"Now, remember what I told you." Kacper drops his voice to a whisper, reminding me of how we're cheating. The other two men he's employed huddle behind us as we walk to the dwindling line to enter the Collection Cave. "Left. Follow every left possible until you reach the room from seven years ago. You must check every room there for the oil can—he doesn't know where it was buried, only the approximate time. He didn't tell us what it looks like, but it's there. You must bring it out."

He turns back to the men behind me. "You must also go to the left but stop at the third door. There is a key he hid—you must find it. Issac said it will make all the difference to taking control of the ship."

The man nods, confirming his mission buried somewhere deep inside the cavern where no other contestants would dare to go for fear of being lost forever in the darkest depths of the Collection Cavern.

Kacper eyes the third man. "You know what to do."

I'm guided into the line, Brodham and Ren behind me. I watch closely as the men slowly allow one contestant in at a time. They continually check their watches. Finally, I step to the front of the line.

"Any tips?" my uncle asks as he pays the entrance fee.

"No, sir." The guard doesn't look amused. Kacper flashes a copper and the man's eyes widen slightly. "I said I know nothing, sir."

His eyes flicker as Kacper pockets the money. I'm sure he's disappointed. He turns, glaring at me as he points me toward the wall for a photograph.

I purse my lips, smirking while trying to still look serious—when I win, everyone will see this photo, I imagine. My hair sweeps over my eye, leaving only one partially revealed—I don't bother to fix it.

The camera flashes, a small puff of smoke drifting away. I nod to the man working the contraption and turn toward the entrance.

The tunnel glows blue, a far cry from the yellow-gold glow of the streets of Horallen's industrial cities. It's a shame the girls can't see me now—they've always latched on to how blue my eyes are and I'm sure the blue lights are only intensifying my look.

The men warn me about being out in half an hour, but they have no idea the depths I must travel to retrieve the trinkets Kacper bribed Issac to tell us about. It's late afternoon, but I'm hoping to be out long before the sun sets.

Before moving to the left to follow my instructions, I peek at the right side, just in case Issac lied to Kacper for some reason. The entire tunnel is closed off, a massive landslide destroying the entrance. I nod to myself and hurry to the left.

Tunnel after tunnel flashes by and I notice all of the beautiful scrap metal people just threw away. Broken inventions lie everywhere, and I wish I could sit and tinker with them for a while to see what I could get to work.

Trails of blood guide my path. The main tunnels are devoid of metal and trash, making the blood easy to notice in the dirt. Much of it has been stepped on, leaving partially-bloody tracks all over. I try to avoid it as much as I can.

Inside the rooms and following tunnels, metal covers everything. In the closer paths, I can denote the tracks where machinery rolled in and out, moving piles from one place to the next to make room for more. The farther I go, the less evident it becomes, but I still catch sight of puddles of red everywhere.

I cringe when I notice a detached finger mixed in the metal. The severed part is clean-cut and I'm grateful on behalf of the former owner that it came off easily—it would have been much worse if it hadn't. My stomach drops, making me queasy at the thought of losing a finger in this place. None of us will be given medical help after this, so whoever that finger belonged to will now also have to contend with whatever infection they may get from the wound.

The farther I walk, the quieter it becomes. The hum of machines left running in tunnels blocked off to us where men are working fades into the background. Only the soft whir of ventilators against the walls that pump in air and keep things moving catch my attention—at least the officials were smart enough to listen to the workers when they demanded an air supply inside the cavern.

I think over how many people must have died in this place. Certainly, there were people trapped on the right side of the tunnel—I wonder how much Issac will be fined for causing an entire half of the Cave to become inoperable. I've heard stories about workers who died here, either from getting lost, being caught in landslides or from injuring themselves. Some even say that men have been sliced in half by sharp sheets of metal that slide when they weren't supposed to.

I'm actually shocked I haven't found any bones yet. A skull or two would definitely fit the décor theme here.

When I reach the far tunnels Kacper directed me too, the paths become so indistinguishable that I'm forced to crawl over piles. I test each step, taking my time. Considering my options, I scale each mountain at an angle, ensuring that anything loose I step on will shoot to the side and not at my other leg where it could slice into me —or *through* me.

The farther I go, the darker it seems. I can't tell, but I almost wonder if the lights are dimmer in the older areas because no one goes there anymore. Once I reach a certain point, the other competitors seem to vanish.

The men outside had said it was late and that most had passed through already. I'm sure tomorrow they'll see a new influx of competitors who realized the errors of their ways and will come begging for a chance to find something to help them inside the dangerous Cave.

Metal clinks against metal as I climb.

"You couldn't have picked something a little more helpful, Issac?" I mutter to myself. "A mansion maybe? We couldn't do this little scavenger hunt inside of the Hall or something?"

I lean back, testing my step as I crest a pile of metal. Footing secure, I begin my descent, grateful I was smart enough to bring work gloves and not just my fingerless ones. I wish I had been given time to retrieve my arm gear from home though.

My finger taps my tincture bottle on my hip holster as I bend, twisting around to make sure I'm holding something secure before moving my feet again. It would be easier to find a sheet of metal and ride it down the pile of things people threw away, but I have nothing to stop me from colliding into another pile of trash at the bottom.

Once I reach the ground—or what passes for ground —I look around, hoping to find something useful in the new room. A pair of scissors rests open. Several springs coil out of a pile of metal, one stretched and collapsed as if something fell on it and rolled off.

I pick up a screwdriver and attach it to a loop inside a pocket on my holster—they'll never know I didn't have it on me before. I examine a few nails, wondering if I can use them as a pick later, pocketing those too, this time in my cargo pants.

"A shattered clock," I say to myself. "Don't need that."

I toss it, cracking the glass even more. I duck at the sound. Sighing, I scale the next mountain of scrap metal and crawl down the other side slowly.

I'm sure Brodham and Ren have entered the Cave by now. I'm even more sure that Kacper must be outside, rocking on his heels and stroking his chin with an arm crossed over his chest as he waits agitatedly for our return.

It's likely that Brodham and Ren will exit before me, given their missions are closer to the entrance. At least, Brodham's is. I'm still not sure what Ren was assigned to retrieve, but I'm positive it's just as valuable.

Dropping down off a ledge, I risk injuring my ankle for the sake of speed. It nearly turns when I hit the ground, but I keep myself upright, avoiding any pain. Two steps later, by footing falters.

My arms shoot out to my side, steadying myself as the metal trinkets roll under my feet. Once I'm sure I'm stable, I look down—another screwdriver. I bend down to pick it up and throw it aside, carefully avoiding hitting anything but the ground a few yards away, but something else catches my eye as I move.

Reaching down again, I pick up a key. The main part of the key is silver, but a golden cog with a diamond sits in the center of the round, top piece. Off to the side, a small, bronze cog rests, attached by a thin bar to a slightly larger cog further down the key near the part that opens the lock. It looks as though, perhaps, the cog on the shaft fits with another cog on the lock, wherever it might be.

I turn it over, examining the backside. It's blank, save for a few markings. The lines curve and bend, forming a face of sorts, possibly an animal—a lion. The end of the key has a series of seven bars, all connected. Three sit on top, while four rest under it, forming a pattern at the ends that will fit inside whatever lock it goes to and open it.

My curiosity gets the better of me and I decide to take it with me as something to explore when I have some downtime later—it will give me something to do as I fall asleep while I'm without an actual bed during this competition.

I scale another dumped pile of metal pieces and drop down on the other side, searching the room for anything to keep my mind engaged while I'm trekking through the wasteland. I'd enjoying kicking some of this junk to get some energy out, but I don't want to cause anything to tip over and slide.

When I reach my final destination, I begin checking rooms, searching for the oil canister. It would have been nice if Issac had provided us with a picture of it, or at least a description. Instead, I'm forced to look for a container of unknown size, color, and shape in this mess. I hope it's small enough to loop on my holster, but chances are that it will be big enough that I have to lug it around with two hands—another reason Uncle likely assigned this particular job to me.

"What if it's inside a pile?" I ask no one in particular. My mother has taken to pointing out when I talk to myself, and I frown, realizing I'm doing it again. Usually, I shove my hands in my pockets and walk away, but I can't exactly leave myself behind.

I duck my head, flipping my hair out of my eyes. It's interesting how it usually only covers my right eye, leaving my left visible. I push the sleeves up on my arms, exposing the skin between where the gloves end and the fabric of my shirt begins.

The search is particularly uninteresting, but I pick my way around, moving from room to room. Three down, four to go.

Just as I'm about to leave, I see the spout of something

sticking out of a small pile that looks like it toppled its way off of one of the mountains. It's not big enough to fall on me, but there could still be hazards hiding inside, waiting to cut through me like my uncle's words.

Bracing one hand against the pile to stabilize it, I pull on the long spout. It doesn't budge the first few times, but slowly, I start to work it out. I take my time, being careful to move it only an inch at a time to keep everything from falling. Slowly but surely, I force it out of the pile of junk, only toppling a few pieces that ping off of other objects and eventually roll away.

Holding it up, I discover it's a watering can.

"Great," I mutter. "Just what I need. For all the trees I'm growing down here."

I doubt anything could grow in this dump anyway. I toss it away. Turning back to the pile, I investigate the hole I created by removing the watering can. Inside, a pipe blocks the way.

I could let it go; I could walk away and no harm would be done—there's likely nothing in there anyway, but I can't help myself. If I can push the pipe away from me, it might knock everything in the opposite direction.

Reaching in, I grab onto the horizontal bar. If I miscalculate, I could lose my arm.

The risk is what makes it worth doing.

I push, jolting the metal forward. It barely moves, but I throw my weight into it a second time, toppling it.

There, sitting in the pile of fallen metal is a canister. It's smaller than I pictured, yet if I were to attach it to my holster, it would reach nearly to my knee. It's long and skinny. The entire thing is dented and rusted, but it's there—an oil can.

Picking it up, I use my glove to brush of flakes of rusted metal. It has an inscription on the bottom, but otherwise, nothing else is remarkable about it. Still, it's the only oil can I've seen in this entire Cave. It has to be it.

Brushing it again, I try to remove the debris and rust on it to reveal the silver metal. It sounds empty as I move it around, and it's light enough that I'm sure there's nothing inside. I suppose we'll have to find oil for it if we're going to use it on the airship.

"What do you have there?"

I spin, finding Ren staring at me from atop a pile of trash. Somehow it looks fitting.

"I think I found it," I answer, holding up the mangled metal.

"Yeah? Let me see. Toss it up." He holds out his hands for the oil can. "You about ready to go?"

"Yeah," I reply, throwing him the metal. "Did you find…. What *were* you supposed to find?"

He catches the oil can with a loud clank. He moves it around as he examines it. "Really? *This* is what Kacper sent you after?"

Ren tips it over, holding the handle with two fingers. He tips his head as he inspects it. "What's your deal with Kacper anyway? He didn't seem thrilled with you when we left."

"He's my uncle," I inform him, certain Kacper already told him. He's likely here to keep an eye on me. "He wanted to give me a job."

"I see." Ren muses still focused on the can. "Well, I suppose it explains a few things."

He looks down at me finally.

"Like?" I ask.

"Like why he wants you dead."

Cold runs over me. *It's a trap.* This has all been a trap. Ren's mission was to kill me.

"Seems like you figured it out, kid." He tips his head. "I was supposed to make it painful, but it sounds like Kacper's just being a wooden spoon. I still have a job to do, mind you, but I'm not going to slice your hand off or run you through with any of this mess."

"Kacper doesn't have to know." I hold my hands up meekly. "I can just stay here for a while and sneak out once you're gone.

"He's watching. You have to die, Aladdin. Sorry."

"We can make a deal!" I'm not above begging.

"I have what you came here for. We're done. Sorry." He shrugs, then turns sideways and aims a long weapon at the far ceiling halfway between him and the entrance.

It strikes, creating a line for him to swing on—an escape.

Ren kicks the pile, starting the avalanche. I have no choice but to run. If I can make it to the far exit, I might be able to find a pocket between piles of metal to hide in while I pray the debris cascading down doesn't reach that far. It shouldn't unless it takes down other piles with it. There's no telling how far it could reach if it does.

It will. *Of course*, it will.

Ren disappears as I turn to run, avoiding the metal falling toward me. Images of Kacper flash through my mind as I indiscriminately pick my way around mountains of metal. It seems like the entire world is collapsing around me.

My emotions run through anger and sadness in short, quick sparks of energy as I nearly fall, catching myself with a gloved hand before propelling myself forward.

If I escape, I'll kill Kacper. He'll never touch my family again.

Falling metal gets ahead of me on one side as a pile crashes down, flipping sheets of metal in the air, crushing steel boxes, and crumpling everything in sight. My movements are frantic and my head darts from side to side as I look for any hope of survival.

The metal grates against other pieces in an ear-shattering cacophony of crushed objects, caving in and flattening out. I can't hear. I can't think. I can barely see.

The entrance is ahead, but there's no way I can reach it. My legs are giving out and metal is licking at my heels like a dog chasing after a man holding the only piece of food it's smelled in a week inside of his shoes. Metal slams against the backs of my feet, tripping me every few steps.

I yell, calling out. I don't know what I say—I think it's just gibberish at this point—every instinct inside of me screams to say something to someone that will remember my final words and pass on my message.

But I'm alone.

No one hears my cries. No one will know what became of me. I'm just another foolish boy who wandered into the Collection Cave to play a stupid game that got him killed, or worse, lost.

I catapult over more metal, trying to survive.

The crunching metal makes a horrific sound. It rattles in my brain, overwhelming my senses. I can't think, much less comprehend what is happening.

When I look behind me, all I see is a waterfall of metal about to rain down on me and wash me away. I pray it's quick and as painless as possible. I don't want to be sliced in half, dying in two pieces.

"Stop!" I beg. "Please, I'll do anything!"

It doesn't relent.

"Please, I'll do anything, just wait a minute. Just give me another minute." I find my words again. Tears stream down my face in utter terror. A man facing his death has many things to reckon with. "Please, I just want to see my mother again! Please!"

I trip, falling flat out on a sheet of metal. My hand grips something and as I pick myself up, I turn, flinging it at the incoming storm, hoping the simple act convinces it to turn back.

It's ridiculous to think it might work, but a desperate man does irrational things. I fling anything I can get my hands on at the metal hurdling toward me.

I make it through the entrance and dive around the corner, flattening myself against the wall. Throwing whatever I can snatch up at the wave rushing past me, I finally grab a sturdy sheet of metal that tips beside me, settling from its ride on the wave. I use it like a shield and huddle in the corner, scrunching myself up.

The sheet sways and objects beat against it. I offer it my weight, shouldering some of the blows to keep it upright. The metal tears past me, ripping and shredding everything not strong enough to withstand it.

My breath slows. My heart pounds in my chest as I struggle to keep the metal in place, but I've found peace. I close my eyes and lean against the metal—it's the only thing keeping me grounded to this earth—and I wait.

Everything is dark through my eyelids and I fall into the rhythm of listening to the metal rush by me. I focus on the air I'm breathing in. I center myself around the way I'm leaning against the metal that keeps creating new dents to pierce me with. I pretend I'm among the noise on the other side of my safety wall.

Eventually, the sheet curves in on top of me as heavy objects force it to bow its head. I sink down, still bracing myself—both for the impacts and for death.

When I wake up, it's dark. It's hard to breathe, but I can feel every limb and taste every bit of blood that has pooled in my mouth from where I bit my cheek. I spit it out.

The metal wall did its job, protecting me from the avalanche at the cost of its own life—no one can use it again. I push on it, trying to move things enough that I can slip out from the corner. Unable to move it, I try creating a bigger space around me, throwing one item at a time over the small crevasse between the sheet metal and the wall.

My hands scrape against things in the dark. I shudder each time I brush against something, reliving my trauma, but no one is here to see so I don't bother to hide it.

One object at a time, I throw them away. Some I have to force through. Some I have to mangle to force past the opening. I grab a wrench and throw it, listening to it clink farther away. It becomes a game, something to keep me sane. How far can I throw without seeing?

Next is a sprocket of some kind, followed by a bottle of some kind. Then I pick up a gravy boat that feels similar to the one we had back at my father's house before we lost it all. I have to manhandle it, turning several cogs on it to get it through the opening. My fingers trace it just before I let it go and it pathetically topples down the pile that has me buried. I sigh, listening to it clink. It makes a strange sound as it topples down the hill of junk holding my barrier in place.

I pick up a spring and add it to the pile outside.

"Glad that didn't catch me in the eye."

"I'd like to say that would make for a strange eye, but I've seen worse when men get it in their heads to be *unique.*"

I slam against the wall as the new voice fills the room.

"What?" the question is automatic, and I give myself a dirty look for speaking. This could be one of Kacper's men. But then, Ren closed off the room, so if it *was* Kacper's man, he would have had to have already been in the room.

My head spins.

Besides, Kacper trusted Ren to do the job—and he did what he was sent to do. Why check up on him?

But if it's not one of Kacper's men, who is this man? I

feel dizzy and raise a hand to my temple, trying to puzzle out the answer.

"Who are you?" Whether he's here to hurt me or not, he knows I'm here and can do as he pleases.

"Javed."

"What?" I ask, confused.

The metal on top of me starts to move, peeling back to reveal blue light. My hand shields me as I turn away from the brightness of the dim room.

"My name is Javed."

A hand reaches down to me. Now or later, it doesn't matter if he's going to kill me. If he doesn't mean to harm me, this could be my escape. I take it.

He helps me climb over the rubble and I realize just how bad the avalanche had been. The room is like a flat surface, covered in a single layer of metal that shortened the room by well over half. I could stand on the tall man's shoulders and touch the ceiling now.

Glancing over, I look closely at the man. He wears a long brocade jacket without sleeves over a black shirt. The design is sewn on in copper and bronze which stand out against the darkness of his shirt and the base of the jacket. One hand is wrapped in a glove similar to mine, but longer. The other seems to be made of metal extending up to his elbow, though I can't tell if it's a device he's wearing or if it's a replacement arm.

"What are you doing here?" I ask, taking in his top hat

and goggles. His beard is long and nearly matches the brown-tones on his jacket.

"You summoned me," he says matter-of-factly. He steps back, both hands on his wide hips. He's a giant—a man the width of three men and taller than even Byron.

"Summoned?"

He bends, picking up the gravy boat I threw earlier—at least I assume it's the same one. The man hands it to me.

But it's not a gravy boat like I pictured in the dark. The metal piece is covered in cogs of all shapes and sizes, working in an intricate pattern, all connected. I move one and they all spring to life.

"You summoned me," he repeats, his voice low. "You called me from the lamp."

An *oil lamp*.

"What are you?" I know before I ask.

"A genie," he says gently as if speaking to a child.

Issac knew. He sent me here for *this*—not that oil can Ren stole. That's why he didn't know where it was, and probably why he couldn't give us a description. He was searching for a genie—I bet this is the entire reason the competitors were sent to the Collection Cave.

"What is your name?" The genie smiles at me, crossing his arms jovially.

"Aladdin," I reply. "I was sent here to find you."

The genie's face falls. "Who sent you?" he whispers, clearly afraid of the answer.

"I was sent here to die," I preface my answer. "My uncle wanted to be rid of me and he had one of his men cause the collapse that has us blocked in here. He sent me in here to find an oil can—which I suppose means this." I hold it up. "Genie—"

"Javed," he corrects. "Who is your uncle?"

"I believe my uncle is working with a man called Issac Von Hinten. I don't know why he wanted you, but—"

"I know why." His voice is grave. He looks like he wants to run from me.

"We're trapped here; I can't give you to him anyway." I attempt to calm his fears. I have no intention of handing a genie over to either my uncle nor Issac.

"You can't anyway—you're my new master now. You must request your three wishes first, unless of course, the lamp is taken from you, but be careful—once you wish, it cannot be taken back."

"Maybe I should wish us out of here?" I say it like a question.

"I wouldn't." He shakes his head. "There's another way out. I've been trapped in here a long time. I can slip out every now and then, but unless I have a master, I can't move my own lamp, so I've been tethered here for the last few years."

"Well, you can explain it to me on the way. Show me

the path out, Javed, and we'll figure out the rest of this together. I have a feeling you're going to be impressed with Issac's plan." Then I mutter, "So am I."

"I imagine so, Master."

"Aladdin," I correct, smiling.

I've either hit my head so hard that I've lost it, or I just met my savior.

Chapter 6
Cyra

Issac will make an announcement sometime overnight. He'll send it through whispers on the streets, confirming it with propaganda he'll have tacked up along the halls and walls of Horallen. Our job is to guess where he's sending us so that we're closest to that location when the announcement trickles out so we can beat the others there.

Last year, he had us running all around the city. This year, I intend to conserve my energy. After all, it's not like it's an actual competition that we have to complete tasks during. The entire object is to get to the airship first and get away. He's just sending us after clues.

If it's like last year, Issac will send them to one end of Horallen and then force them to run to the other. If I skip a few steps and jump back in somewhere in the middle, it won't matter. Wherever he sends us first, I'll go in the opposite direction and catch them as they attempt to fly by me.

The night is cold. I can see my breath as I sigh. I tuck myself under cardboard, wrapping faded newspaper around me in the corner under the stationary fire escape. In the upper echelons of Horallen, people don't want unsightly, squeaking fire escapes. Theirs are wrapped in brass and steel, forming a garland of cog-flowers that wraps and cascades down the railings. It's a *part* of their homes, not merely a mandate.

The garden box blocks me from view, keeping me concealed from the street. The owners have no reason to be out at this time of night, but most would understand if I explained I was a part of the hunt for the Stourbridge. Some might even allow me to stay.

I shift, tucking my head under the collapsed box. Having lived in a bed since my time in the competition last year, I find myself regretting the decision to face the cold night.

Sleep comes quickly, knowing I'm relatively safe in my little corner as I hide from the world and await my victory…again.

A few hours later, I awaken of my own accord, though it's still dark out. I climb out of my corner as the sun just starts to peek up somewhere over the horizon, offering a sliver of light once I'm no longer next to the garden box.

I adjust my cape and veil, ensuring no one can note my identity. I pop open the pocket on the vambrace I'm wearing around my forearm and fish out a small clip to help hold my hair back. I poke it in, banishing my overly-long bangs from falling in front of my face.

It's quiet in the streets as I move. I decide to head toward the Industrial District, hoping to find a place to hide out in a warehouse there or meet one of my contacts. I may not know much about Issac, but if I were in his place, I'd want to put on a good show. I'd test them first, sending them to one of the harsher cities before moving on to the factories, and ending with a chaotic run through the main city for all the officials to watch the spectacle.

Last year, Issac and the officials wanted a show. If Issac is trying to show off now that it's in his own hands, I'm sure he's even more adamant about parading us by the people he left behind when he took his game back.

Bridges will be burned this year. I'll happily be the match.

I made friends last year. I made those friends promises...which I kept. I should pay them a visit and keep them on my side. Should I win, I have more to offer this time.

It takes an hour's walk, and several rides under transportation vehicles the drivers didn't know they were giving to me to reach the industrial district, making me wish I had taken the train instead. Smoke plumes in the air and everything smells.

Here, the streets are encrusted with cogs of different shapes, sizes, and colors that help denote where workers should go. Frequently, they're sent to different factories to perform different—or the same—jobs, and explaining directions takes too much time. Instead, they are directed to follow a path in the ground to reach their destination.

Simon is at the end of the path with the brass cogs with short, square edges. They're my least favorite of all of the types of cogs, but it's an easy way to remember. I follow the path, winding down the streets.

The building is tall and made of brick. Outside, tall poles of black metal arch into lamp hooks outside of the building. I still don't know what happens inside or what job Simon does, but if he's still here, it will be a place of rest for me where I can scout the other players.

"We don't like your kind here," a man calls to me. He pulls a pipe away from his mouth.

"Come now, Taren. Be kind to the lady. I know you don't see them often but be a gentleman." Simon rounds the corner, flicking something on the ground casually. "Let's see what the lady wants first."

"How generous of you, Simon," I shout, strolling toward him. His eyes grow wide as he recognizes my voice.

"Well, see now!" He slaps Taren with the back of his hand, making the man grunt. "I knew we could trust the pretty lady."

"You can't tell if she's pretty or not—you can't see *anything*."

"Don't insult the lady's wardrobe, you shabbaroon." He bows to me grandly. "I was wondering if I'd see you again, my love."

He holds a hand out to me and waits for me to approach. Simon nods, in his own way confirming that he hasn't mentioned me to his coworkers, though I've assumed as much from his friend's reaction.

I allow him to lead me around the side of the building where he had just appeared from, putting distance between us and Taren. The goggles over his eyes reflect the sun that's just starting to come up over my shoulder as he turns to face me.

He nods, sending his black braids to fall over his chest from one side of the giant collar he wears as part of his coat. The same as last year, a brown, leather holster sits on his belt, holding his teacup and saucer in place. He dabs his mesh strainer that looks like a spoon with a closed circle at the end in the air, his loose-leaf tea in a vial on his hip. Simon purses his lips at me and takes stock of my vastly different outfit.

"Fancy some tea?" he asks, not commenting on my wardrobe.

"Are you going to let me in, Simon?"

"We're not supposed to help you, you know." He raises an eyebrow. "It's part of the rules."

"You were pleased to break the rules last year."

He places a hand over his chest, feigning shock. "For a lovely lady like yourself, a man is willing to break a few rules, Cyra, but I don't actually know anything that can help you."

"You didn't last year, either." I mimic him as he crosses an arm across his chest to grab his elbow. Tucking his head down, he hooks the tea strainer back in his holster. "But then, *suddenly*, you knew a *great deal*, didn't you, Simon."

"For the lady, a man finds out." He reaches out, grabbing my elbow to spin me as we continue our walk toward the back of the building. "Now, why are you here? I thought you were banned from the competition."

His top hat swivels on his head as he turns to glance at me, arm still looped through mine. I tuck myself in close to him, glad to be near him again. Simon has always had a way of lifting my spirits with his strange mannerisms.

"I can't play for the same benefactor, Simon. I'm free-lancing."

His eyebrows shoot up in delight. "*Well*," he drawls. "Our girl grew a spine. Saucy."

"Oh, I'm still playing by a code, Simon. It's just that this time, instead of *having* a benefactor, I *am* the benefactor."

"To whom?" He nearly giggles his words. Simon leans toward me, tapping his fingers together gleefully. He's only slightly taller than me but the hat makes me feel like he's towering over me.

"Telling you wouldn't be any fun, Simon."

"Oh, indeed not. Indeed not." He plays along. "So, enlighten me… Where am I to hide you?"

"Near the boiler room. I need to warm up."

Simon turns to me, frowning before clasping my hand between his, our arms still looped together. "Oh, my dear, yes, we need to thaw you out. Come, come. To the boiler room it is."

I follow him inside and he guides me down the some-what-familiar halls of the factory. He moves as if he's unconcerned about anyone seeing us, but I know he's too keen to allow us to be noticed. I saw what he was capable of last year.

"There you go, my dear." He points to a chair he dragged out from the corner once we arrive. "Food? Information? Both?"

"Both," I confirm. He pauses while I explain my theory of how Issac is working the competition.

"Very interesting indeed. I wonder what dear old Von Hinten is up to." Simon taps his coarse goatee, which is surprisingly red, unlike his braids. "I'll return."

Spinning promptly on his heels, he retreats, leaving me alone. I take a deep breath, closing my eyes before sinking back against the chair that clearly once belonged to a table set. The armrests are covered in intricate carvings, though I don't bother to inspect them.

The warmth seeps into my skin, refreshing me. I wasn't made for cold nights.

It isn't more than twenty minutes before Simon returns. He tsks at me for not carrying my own teacup, producing one. Slipping behind one of the energy-generating machines, he produces a tea kettle and sets it nearby to boil. "Ready in a moment, love.

"Now, about your race. Who are you working with?" He flounces over, pulling up another chair and takes a seat, flipping his coattails out of the way as he does. Leaning forward, Simon rests his elbows on his knees, and his chin in his hands.

"You, so far."

"And you're hedging your bets that Issac is going to play the way you described and send everyone on a run about town?"

"I am."

"I see." He leans closer, observing me. Then, he leaps out of his seat to check the kettle. "Not yet, I'm afraid. I always get antsy when a good cup of tea is involved, you see."

"I'm aware, Simon." I raise an eyebrow at him as he walks back and hovers by his seat. "Now, my friend, tell me what you learned."

"It seems you're correct, love. Issac has them running the length of the city, but a tip has told me you'd do best to move to the outskirts of the Hall."

I don't ask him how much the tip had cost him—he knows I'll pay him back later. I'm sure it was pricey.

"A man who knows a man, of course," he says by way of explanation. I don't need to know his source and he doesn't want me to—his ways of getting information are what make him useful to me…and others. "Do you know where you wish to go?"

"I know enough about the Market to get by, thank you, Simon. Perhaps I'll even pay Issac a visit while I'm there—he can't very well turn away his former victor."

"*Still* the victor dear, at least until someone else takes your place." He shakes a finger at me, smiling. "Act like the victor you are, and you'll be treated as such."

The kettle whistles, enticing him to his feet again. He brings it over, pouring water in the cup I hold out to him. From under his coat, he pulls a second strainer and offers it to me. We talk through my plan as it steeps. When I taste it, it has floral notes to it.

"Time to get back." He finally stands, dropping his voice to its normal pitch—he's concerned for me enough to leave the personality behind. "Will you be okay?"

"I'll be fine, thank you, Simon. I appreciate your help."

"Come back anytime, love. And take this." He reaches back under his coat to his hip. "It's a monocle. Strap it on like this, and then flip the levers for different magnifications. Perhaps it will come in use when the time comes for that wrench."

He quickly demonstrates, flipping the levers and then hands it to me. I pat his upper arm in thanks. "See you soon, Simon."

"I'll be watching, love."

He ducks his head and slips out of the room, leaving me to find my own way out. I finish my tea and leave the cup and saucer on the chair for him to collect later.

I nearly slam into a man wearing a gas mask as I try to slink across the bridge to the market place. It's decidedly less crowded than I thought it would be. A few school children wander around, and a few competitors who have no idea how the game works and are flailing about trying to guess where they're supposed to be for the next announcement.

Rich children should not be allowed to play games until someone has educated them. They bumble about, trying to buy clues off of merchants who are only too happy to sell them falsities.

"What can I get you, honey?" a woman asks, leaning over from her table watching me reel back from the man. Her hair is pulled back and she wears a kerchief around her neck that buttons to her chin and topples back over on itself. Instead of food, the entrepreneur has a table littered with tools. Wrenches, knives, guns, pliers fill the flat surface. She twirls a tincture bottle in her fingers.

I hadn't intended on buying anything this early in the competition, but I stop to seriously look at her wares.

"How many of these have you sold?" I laugh, holding up a piece designed with so many flaws that it would break after the first use, if not before.

She raises a satisfied eyebrow to me as if to say *cheers*. "Enough." Her smirk makes me grin in return, though she can't see it beyond my scarf.

"And what *does* work here?" I ask, browsing again.

"Most of it." She stops as I give her a knowing look, correcting herself. "Some of it."

"How much would it cost to dump all of the good into the waterfall?" I question. It might be worth it to do a little preemptive sabotage.

She laughs, mocking me. I pull out a high-end copper, sobering her. She considers my offer for a moment.

"And this." My hand darts out, taking up a set of pliers I had been eyeing.

She finally nods, holding out her hand.

"Tools first," I instruct, pulling my coin back. She frowns—she had intended on cheating me. I nod to the waterfall.

Reluctantly, she begins gathering the pieces that would actually work and places them in a box. I stand by her table, guarding the broken materials as she makes her way to the waterfall. She stands aside, showing me she's dumped them all into the rushing water. Turning the box upside down, she proves nothing is left inside.

I had watched carefully as she walked, making sure she didn't pocket anything I had purchased. When she returns to the table, she drops the box and holds out her hand.

"Not bad for a day's work," she murmurs, admiring the copper.

"Yes, and now all you have to do is sell that junk to the competitors who come by. You'll have even more money in your pocket."

"This is true." She pockets the copper. "How did you come about this?"

"Does it matter?" I challenge. "If it *does*, I should *also* have to ask how you happened upon all *these* lovelies."

I point to the broken tools pretending to be gadgets that will turn the tides of the game in competitor's favors.

"Fair point," she adds. "It was nice doing business with you. Hope to see you around again."

"Not during this race," I reply. "Make sure you don't sell anything else useful for the duration and there's another copper in it for you after. I'll know how to find you."

She appraises me, looking excited at the chance for another high-end coin. She nods.

"And I'll know if you lied and sold it anyway," I add. "I have eyes everywhere, my friend."

Her face drops a little, but she stays composed. "All right."

"All right," I repeat. "Enjoy your day. Best of luck on your sales."

I wave the pliers, moving them to my temple in a mock-salute before swerving away. I hadn't wanted to waste my money but keeping her from helping others was too good of an opportunity to pass up. She'll understand when she discovers who I am after this is all over.

Contemplating what to do next, I continue to stroll forward, almost wishing I had a parasol with me. I could try to approach Issac, but do I really want to give myself away so early? And worse, would he tell the Governor where to find me.

Oh! The Governor.

I had forgotten about him this morning. He's surely realized I'm gone by now. He's likely scouring Horallen looking for me. His men won't find me dressed like this, but I'm sure I've caused him quite a bit of panic despite the note I left.

One day he'll understand. I feel bad for concerning him, though.

The platform in front of the Hall seems quiet. It's strange to think I stood there only yesterday with Issac, the Governor, and the officials. Everything feels so different today.

I turn to walk away but slam right into a man's stomach.

Apparently, Issac has found me.

Chapter 7
Aladdin

"HOW DID YOU FIND THAT AGAIN?" I ASK AS WE STEP OUT into the daylight.

"I had time to wander," Javed replies.

"I thought you couldn't leave your lamp." I wait as he closes over the secret entrance at the back of the mountain.

"There are other ways of exploring, my new friend. A genie can see many things, even while tethered to a lamp, even while under the care of a new master."

His coat sways behind him as he walks, leading the way. The genie's lamp bumps against the front of my leg as I walk, ensuring me it's still strapped to my belt.

"Have you considered your wishes yet?"

"No, but this is the fourth time you've asked me since

we left the avalanche," I grumble at him, quietly. "Aren't you the one who told me I had to be mindful of my wishes?"

"I'm required to ask, friend." *Great.*

"I'll think about it," I relent. "But thank you for getting us out of that cave."

"I've been wanting to leave for seven years, Master. Thank *you* for allowing me passage." He turns to look over his shoulder, bowing his head to me respectfully.

I grin involuntarily as he turns back around. No one has done that to me before.

"What is this competition you mentioned?" he asks, continuing the conversation.

"We're on the hunt for an airship. Last year, Von Hinten created a ship called the Empress which Horallen's officials bought as a showpiece to turn into a prize for some game.

"This year, Issac took back control and brought in an even bigger ship—the Stourbridge—and has coerced Horallen to play. I'm assuming this is more about *you* than me though." He cringes as he hears the word *Stourbridge.*

"I would imagine so, Master," the genie agrees. "Issac has been trying to find me for a long time."

"Why?" I have a million questions for him, but that seems to be the most pressing.

"I have answers he wants," Javed says slowly. "And

magic. A man like him could do well for himself if he had my magic."

"I'm sure my uncle doesn't know about this, or he would have double-crossed Issac for sure." *And he wouldn't have needed to kill me.*

"I do not know, Master."

"Javed?" I pause. "Do you really live in the lamp?"

"Do you need me to show you how I enter it again, friend?" He laughs at me.

"No." I was still shocked from the last time he showed me. I was terrified he wouldn't come back out or that it had all been a dream. "I prefer you stay here. But, Javed, why aren't you more nervous around me knowing I have control of you?"

"Ah, my friend, a genie can tell what is in your soul. I knew from the moment I pulled you out of that pit that you would not threaten me. You'll bide your time, make your wishes, and we'll go our separate ways, but I have no need to fear being mistreated. You have a greater purpose in this." He knows something he's not saying… I'll get it out of him at some point.

Grass covers the dirt we walk on. It's unusual to see grass growing outside of designated areas, but it's not uncomfortable to walk on, so I don't complain.

"Can you read everyone like that?"

"No, Master. But there is a special connection between Genie and Master. Should I need, I can know your heart. It helps me to illuminate your wishes to you."

"You're going to help me make my wishes?" I ask, utterly astounded.

Javed ducks under a wire hanging from two posts outside of the mountain that mark of sections for machinery. "I do not help everyone," he admits. "I leave some to suffer from their own devices.

"But those like *you* I chose to help. Three is a finite number and each wish has the potential to do more than you might imagine, young lad. I will help you because I feel as though you will make wiser decisions than most."

I mull over his words as we continue. We avoid the Cave entrance, agreeing that there's no need for the people to see either of us and know we got out another way, especially since Kacper is careful and will be keeping an eye out for me despite Ren's assurance of my death.

I decide to avoid my home and the Hall, leaving the industrial district, the outskirts, and a few other places for us to hide. I need information though, and I'm sure by now, Issac has released clues on the next location to go, meaning we need to find a town that gossips more than it watches.

Along the way, I fill Javed in on what's changed over the last few years on Horallen, and he explains that he was only in Horallen for few years before being trapped inside of the Collection Cave. He's quiet about his past, but I resolve myself to learn more later.

I'm exhausted by the time we see the town in the distance. I haven't slept since my brief blackout inside of the Cave, and before that, it hadn't been since the night before. My eyes are heavy and I find myself blinking to keep focus.

"Are you all right, Master?" Javed places a hand on my elbow to steady me as I sway.

"I think I should sit," I reply.

"That might be wise." He flicks his hand and conjures a chair next to me. My jaw drops open.

"It was a kindness, not a wish, Master."

"I—" I didn't know what to say. I hadn't considered that he took that as a wish, but mostly I was just stunned that a chair had appeared out of nowhere.

I let him guide me into sitting.

"So," I stammer, pausing. "What else can you do? Can you create more things just to be nice?"

I blink, realizing how that sounded. "Not that I'm asking you to give me a bunch of free stuff, of course, but—"

"You are confused," he says, bending down in front of me. The genie pats my knee. Behind him, another chair grows and he lifts himself up and back just enough to sit in it while still leaning toward me. "Yes, from time to time, I am permitted to create small things. Chairs are a good example.

"Should we be in a dire situation, I can conjure a limited amount of food for you. I can create small things like a tac to put paper on a board if you don't have one. I can create—"

"Tools?" I interject. "Should I need tools to steal the Stourbridge, can you create those?"

"It depends upon the occasion and need, but yes, I can conjure some."

"What about locating the airship?" I ask, noticing people walking around the town ahead of us. They haven't noticed two men in chairs in the middle of the dead field yet. "You said you can see things without actually being there. Do you know where the airship is?"

I lean forward in my chair, eager for the answer. If the genie can find the ship, the competition will be over and I can rescue Mother from Kacper and get us both somewhere safe.

"Sadly, no, I do not have that information at this time."

"But you *could* at some point?" My fingers curl around the arm of the chair gently.

"Perhaps," he agrees. Reaching up, he touches the brim of his top hat. "Some of that is up to you, some of it is up to fate, and some of it is up to the lamp."

I sink back into the chair, pondering what that means for me.

"You'll figure it out, Master. You should rest now." My eyes grow heavy at his words as if the very thought had drugged me.

"They'll see us," I protest as he lifts a hand to hold me in place.

"Then I shall handle it. They don't know what I am, and I'll wake you if anything should happen so you can protect the lamp."

"What if Issac—?" My words fade a little with each syllable.

"In a field in the middle of nowhere?" he teases. "Rest, young Master. Just rest. When you wake, we'll find the Stourbridge—it's the key to everything."

True to his word, I find Javed staring at me as I wake. I startle, nearly falling out of the chair, and clutch my chest as he laughs. It's going to be an interesting experience having a genie.

My mind is foggy as I come out of my sleep, but something pulses in my mind—something Javed said—forcing me to figure it out before I can do anything else.

"Javed?"

"Yes, Master?" he replies, leaning back in his chair.

"You said that finding the Stourbridge was the key."

"I did, Master."

"What did you mean by that?"

"All I know, Master," he says softly, "is that your purpose is to find the Stourbridge. We must find the lion, for that is where your destiny awaits, Master. That, however, is all I have seen. We must find the airship."

Only the lion can win.

"I can't win the airship—if I do, my uncle gets it as my benefactor."

"There are other ways, Master." Javed turns, looking over his shoulder to the town. "We simply need to ensure you are there to find the Stourbridge. That is all I am privy to at this time."

I ponder the idea of having the Stourbridge to myself. What would it be like to own an airship worth millions? And how would that play into getting my mother away from Kacper?

"Time to listen for whispers, Master," he informs me. "A collection of men and women is growing in the streets; I think they have news."

I stand and the chair disappears. Magically, I feel refreshed. The sun is overhead, but to the side—mid-afternoon. I've been sleeping for at least two hours.

The town is cluttered with people who all have their own jobs instead of having to beg and fight for work each day. The homes are built with intricate designs and the metal work is far cleaner than what we have in my rundown alleyway, though it still doesn't measure up to the life I lived when my father was alive.

Looking around, if I saw the right target, it wouldn't be the worst place to steal a meal from. I wonder how thievery plays into the genie's code.

People glance up when they see Javed coming toward them. He lumbers several heads taller than me, swinging his arms as he walks. The genie nods to the people, greeting them.

"We should probably try to be less noticeable," I whisper harshly.

Javed looks at me for a moment before nodding. This time, he doesn't make eye contact with anyone, nor does he speak to them.

Around the corner, we find a congregation of townspeople gossiping about the competition. Neither top hats nor petticoats turn to engage with us as we walk near them.

"I've heard it's hidden under the waterfall," one man says. "Does anyone truly know what's down there?"

"For that matter, why don't they hide it under the gardens?" A woman mocks him, shaking her head. "I'm sure the flowers have some spare dirt they could hide the Stourbridge in!"

I step up to a vendor, pretending to look at rolls. Javed hovers behind me. The merchant glances up, gulping at the sight of the extremely tall man. He blinks, unable to tear his eyes away.

I scoop two rolls into my hand, holding them against my stomach until I'm sure no one saw.

"One please," I say, calling the man's attention away. He still doesn't look at me. "Sir?"

I pocket the rolls, asking again for the merchant's attention. I had intended on paying for a third, but if he wants to give me a reason to escape without parting with the coppers Kacper gave me, I won't argue.

"Fine. I don't need these anyway." I turn, making a show of leaving. Javed follows behind me without asking questions.

Finally, I ask, "Is it against your code, or something?"

"Is creatively providing for yourself against my code?" He laughs. "No, my friend, not for you. Others, perhaps, but not for you."

Javed had said he could see into me…I wonder if that has something to do with giving me a pass for something he otherwise might not have forgiven. What does this genie know that I don't know yet?

I reach into the pocket on the side of my pants right above my knee and pull out the food once we're far enough away. I offer one to Javed.

He takes it, pulling a piece off.

"Do you eat, Javed?"

"On occasion. I don't need it, but I still find pleasure

in the tastes of certain foods. Your willingness to share is appreciated, Master."

The genie has a lot of faith in me. If he weren't about to give me wishes, though, I doubt I would be so kind. He's bound by the lamp.

We mix among the crowd, looking for answers. I instruct Javed to walk several paces away and listen. I keep an eye on him, but he's assured me that should anything happen, all I need to do is turn the cogs on the oil lamp and he will be forced to return to me within two minutes.

"They say Von Hinten has hidden a code somewhere in the Industrial District," a man exclaims to a group of men wearing long coats and carrying pistols. "I say we storm the factories and force them to tell us where it is. If we share our information early on, we can get a lead before going our own ways."

"How are we supposed to solve a code?" one argues back.

The conversation devolves into mindless banter about which has the smaller brain. I loop around them to a group of teenage girls hanging off slightly older men.

"We can talk our way into the factory," the tall one says. "The girls can do it." The rest of his words fade as I move around them, too.

"If everyone is standing around talking about the Industrial District, we either need to go, or figure out how to skip to the next step," a woman informs someone who looks to be her sister. She nods back.

"So, it really *is* in the Industrial District, then?" I interject, leaning in. I look out from under my bangs and give the girls a half smile. The younger one nearly swoons on the spot, so I focus on her sister. "Hi."

"We're not working with you," the older girl says, clearly unimpressed.

"I wasn't asking you to. I was just making conversation." I turn, looking at the sister, and she melts in front of me. Her sister elbows her, but then she really looks at me. She bats her eyelashes as she takes in my face. "I just wanted to know your opinion, that's all."

I turn to walk away.

"Yes, we think it's true," the younger sister stammers. "And it wouldn't be the worst thing to work together… for a bit."

"Oh," I drawl, turning. "I wouldn't want to impose. But I appreciate your honesty. It's so refreshing to meet people like you lovely ladies."

I grin and they smile back. "Do you also have an opinion on where they might be leading us to *after* the factories?"

They falter, searching for an answer.

"Well, if you come up with anything and run into me again, I'd love to talk with you two beautiful women again." I take a step back. Reaching up, I grab my goggles and tip them as if I were wearing a hat. Before they can say anything else, I turn and stroll around a rather large group of people blocking the path. As soon as I'm out of their line of sight, I run for Javed.

"Time to go, Javed!" I grab his arm, spinning him away from the men he was conversing with. He stumbles for a moment but then keeps step. For someone his size, he has no trouble keeping up with me.

"Genies are not bound by gravity or the laws of this physical world," he says as if reading my mind. "I believe we need to go to the Industrial District."

"So do I."

We rush down the streets, earning glares from many of the women as we hurry around them. Several of them shout rude comments about us while turning to each other, but I block them out. Javed doesn't seem to notice.

"Here?" he asks, turning before I do, nearly cutting me off. Clearly, he remembers the streets from before, so I'm not sure why he's checking with me.

"If you know, Javed, then don't ask."

Along the walls of buildings drawings and sculptures of lions have emerged. The residents either want to celebrate the competition or they want to throw the competitors off. I'm sure at least some of the crude sketches are from others participating in the game.

"I haven't been through much of Horallen, Master. It is better to check and be sure."

"Have you been *here*?" I ask, arms pumping in the air beside me, but then lean back suddenly, slowing myself. I come to an almost complete stop, nearly losing my balance as a small boy darts across the entrance to the alleyway I'm about to exit. Javed appears to have leaped over the kid, though I can't be sure.

"No."

"Then how did—?"

"Intuition, friend. All genies have it; it goes along with that *knowing things* thing I mentioned earlier," he yells over his shoulder as I race behind him.

Javed is a puzzle.

I hurry to catch up with him and the genie slows a bit to wait for me. I envy his ability to run without tiring.

"If I wished for the ability to run without getting tired or slowing down, is that something you could do?" I ask when I catch up.

He scrunches up his face. "Yes?" He says it like a question. "But why would you wish for *that*? Your requests are limited and there's so many *other* things that could benefit you more."

"I suppose you have some suggestions?"

"In time, my friend." This time, he turns down an alley without asking first. I hadn't expected it and continue running straight for a moment before turning to look at him. My feet stay in place, but I lean with my back at a strange angle, arms still in the air.

"Where are you going?"

"Here, Master." He points, arms still raised as if we were running. Only one finger moves.

"But *this* is the way." I point in my direction.

"Yes, but *this* is the way we need," he counters, nodding in his direction.

Something snaps above my head—a carpet...a sheet... some husband's long underwear—as a housewife leans out the window and shakes it out. A rope squeaks as the person above me clips whatever it is to it and moves the clothing line along.

"No," I challenge. "I'm the one who knows Horallen, remember? We need to go this way."

"Friend," he addresses me, starting to rush his words. "I think it would be wise to go—"

It's too late, though. I hear the group of rowdy young men step into the alley before I turn. It's going to take some getting used to if I'm going to remember Javed can sense certain things before I can.

"Oh, he's *definitely* a competitor," the one man announces. His red hair gleams as it sticks out from under a cap. He taps the pistol on his hip.

"He must be here to pay his passage," his friend suggests, holding out a hand to gesture toward me.

I hold my ground as Javed steps up next to me. He mutters without moving his lips, "If a powerful genie tells you you're wrong, next time, listen."

"Any chance you can produce a couple of chairs to throw at them?" I mutter through one side of my lips.

"The only way chairs will appear here is if you lay them like a chicken, kid."

I look at him abruptly, startling the crew of boys walking toward us. Their feet hover in the air mid-step for a moment before walking swiftly toward us, not having heard Javed's sarcasm.

"Pay up and we *might* not beat you," the red-head addresses us.

"If he pays *high enough*, we won't beat him." The second-in-command turns to his boss to speak. Then he faces me. "If you went to the Cave, we want what you took."

"We're not a part of the game, and we haven't been to the Cave." I raise an eyebrow at them. "Though, my friend and I recently acquired a tip that we would be willing to part with...*for a price.*"

Folding my arms over my chest, I wait.

"Tell us what you know, and we won't leave you dead in the street, *boy.*" He uses that term as if I'm younger than him—we're definitely the same age.

"This is worth seven coppers at least," I shake my head.

"Eight." Javed elbows me, playing along.

One of the guys pulls a faux-jewel encrusted dagger out from under his jacket. The way the goggles over his eyes reflect the light makes him look a little insane.

"If you kill me, you'll never find out where the airship is," I remind them. I don't make a move, waiting patiently.

"There are others who will pay for our information," Javed says, tipping his head. A few of the boys look up and realize just how tall Javed is. They shrink back slightly.

"You know where the Stourbridge is?"

"I've heard rumors—"

"Credible rumors," Javed adds.

A few of the boys cross their arms, and I move at the same time, testing their resolve. One of us will break first, and if it's them, I either have to have a good lie or I need to run.

"But I'm only telling you if it's worth my time. There's a group of people waiting up there and any one of them could be my meal ticket. I'm not above selling it to as many people as possible, so if you start running now, you'll have a head start." I tap my foot once.

"You can't sell it if you're dead," the red-head counters.

"You can't kill him." I jab my thumb at Javed. "At least one of us will make a killing on this. You can benefit from it, or you can find the ship on your own."

He looks torn between his options, face twitching back and forth so much he almost looks like a rat searching for food in Mother's kitchen last month. I removed it for her, but I've been nervous more might return ever since.

"Tell us and we won't hurt you," he finally offers, stepping forward to try to intimidate me. As he moves, he lifts the mask that had been dangling to the side of his face, revealing a bronze, sculptured piece that covers his nose, upper lip, and jawline while still exposing his chin. It's shaped to look like a lion's nose and lip. He's taking Issac seriously, I see.

"My friend can take out all of your friends," I counter. "Eight coppers or I'm walking away."

"Five," he counters as I step to the side.

"Nine." I tip my head, raise an eyebrow, and wait.

"Six."

"Ten." This is ridiculous.

"Fine, I'll pay the eight." He seems nervous. *I like nervous.*

"No, you won't. You wasted my time, then you tried to haggle with me. I don't have time for this, and it seems like you're clearly not serious about finding the airship anyway, so I'll take my trade elsewhere."

"Fine!" he shouts as I start to leave, but no one makes a move to stop me. "Ten."

I pause, hovering in place for a moment before turning back. Slowly, I walk back over to him and size him up. Holding out a hand, I wait.

Ten coppers clink into my hand. I make a big show of inspecting each one to ensure their value. When I'm satisfied, I tuck them into one of the inner pockets of my vest.

"The airship is hidden in plain sight, my friends. My information tells me it's in the heart of the city, right in front of the officials."

"Someone would have seen—" a boy rushes to cut me off. I slice a hand through the air, silencing him mid-sentence.

"I've been told it's there, where no one would see it."

"Where—?"

I glare as the ringleader interrupts me. "Think. Where could Von Hinten hide an airship inside the Hall and Market areas? What would be a grand spectacle?" I pause for dramatic effect, then gesture grandly with my hand. "Behind the waterfall, of course. You actually have to pass through the waters and—"

"We'd die!"

"The water is far too strong to go through it—it's a suicide mission."

"And I'm sure Von Hinten intended it to be. Now you know why *I'm* not risking my life for it." I shrug. "But I'm sure you boys will figure it out."

I salute them and turn to walk away, calling *good luck* over my shoulder. The last I see of them, they're looking at each other, pondering how to make it past the tremendous falls.

"A ship like you say would never fit behind a waterfall…" Javed comments when we're far enough away.

"And no idiot would survive going through it," I reply. "They'll work on a solution for a while and then they'll get another tip and forget about it. No downside."

"It was a pretty creative lie, but it was also very bold, Master. They easily could have called you out for that."

"And if they had, Javed, I'm sure you would have helped get us out of there."

Claw marks wrap around the corner of a building as we step out onto another side street. People are getting far too literal with this lion nonsense.

"You know, I still feel pain, even if they can't hurt me." Javed looks annoyed, the skin around his eyes pulled tight.

"I didn't know that." I assumed that if Javed could run without tiring, he also didn't feel pain.

A bullet's crack erupts next to us. It pings off a nearby pole. Wrenching around, I see the boys have followed us, pistols in hand.

"Time to run."

Chapter 8

Cyra

"CAREFUL," ISSAC SNAPS, GLARING DOWN AT ME AS I GAPE up at him. I hate those ridiculous stilts he's constantly wearing. His body bounces slightly as the curved leg extensions take on the shock of the collision.

His eyes widen as he sees me. Bending down, he examines me as I realize my scarf has been knocked from around my face when I ran into him.

"Cyra?" he asks in surprise. After a moment, rage washes over him. "What are you doing here? You can't be involved in the competition! What is Alias trying to pull here?"

The hand holding his walking stick lurches out to the side as he attempts to talk with his hand, clearly forgetting he's holding the device that helps balance him on his extensions. One side of his coat flops back behind his arm, hanging open at an odd angle. In my peripheral vision, I can see the top of the metal binding on the stilt that is now revealed by the open coat, but I force myself to focus on the Proprietor of the competition.

"I'm competing as a private entity," I respond. I reach up to move my scarf to cover my face. "The Governor is sponsoring Levi this year. He knows he can't be my benefactor."

"And yet here you are…" He looks at me skeptically. "You're dressed differently too."

"Wouldn't you too, if you had won the previous year and knew everyone would try to take you out of play if they recognized you?"

He raises an eyebrow and rocks back on his leg extensions slightly. "A valid concern, I suppose. Still…no one knows you're here?"

"I hope not." I hold my ground, refusing to waver as he looms over me.

"And why are you *here* instead of playing the game? This isn't where I sent you."

"I didn't win last year by being stupid, sir. I'm trying to stay a step ahead."

"You think you know my plan for this?" He gawks at me.

"No, sir," I reply. People shuffle past us a few feet away, ignoring our interaction. "I think at some point, you'll be bringing them around to where they can put on a show for the officials. Why waste my time across Horallen if I'm just going to end up here anyway?"

"Wise."

"I was also hoping I might run into you." I offer him a smile. "I'm sure you can't tell me anything, but I thought if I *watched* you, I might learn something."

"You think I'm dumb enough to give something away?"

"I think," I challenge him, "that unless you totally remove yourself from the competition, at some point, you have to be involved. You'll go to a venue you're directing the competitors to, or you'll speak to someone who is delivering instructions for you that I can cut off before they announce it to everyone, or, if I'm incredibly lucky, you'll visit the Stourbridge and lead me right to her.

"I think," I continue, "that you're not one to be completely hands-off on your projects, and even for as careful as you are, I can learn something somewhere."

"And now that I've seen you?" He leans more weight onto his walking stick, teetering slightly on his stilts.

"I think you find me intriguing. I think perhaps all through this conversation you've been dropping hints for me, or that you will before this discussion is over. I think you want to see how smart I really am. You *want* me to win," I suggest. "I think you're going to see if I have what it takes to figure out your riddles."

I've set the bait. Now, I have to wait to see if Issac is going to take it.

He stares for a long time. I try to decode him as much as he tries to decipher me.

"You're right. I *do* want to see if you have what it takes to win, Cyra. But I have a different kind of deal for you." I perk up at his words. He has my full attention and I block out everything else around me. I'm safe while standing by the Proprietor anyway. "Have you gone to the Collection Cave yet?"

"Yes."

He frowns. "I see." Issac pauses. He adjusts the goggles on his head. "I'm glad to see you fared well. I'm sure you found something marvelous?"

He waits for me to pull it out, but I don't.

"Oh, Mr. Von Hinten. I know better than to show the game master what piece I collected from his board," I tease. I know full well that he could take my wrench out of play the moment he walks away from me.

"I can't tell you if you were right or not if you don't show me, Cyra." He tries to entice me into showing him. I won't give in.

Suddenly, my body lurches forward without my consent, nearly causing me to collide with Issac again. A girl with colorful hair, dangerous-looking boots, and a gun bigger than her arm turns to glare at me as if I was the one who slammed into her as I walked by.

"Come," Issac says, taking my shoulder.

He guides me to the end of the Hall building where a car is waiting for him. It's covered in brass cogs and pipes. The cab of the vehicle has a single, circular window on each side. The front is made entirely of a sheet of rectangular glass, save for the frame. Two lanterns hang from hooks off the roof in front of each side of the frame.

Issac walks over to the front of the running vehicle and leans back, sitting on the wheel that's tall enough that I would have to jump a little to reach the top of it. The back wheels are decidedly smaller.

He nods to his driver to step away before signaling me closer. I stand in front of him while he sits. "Now, why don't you show me?"

"I know better," I remind him.

"Fine." He rests the walking stick against the vehicle. "I have a different proposition for you, in that case. Leave the game and help me with something else."

"I need—" My protests are cut short.

"What? Money? I can give you money."

"No—"

"The fame?" He scoffs. "You're already famous, Cyra. The world knows your face."

"It's not about that," I jump in calmly. "I want the Stourbridge."

"To do what with?"

"I have a plan."

"You'll do better with my plan. I'll make you the richest person in Horallen."

"I'm already rich." He glares at me. "The Governor has provided me with everything I need. I'll inherit every-thing one day."

"I can make you rich *now*. You can afford your own Stourbridge and more. You can even help me run the competition next year if you like." He offers more and more to entice me.

Money isn't terrible. I could help the children if I had that kind of money. He takes my pause for curiosity.

"All you have to do is help me retrieve something from the Collection Cave."

"You expect me to go back there? I nearly died in there."

"I'll have it blocked off. No one will go in or out." He moves his hand out from his side, gesturing while he speaks. "Or I can send a team with you. It shouldn't be terrible to find one little oil can...especially since I have the location narrowed down to just a few rooms."

"You want me to find a *can*?" I look at him incred-ulously.

He nods slowly. "And if you do, you'll be richer than Alias."

"You're willing to pay me millions to retrieve an oil can from a dump?" Skepticism floods over me. "*Why?*"

"It has sentimental value to me." He adjusts the goggles on his head, messing up his hair strangely. "I'd like it back. I lost it several years ago."

"Why not hire a crew to find it?"

"The officials wouldn't allow me near it until I drove the competitors there." He shrugs. "I wasn't allowed in, but they couldn't stop me once I announced it was a part of the game. I forced their hand."

"You could have had us *all* scavenging for it," I lead, pushing up my sleeves.

"I don't want the officials to know what I'm doing. This piece has value to some of them too and I'd prefer to keep the acquisition quiet.

"Besides, what if one of the competitors found it and tried to use it against me to get more than we bargained for? I'd rather strike a deal with someone I know can get the job done properly. I'm willing to pay for your time and skills, Cyra. You'll be much better off partnering with me, than whatever your plan is. I can help you. Perhaps we can even come to another arrangement."

Something prickles at the back of my neck.

Don't do it, my inner thoughts whisper.

"And none of the people from the competition found

it?" I ask. I wish I could question him about the symbol I found on the wrench to see if I was correct, but I can't.

"No one emerged with it. I had a few men I trust watching for it among several things. That's why everything was logged when people left the Cave. A few of my hidden tokens of good faith were found though, I hear."

"I'm not going back into the Cave, Mr. Von Hinten. Sorry." I take a step back.

His smile fades. Issac lifts himself up off of his car, signaling his driver. "Perhaps I'll have to employ other ways of getting it back then. Good luck with the rest of the competition, Cyra. If you reconsider—and I think you might—come find me."

I have a terrible feeling that the competition might drive people back to the Cave at some point. I hope he remembers my plan about avoiding the majority of his game—I'd hate for others to be forced back into that death trap just to get me to go there for him.

The driver slips onto the front cushioned seat and settles onto the red velvet. He nods to me before putting it in gear and driving off, Issac refusing to look at me from inside the cab.

I step back, assessing my next move. Issac is gone. He didn't have time to warn anyone inside the Hall to watch for me. I could break into the small room they gave him for his own personal use last year after he sold the officials the Empress. I've been in the office before—right before I was paraded out for the Stourbridge announcement, in fact—and the Governor has brought me to the Hall a few times before that. I could probably break in without getting caught.

I don't know what information will be in there, but it's worth a shot. If I get caught, maybe I can claim that I'm running errands for the Governor.

Maybe.

I just have to make sure he's not there, though I have a feeling he will be out looking for me instead of working. I'll avoid his office at all costs.

I round the corner and take the stairs up to the Hall deck. Everything is quiet in the late afternoon. Not too much longer and the officials will be going home for the evening, which could give me the perfect chance to snoop.

The doors are open. I walk past the lobby where no one waits to greet the visitors—the Hall rarely gets any without an official acting as their escort inside. A small steam-powered robot waits at the end of each hallway. I bypass it without engaging and it does nothing to interact with me.

I take the first right. Issac's office is halfway down the hall, but unfortunately, several men stand just beyond it. I turn on my heels as if I accidentally turned too early, hoping they don't take notice of me. Once out of sight, I stand around the corner, back pressed against the wall. A mural made of copper pipes stares back at me on the opposite wall as I attempt to listen to the conversation.

"This is ridiculous. Issac never should have—"

"Did you really expect Von Hinten to listen to us?" a man interrupts angrily. "He never takes us into consideration."

"I still can't believe he took the game out of our hands." The voice is too deep not to be Mr. Rodemier, one of the Governor's co-chairs on the committee.

"Oh, believe it. Issac has an agenda." The first voice sounds unamused as if he's tangled with Issac before.

"And now we have to go through all of these precautions!" the second man audibly cringes as his hand smashes into the wall. That will teach him to talk with his hands.

"What do you care if we have to post extra guards here at night?" Mr. Rodemier questions.

"*We're* the ones who have to *pay* for those guards."

"You don't think we could just pull some of those men who congregate at the Market every morning—?"

"Do you honestly think they'd do a good job of monitoring every single door all night long?" the first man interrupts.

I jump as I hear someone in the foyer about to enter the hallway. Turning, I walk, acting like I'm supposed to be there. I take the next hall and wait until they pass to loop back. I knock my scarf and hood off, just in case anyone spots me—I'm less suspicious as Cyra than I am as the hooded girl.

I listen for the men before stepping into the hallway, pausing until I'm sure they're gone. Issac's office door is closed when I reach it—and, I'm sure, locked—but breaking in shouldn't be too hard.

From the top left pocket on my corset, I pull a hairpin out. Working it into the lock, I attempt to pop it. It takes longer than I'd like, but eventually, I force my way in.

Once the door is closed behind me, I begin my work.

"Ten minutes," I whisper, reminding myself I'm on a deadline. Half an hour isn't nearly enough time to search a man's entire office. I haven't found anything particularly useful yet.

There are some drawings and plans sitting on the table. He has extra stilts and accessories laying around. In fact, the entire office seems like it's just for show. I wonder if he does any work here at all. The desk drawers are empty, save for a random stapler, a few snacks, and a number of empty file folders.

The entire thing seems to be laid out to look impressive even though there's nothing of value inside. Perhaps he exclusively uses this for meetings. But why?

I wouldn't put it past Issac to use this as a show of

power. From what the Governor says, he's only here a few times a week at most, and he never invites anyone in if it's not for a short meeting. What is he hiding?

Despite finding nothing, I open every file as I sort through the cabinets and drawers. Getting down on the floor, I check under the desk, hoping a paper fell out somewhere.

Five minutes.

My hair flops in my face and I brush it back, annoyed that it's no longer cooperating. *Oh, for a warm shower!*

I run my hands along the bottom of the desk drawer, inching it out with my fingers to feel behind it. "Come on, come on," I whisper over and over as if cheering myself on.

Just as I'm about to sit up, my finger grazes against something. At first, I think I caught a sliver in my finger. Pulling it back, I discover it's a papercut. My skin starts to bubble with a faint line of red blood as I reach back up with my other hand. I wipe the cut on my pants, hoping they aren't too dirty—I should use Issac's personal washroom to rinse and clean it before I leave.

The paper is thicker than usual as I try to work it out of the crevice. It's been hidden well, obviously intentionally placed there.

When it finally comes free, I discover a picture of a woman. One side is faded a bit and greasy where the oils from someone's skin has damaged it over time. My guess is that Issac hid it here where he thought no one could find it, but instead of working it out to look at it each time, he simply reached under his desk and touched it.

She's much younger than Issac, at least in the photo. She obviously means something to him.

Time to go, my head sounds off as a man walks by the door outside. *It's closing time.*

Looking around quickly, I find a heavier stock of paper and hurriedly cut out the same square shape as the photo. I tuck the paper where the photograph had been, slipping the girl's portrait into one of my pockets.

If she means something to him, she might mean something to me too. I'm going to try to track her down —whether to help me or to leverage against Issac if he tries to push the Collection Cave mandate.

I resolve myself to think about her later, though. Escaping without being caught is more important. Resting my ear against the door, I try to judge if anyone is in the hallway.

Unsure, I gently push the door open a crack.

"You can do this, Cyra," I whisper to myself.

This time, I push the door open confidently. Last year, I snuck into several locations I wasn't allowed in for the competition, and in all but one of those, pretending I belonged was what prevented me from being caught. Simon's words echo in my head—act like the victor.

Funny *he* should be the one giving me that advice—he's the only one who caught me.

The foyer is filled with officials and a few guests preparing to leave. I could wait until they're gone so they don't notice me, but that might mean the *guards* would take notice.

I walk up to the group as they turn to the doors and follow them out. Surprisingly, no one says anything to me. They're all too absorbed in their own conversations to worry about anyone outside of their groups.

The doors open and we file out. I keep to the back of the line but make sure I'm not the last one out. I follow them down the steps and then turn right to where Issac's car had been waiting for him. I walk to the back of the Hall building without stopping.

Once out of sight, I lean against the building. I made it out without being caught.

Counting to thirty, I pop back out and take the stairs to the lower level, walking directly to the Market to find food for the evening while I planned my next move.

I step into the market place and look around at the vendors. The smell of food is overwhelming and my stomach grumbles loudly, begging for more than tea.

Just as I reach to pay a merchant for my meal, I'm slammed forward, toppling over the table.

JAVED'S EYES WIDEN AS HE REALIZES WE'RE BEING SHOT AT. I duck as the second shot rings out.

"*Ah!*" Javed grunts. He lets out a few short breaths. "I'm fine."

"He *hit* you?" My voice rises in pitch.

"Pain. Not damage," he reminds me. "We need to move."

I scramble around a corner, furious that Kacper had made me give him my pistol before entering the Cave.

"We need weapons," I inform Javed as if he doesn't know.

He shakes his leg as if the motion would toss off the pain the bullet caused. Apparently, it works because he keeps running.

"How about an escape instead?" Javed grins as he races ahead of me to the main street. "Hurry, friend."

I push harder, straining my muscles to keep up. Just as we burst out of the alleyway, Javed jumps into the air. He grabs on to the back of a tall vehicle with a long bed on the back. The genie reaches for me, grabbing my wrist.

I let him pull me up onto the steam-powered truck as it picks up speed. The boys take aim at us but don't bother to pull the triggers as the truck rounds the corner.

"You conjured a vehicle?" I demand answers, turning on Javed.

"I slowed the truck down so we could catch it, that's all. The man driving has no idea we've caught a ride."

"Where is this going?" I look around at the metal in the bed with us. I feel like we're back in the Collection Cave.

"Judging by the pipes and gears wrapped all around the sides, I'm guessing this is an official vehicle that collects unwanted materials for the Collection Cave." Apparently, I had guessed correctly.

I huff. "I'm not going back there." Crossing my arms, I realize I look like a petulant child. I don't let that stop me.

"I believe they're collecting things. We can get off at the next stop before they notice us."

He sits back, relaxing against the metal that's still in surprisingly good condition. It won't stay that way once it arrives at the dump site. I watch Javed for a minute as he closes his eyes. I lean back, finally, and rest against the metal leaning against the side of the truck.

Studying the mechanics of the system rigged to the back of the vehicle, I occupy my mind with trying to figure out how it works. My eyes trace over each cog and gear, following everything that connects them.

"Your time might be better spent pondering your wishes, Master." His eyes are still closed as he speaks to me, snapping me out of my invention-induced haze.

"What exactly am I supposed to be doing about these wishes. Javed?" I ask.

"You're supposed to ask for three wishes, and I'm supposed to grant them no matter the cost."

"Yes, but how do I know I've picked the right wishes?" I want to ask what else he knows about why I need to get to the Stourbridge, but one thing at a time.

"Well, you must keep in mind, Master," he replies, voice jumping as we hit a bump in the road, "that you also have to *make* your choices. You can't just let this go on forever because you're indecisive. You need to come up with a plan."

He's the one who keeps telling me *not* to use my wishes.

"Are you being like this on purpose?"

We slam into another bump in the road, this one shifting the metal around us.

"Yes."

I do a double take. "*Yes?*"

"You'll figure it out. In the meantime, we could talk over a few wish ideas, if you like," he suggests.

"I'd rather discuss where we're going," I reply, pursing my lips. I catch the final glimpse of the steam engine train between the buildings we're driving by. If I could catch it, I could get close to home without having to run. Of course, I'd be stowing away so that they didn't ticket me, but I've been known to ride on top of the trains a time or two.

I'm not going home though. I'm going to the Industrial District to follow a game I have no way of winning, despite the genie's insistence that I need to find it.

"We're going to the airship, are we not?" He tips his head to the side inquisitively.

"Why?" I act like I'm changing my mind, hoping for more information. "It's not like I can steal it. Even if I *did*, I'm still sponsored by Kacper. They'd give it to him."

"It doesn't have to be that way." His voice takes on a different tone as if he's offering me a contract where I sign my soul away for something shiny. "Wishes are a wonderful thing, Master."

Javed has yet to address me by my name. It's always *Master* if he's reminding me of something, and *Friend* when we're in public. I wonder if he realizes he's doing it.

"You're saying the Stourbridge could be *mine* if I wish it to be?"

"Well, you'll have to do some of the work, of course, but yes, there might be ways around that. I have reason to believe continuing the competition is in your best interest—how else will you save your mother from your uncle?"

I haven't told Javed about my mother yet, just that Kacper was trying to get rid of me.

"Looks like this is our stop," he announces before I can comment. The genie launches himself from the back of the truck as it slows.

I could crank the gears on the lamp and call him back, but if the truck is slowing down, that means we're likely to be caught anyway, and hitching a ride without permission is grounds for some pretty nasty retribution in Horallen, even during the competition. I'm more likely to be shot on sight and dumped in an alley than to have to go before a committee for a trial.

I let Javed guide me backward as I continue to stare at the intricate design of the truck we just jumped from, studying it. It stops in front of a house and begins to load the throw-aways by working a system of levers and pulleys, but before I can examine it more, Javed forces me around a corner.

"I see you're curious. My last mistress was too. It

didn't end well for her." His warning is dark and ominous, accentuated by the look on his face. Remorse? Regret? Fear?

Looking over my shoulder, he sucks in a deep breath and then vanishes. It takes a moment to register that he's no longer standing in front of me. A puff of smoke appears in his wake, quickly dissipating.

"Javed?" I call.

Just then, a car drives by. Two lanterns on the front swing as they slow around the curve. The car suddenly jerks to a stop in front of two men who are clearly competitors.

The men pause to look at the vehicle, awe washing over their faces as they see the man get out and walk toward them. Issac springs in their direction, still wearing his leg extensions.

No wonder Javed vanished.

I back up into the shadows created by the late afternoon sun, ensuring I stay out of the glare the mural some tagger built out of bars of metal on the wall across from me is creating. I'm too far away to hear and I can't risk getting closer—I don't know how much Kacper has told Issac about me. He could know my face at this point for all I know.

One step at a time, I creep back, trying not to draw attention. I could be in their direct line of view if any of them turned slightly. My hand scrapes along the wall behind me, helping me judge when I've reached the end of the building to duck behind it. I finally find it and sidestep around.

Letting out a breath, I turn to find an escape. The streets seem dangerous at this point—there's a fight further down the street between competitors where a girl is destroying the man she's with—but the fire escape a few feet ahead of me doesn't seem nearly as concerning. It's *familiar*.

I run, springing up to catch the collapsible platform and swing my legs up on it. As long as I don't run into any people or pass any windows where the curtains aren't drawn, I should be okay.

Making it up two flights, I decide I need to move over instead of just climbing up. The distance between the buildings isn't too far, so I run, kicking my feet up to the railing. Leaping off it, I fly toward the fire escape on the building next to me.

I grunt as my stomach slams into it, but the momentum flips me over the bar, dropping me down on the platform. Sitting upright, I run my fingers through my hair, knocking off my goggles. I remove them as if they had been the reason I nearly fell and hook them onto my holster.

The railing above me is higher than I expected, but I grab the bar and haul myself to my feet. "I hope you're appreciating this, *genie,*" I hiss at the lamp. I suddenly wonder if I damaged it in the jump.

Scooping it up, I look it over, but everything appears to be in working order, so I don't bother cranking it to summon Javed.

This time, I decide to make it to the roof before I leap again. I take the stairs up to the top of the building and assess both my jump and the possible fall. I've never been one to take so long to make a decision, but something about having Javed around is forcing me to think things through differently. *I don't like it.*

I run. It doesn't matter. Everyone thinks I'm dead. If I die here, it won't make any difference.

I focus on the way the air feels against my skin as I leave the building. It pushes my hair back and tears at my clothes until I slam into rock. My feet keep running with the momentum, but I'm back on a rooftop. I slow, turning to see where I had leaped from.

"So, I *can* do this."

The train whistle blows as if cheering me on. It's times like these that I wish it ran all around Horallen—if I could jump on it now, it would save me a lot of trouble. If only I were going in the opposite direction.

I take a deep breath and run again. Each time I throw myself off of a building, my feet continue to run as if they can keep me from falling. I don't try to stop them, eventually gaining the confidence to not stop at all between jumps—the less hesitation I have, the farther I can jump.

By the time I reach the end of the row of buildings, I'm exhausted and my heart is hammering in my chest. I wander to the edge of the roof, only to have my heart drop into my stomach when I realize there's no way I can jump down. I'll have to swing down the fire escape.

The fire escape isn't there though—at least not one that I can get to from the roof. The tenant has it blocked.

I can jump back to the previous building or I can find another way down. Knowing my body can't take another jump, I begin to search for an alternate route to the ground.

The lamp bumps against my leg as I pace, searching for an answer. *The lamp—of course!*

I crank the lever, turning the cogs until the lamp begins to shift. It's the first time I've seen Javed come out of his container and I wait for something mystical to happen. When nothing does, I turn the level again.

"What?" Javed's voice behind me startles me, making me jump in the air. I try to disguise it as a turn but he seems unimpressed. "What?"

"We're stuck."

"Stuck?" the genie repeats.

"On a roof." I point around us. "I can't get to the fire escape and there's no other way down."

"And what would you like me to do about that?" He crosses his arms, ruffling his jacket lapels.

I think about it a moment before answering. "The ability to fly."

"People can't fly."

"*You* can defy the laws of nature, but *I* can't fly?" I nearly shout. It seems I can't make any suggestion of a wish without being told no.

"I can only help with things of this natural world. Not even *I* fly, Master."

"This is ridiculous." I cross my arms in front of me. "I command you to get me down."

"A command is not a wish."

If I could push him off the roof, I would.

"Then what precisely do you suggest?" I glare at him, knowing it's not his fault I brought us up on a roof. "Can I just wish myself down?"

"Waste a wish on that? Hardly. You'll be done before the end of the day and then you'll never find the Stour-bridge and its secrets."

"Secrets?"

"You'll figure out a way down," he redirects, ignoring me. "Let me know when we're on the ground again."

He vanishes again, leaving me alone. Once I figure out how to get out of here, he and I are going to have a very long talk.

"*I probably shouldn't waste a wish on this.*" I roll my eyes, mocking him. If I could wish myself a mansion far away from Horallen for my mother and me, money for the rest of my life, and the ability to fly, I would. Or maybe I'd wish for my uncle to never be able to find us.

Actually, that's not a bad idea, I'm going to have to ask about that.

The side of the building appears to be covered in a mural, this one intentional. It's hard to tell while looking straight down, but I think there are enough elements that I can use it like a ladder.

I swallow hard and then lift myself up on the edge of the wall, dangling one foot over it. From here, I can see for several blocks. The Market isn't too far away. That might not be the worst place to hide for the night since I'm familiar with the area.

My foot comes down on the joint holding two angled bars together, but I hold my weight on the wall until I'm sure it will support me. I have one chance at this, and if I slip or if anything snaps, there's nothing to keep me up.

When it holds, I transfer my weight and grab onto two knobs that act as handholds before finding another place to stretch my other foot down to. I bounce between watching my hands and my feet as each finds a new place to grip onto one of the silver, bronze, or gold colored bars or joints.

I try to avoid dragging my chest against the gears meant for decoration. I brush against a few, spinning them enough to worry about catching my skin on them. Should I slip, I hope to catch one of the stationary bars instead of anything that moves. I keep my focus on my hands and feet and how I wished I had removed my vest before climbing—I don't want to ruin it by catching it on any of these gears.

Halfway down, I've determined that the metal pieces move when it rains, using the force of the water to the building's benefit. I'm sure it looks magical, should someone want to stand in the rain to see it.

The light shifts again, noticeably duller than when I first climbed up on the rooftops. The warmth leaves my back as I finish my slow climb off the building.

"Inventive," a voice says behind me. I turn to find a woman, her withered hand on her cane I can tell doubles as a sword.

"Fire escape was blocked." I shrug, offering her a half smile to test the waters. The train sounds in the background, alerting people to the end of the workday.

"Yes, well, those non-existent fires are true motivators, aren't they?" She raises her eyebrows in a challenge, matching my smirk. The woman reaches up to brush back her aged-white hair. "I recognize you, boy."

My blood runs cold and I reach for the lamp.

"I knew your father quite well; your grandmother too. You're the spitting image of your father. Remind me of your name?"

I search in the back of my mind for anything that would tell me who the woman before me is. Her brown dress with a lace front and bustle in back could belong to anyone in Horallen. If I knew her as a child, her hair might not have been as white, but if she was friends with my grandmother, it might have been aged when I was younger as well.

"You won't remember, child. You were young the few times we met—rambunctious, child, you were—but I saw you last year at Behnam's funeral. I was so sorry to hear of his passing."

I can only nod. I'm still not sure of the woman.

"Competing, I see?" Her smile twists down. "Working for your uncle, then?"

"No," I say, hurriedly. Her eyebrows shoot up again, clearly surprised.

"Good," she declares. "Kacper was never nice to my son while he was still alive, but your father was always kind to him. My son had troubles, you see, but your father treated him well anyway. Hold this." The woman strides over to me and shoves her cane sword at me.

Reaching down, she pulls up her skirt, revealing her tall boots, and she pulls out a pistol. Handing it to me, she switches sides, opening the pockets on her other boot. Her fingers disappear inside, coming out closed around something. She pulls the sword away from me and forces the contents of her hand into mine. When I open my fingers, I find bullets.

"To repay his kindness. Should you need anything on your journey…" She pauses, waiting for my name.

"Aladdin."

"Should you need anything on your journey, Aladdin, I should be happy to assist you." The old woman rattles off an address in the elite section of Horallen.

"Thank you…" I stumble over my words, also waiting for her to give me a name.

She nods. "Lady de Ghent. And now, I have a train to catch. I've heard whispers that there's something hidden near the Hall if you wish to bypass some of this messiness."

Lady de Ghent turns, walking away. I wonder for a moment if a gentleman would help her reach the train, but she cuts my thoughts off.

"Do I look like I need someone to escort me?" She spins, pointing the cane at me as if she had unsheathed it and was preparing for a duel. "Your uncle is lucky he was my friend's child, or else he would have lost a limb harassing my boy like that. Besides, I've been here before— it's not like I'm lost and wandering. I know Horallen better than you do, son of Behnam, and don't you forget it."

The woman chuckles, turning away again. "I'm here when you need me, boy."

I wait until she disappears around the corner as quickly as she appeared before attaching my new pistol to my holster. Cranking the lever on the oil lamp, I summon Javed.

"I knew you would figure it out." He grins at me. It fades the moment we hear Lady de Ghent raise her voice, warning someone off. "Should we assist?"

I don't answer. Javed follows behind me as I dart around the corner to find the white-haired woman holding her sword over her shoulder, ready to defend herself.

"You clearly have enough to spare, ma'am," one of the men says. Lady de Ghent sways, shifting her weight as she prepares for battle and reveals the red-headed man in the lion mask from before. Her sword hovers in the air above the redhead's arms, threatening him.

How did they get here so quickly?

He spies me the same time I see him.

Raising his pistol, he takes aim at me, shouting to his friend. His cries turn into shrieks of pain, though, as Lady Ghent brings her sword down on his arm. The pistol—still in his hand—drops to the pavement, firing a shot. The others gape at him for a moment before turning their weapons on the older woman.

Javed and I rush forward, shouting warnings to the men. I pull out the pistol Lady de Ghent gave me and hope it's already loaded as I lift my arm, catching it in my other hand to support it.

As I get closer, I notice Lady de Ghent has a solid white clock woven into the back of her hair that's piled on her head. The second-hand ticks away, but it's clearly not keeping with traditional time. Two ticks, a pause, two ticks, and another pause.

"Get back!" she shouts, threatening the others.

The red-head has collapsed onto his knees, blood pooling from the stub the Lady left on his arm. He clutches at it, still screaming in shock.

When they notice my gun, the men both turn to me, then panic, turning back to Lady de Ghent. Confused, they finally pick a side and each hold a weapon on one of us.

"If you shoot, so do I!" I caution them. The train calls in the distance. If Lady de Ghent is going to get home, she needs to get to the station before it pulls away, though, I imagine that's not her priority at the moment.

A vehicle screeches to a stop out on the main street. *"What is this?"* The door slams. One of the boys whips around, pointing the barrel of his pistol at the heart of Issac Von Hinten.

"Don't move!" I command Javed with a whisper. His back is to the Proprietor—from his viewpoint, the genie could look like anyone. I hope. Javed shrinks down, trying to make himself less noticeable as the boy jerks his gun away, realizing he's threatening the creator of the competition. Everyone lowers their weapons quickly.

Issac's nostrils flare as he glares at the boy. His gaze sweeps around to all of us, settling on the Lady. "Lady de Ghent?" he asks in shock. "What is going on here?"

The woman lowers her sword, but still grips it tightly should she need to swing it upright and cut into someone's throat. "These men are trying to rob me for your ridiculous game, Issac."

"Gun!" I shout as the red-head makes the horrifying move to pry his pistol out of his detached hand and raise it at us in retribution.

"Enough!" Issac shouts.

I push Javed just as the gun goes off, signaling him to run. He cuts in front of me and the bullet misses us both. I start to move toward Lady de Ghent to make sure she's all right, but Issac propels his walking stick into the air, slamming it into the red-headed boy.

Both of his friends take off after Javed as I hesitate to watch. Lady de Ghent starts shouting, glaring at me once while tucking a hand behind her back and motioning me to go. Issac seems to have the boy under control and is concerned enough with Lady de Ghent that he'll make sure she's safe, so I follow her direction and take off after Javed.

Just as I catch them in my view, they round a corner. I push myself to catch up, but I can't even attempt to shoot them, much less catch them if I'm an entire street behind them. Running faster, I ensure I don't lose them, but catching up seems an impossible task.

We cut around buildings and pull into alleyways as Javed leads us on an insane chase. The boys look like they're having trouble keeping up with the genie. I'm puffing as we race through the city.

The waterfalls come into view and I realize we're on the far side of the Market, leaving only the waterfall between us and the entrance to the trading area. If it weren't blocked, I'd be able to see the Hall.

I veer off on a side street, still following them when I slam into someone. "We've arrived," Javed says, appearing in front of me.

I cough, trying to catch my breath that the collision stole from me. The boys turn around ahead, doubling back.

"How did he—?"

"Just shoot them!" the other shouts, raising his pistol.

Javed pushes me this time and we backtrack, taking the street we had just run down.

"We need to get in a public place!" They can't kill us publicly—there are laws about that. It's closing time and there should be enough people around to dissuade them from shooting us.

A bullet punctures something metallic as we pull around the corner. I take the most direct path to the

Market, slithering along the streets behind the barrier on the back of the waterfalls.

"Inside!" I demand, not bothering to slow. "If Issac saw you, we can't let him find you here."

Javed hesitates, but he doesn't slow. "Won't they see?"

"They saw you disappear once," I remind him. "What's the difference now?"

"I was around a corner and vanished. This is right in front of them."

"So, we'll take a corner!" I shout, adrenaline feeding into my response. "Ready?"

I dart to the right, pushing into him. The second we're around the corner, he vanishes. I haven't thought far enough in advance and topple into the wall, scraping my arm against it as the human-barrier—*genie-barrier*—between me and the building disappears.

Inspecting my sleeve as I run, I'm grateful to discover the fabric is still intact, even though it's covered in black grime now. One last sprint and I'll be in public.

I pump my arms, forcing my legs forward. The men yell behind me, one of them directing the other not to shoot because they'd get banned from the competition. *Wise choice, boys.*

The Market is crowded with people. Merchants try to enchant officials into taking their wares home for their families. Officials mill about, conversing with their friends as they wait for their rides to arrive.

I indiscriminately run into the crowd, trying to blend in. Women shriek as I crash through their groups, while men lecture the competitors about proper etiquette in the Market. One tries to trip me with his cane, but I leap over it.

Stumbling on my landing, I propel myself forward as I crash into someone, flipping us both over the table. The boys cheer behind me, only feet away.

Chapter 10
Cyra

I DON'T KNOW HOW ISSAC FOUND ME, BUT HE SENT HIS men after me. I wasn't careful enough. I let my guard down once I made it to the Market, assuming I could walk away from breaking into the Hall without being caught. Somehow, he knows I stole from him.

The guard's weight is crushing, driving my shoulder into the pavement. Had it been my other side, my shoulder guard would have protected me a little. I can only hope it's uncomfortably jabbing into his face as he struggles on top of me.

The tables crashed with us, sending rolls and breads everywhere. I fight to get out from under the monster, but he's shifting too much to allow me to slip away.

His arms wrap around me, pushing himself up off of

the cog-covered street. Muttering, the man leaps to his feet, legs straddling me. I can't kick him from my angle, so I bring my knee up, slamming it into the back of his knee before he can move.

"Ow!" he yells, pitching forward.

I bring my other leg straight up, catching his backside as I force him to fall forward. He rolls, but I'm up on my feet before he can beat me to it.

Grabbing his arm, I hope to hurdle him back toward the crowd so I can make my escape, but he's prepared for me.

"What are you doing?" he shouts, grabbing my arms and spinning me like I am trying to do to him. I slip on a roll and he holds me upright, ice blue eyes glaring at me. "Stop it!"

He shakes me and I slap him across the face.

Behind me, men are shouting. The officials and some of the women protest the competition coming into the market place, but there are several distinct voices shouting threats at us. I have nothing to do with it, though—I don't know why they're involving me in this.

"They will kill us if we don't run now," the blue-eyed man announces. "You're a part of this now, we have to go."

"No." I try to wrench away, but he's strong enough to force me to stumble forward.

I drop down, scooping up a roll. He growls at me as I launch it at the side of his face.

"Let me go!" I protest.

He's too quick to stomp on his foot, and he's already seen through my act of dropping down to retrieve bread, but I throw myself down once more anyway, not wanting to reveal my pistol yet in case this goes farther than I'd like.

I toss the hard roll under his feet, nearly tripping him. He falters just as a shot rings out.

I whip around, but he pulls me low.

People scream behind us as someone runs toward us, weapon in hand.

"We have to run!"

This time, I listen.

I may not know this man, and he may even be after me, but right now, he's not the one with the gun pointed at the back of my head in a public place. He doesn't let go of my arm as he guides us through the streets, down to the place where men and women come to find work for the day.

It's darker at this end of the Market. I've never been here before—not even last year for the competition for the Empress. The sun is down enough that nothing reflects, leaving the place looking dull.

I'm amazed at the trivial things I'm focused on as two men chase us through the streets. Not having to make decisions about which direction we should take, my mind wanders enough that I have to force myself back to the task at hand—survival.

A shot rings out again and someone cries. I look back to see a guard has shot one of the boys in the leg, dropping him to the ground.

"One down," I inform the man I'm running with.

The second boy doesn't stop now that his partner has been taken out of play. His face fades from angry to scared as he looks for a place to hide. He quickly peels off on a side street as another shot rings out.

"He pulled away!" I shout, but the man doesn't slow.

"We can't let them catch us or they'll pull us from the competition. Keep running!"

He makes sense. I run with him, letting the buildings fly by as we exit the back end of the Market and turn into one of the slums behind it. A stench fills the air, like garbage no one has removed for months. The buildings are even worse than those in the slums I visit to feed Amany and her friends, though I have yet to see a burned-out building anywhere.

"Can you jump?" the man asks.

"What?" In the distance, I can still hear men running behind us, trying to catch us.

"We're jumping onto a fire escape; can you do that?" His words are hurried. He sounds scared.

"Yes!" I shout.

"Okay, up ahead, do you see it?" I nod. "Good, take the first one, I'll take the second."

We rapidly approach the fire escape and he rushes to continue. "Once you're up, climb to the roof and wait. I'll jump over to you once they pass and we'll figure out a plan from there. Now, go!"

He pushes me to give me a head start. I jump off of a wooden flower box that sits empty on the ground, dividing one property from the next. My hands catch the fire escape landing and it jerks under my movements, but I pull myself up.

I scramble as quietly as possible until the men enter the mouth of the street, searching for us. Freezing, I plaster myself against the wall halfway up the building. Holding my breath, I wait for them to approach, but quickly realize I haven't checked on the man I was with yet.

My head moves fast, whipping over to face him. He's a flight below me, but still high enough that the men haven't taken notice as they slow to look for us. He rests against the wall too, breathing heavily.

For the first time, I can assess him. A white dress shirt stands out against his black vest covered in pockets. A holster filled with too many gadgets to count rests against his hip. It sways as he breathes. His dark hair falls in front of his face as he intently watches the men below us. He's my age, if not just a little older.

Just then, he glances up at me. Grinning, he nods once before looking back to the men. Once they've left the street, the boy turns back to me and nods up.

Scaling the steps of the fire escape, I follow his plan to go to the roof. It's still bright enough out to see, but it won't be for long and I need to put some distance between me and the boy with the pistol—I noticed it on his hip as he turned to climb.

The roof is empty save for junk the owner clearly just tossed up here to be rid of instead of disposing of it properly. Before I can make it to the wall, the boy launches himself over. I hurry to him, helping to pull him up, my instincts taking over.

"Who are you?" I demand.

"You slapped me," he retorts.

"You abducted me." I raise my hand, prepared to hit him again, this time hard enough to send him toppling over the edge of the building.

"I saved you!" he counters, raising his voice. He sounds indignant like he can't believe I would challenge him.

"They weren't chasing me until *you* showed up." I point at his broad chest. My eyes dance over his outfit now that I can see it better. Surprisingly, it's the perfect cut for him. Shame he's also covered in dirt and grime.

"Fair point," he grumbles.

He studies my face, making me realize that I've yet again lost my scarf. I fumble to reattach it.

"Really?" he asks. "I've already seen it, so what does it matter?"

Just as I attach it, he jerks forward. "Wait!" He reaches for my scarf and takes it back down. I'm too shocked to step back as he raises and lowers it. He grins. "I know you."

He recognizes me. My heart slams into my chest.

"We met in the alley the other day."

The boy from the alley after I left Amany.

He hadn't hurt me then and he hasn't hurt me now. Maybe he's not a threat.

"And as I recall from the *uncovered* face," he continues, "you're not supposed to be in this competition, are you?"

He knows. *I was so close.*

"Going to try to kill me now?" I ask, preparing to push him. I try to circle around him to distract him.

"I imagine you have quite the story, Cyra." He raises an eyebrow flirtatiously. "But so do I. I won't tell who you are if you don't tell who I am. Deal?"

He holds his hand out to me to shake.

"For that to work, I'd have to know who you are." I fight to keep from crossing my arms over my chest—I need them free in case I have to fight.

"Why were you in the alley?"

"I wasn't, I was in the Market." I know that's not what

he's asking, but I don't like making this easy since he knows more about me than I know about him. I have no leverage—yet.

"You know that's not what I mean." He leans back against the edge of the wall as if he doesn't have a care in the world.

"You expect me to tell you more when you haven't told me a thing about yourself yet?" I reply. "Why were those men chasing you?"

"They were trying to rob an old lady and I intervened. I also had a bit of a run in with them earlier," he answers. The boy reaches up, running his fingers through his hair as he eyes me. *He really knows what he's doing.*

"They tried to shoot you for that?"

"Everyone is trying to kill everyone in this game when no one is looking. *You* most of all should be aware of that. I assume it's where the veil comes into play, right, Cyra?"

"Most people would want to take down the winner from last year. I have to be careful."

"You still think I'm trying to hurt you, princess?" He kicks one ankle over the other as he leans further back. "I'm not."

"I think it's time for us to go." I step away and walk to the adjoining edge. Looking over, I make sure the street is clear.

Slipping back onto the fire escape, I start to walk down.

"Oh, I wouldn't do that if I were you, princess." He follows me.

"Stop calling me that." I frown at him over my shoulder.

"Princess?" He scoffs. "It suits you. After all, you won last year, didn't you…doesn't that make you royal?"

"Won and beat you." I try to best him.

"*I* didn't compete last year," he says. "You don't know what I'm capable of."

"Other than dragging a girl into the run-down part of town?" I glide my hand to the side, hip following it to make a point as I gesture to the buildings that look like they might fall down. I take it back, this is worse than the city I came from. "Why didn't you play?"

"I wasn't available."

I turn around to face him, stopping. "What does that mean?"

"It means I had other engagements."

"Such as?" I narrow my eyes. Now or never. Either he tells me or he doesn't, in which case, I get out as fast as I can.

When he doesn't speak right away, I turn, taking the final flight of steps.

"My father died," he calls after me. "I didn't even know it happened until people started talking about it this year."

"An entire year and you didn't hear about the Empress?"

"I kept my head down." He shrugs. "Don't go that way."

"Excuse me?" I whirl around to face him. He's so condescending.

"You clearly aren't familiar with this area," he continues, mimicking me with a hand out to the side, moving his hip like I had. My eyes widen in annoyance, wrinkling the skin on my nose. "But I am. That way is danger. They don't like strangers around here. Our best bet is to go back."

"They're looking for us back there."

"We'll be fine. I do this all the time."

"You get chased by angry men all the time?"

"When my father died, my mother and I lost everything. I've learned a lot in the last year," he says. I don't bother to tell him I've been training for over five years for this, longer if you count my time on the streets. "Down there, there's only traps."

"Traps?" I don't believe him. I feel like he's trying to keep me here, but I'm not sure why.

"Traps. Vicious ones. And now that the competition is going, it's only going to be worse."

He's definitely trying to keep me here.

"What is your angle?" I put my hands on my hips. I'm done with the games.

"I think we should work together."

"Why?"

He walks over to the side of the building, picking up a small board someone left on the ground. Using the board, he touches it and the entire section of the wall moves as one, cogs and gears turning to force a piece of metal out that looks like an upper and lower jaw. It snaps the board, breaking off the end loudly. The boy looks back to me.

"I think you know things I don't know," he points out, "and I know things you don't. Working together will help us win."

"I'm not splitting the Stourbridge with you." I swallow, thinking about the board as he drops it on the ground.

"Fine. At least let me walk you out of here before we go our separate ways," he offers. "My mother didn't raise me to allow others to do things on their own when I could easily help them."

"You're in a race that's all about looking out for yourself and *suddenly you want to play the nice guy?*"

He motions for me to start walking. I watch him closely from the corner of my eye but he doesn't seem to be doing the same to me. He walks casually next to me—either he's not worried about me or he's a sociopath.

"Why were you in the alley?" he asks again. "I'm from there, but clearly you aren't."

"I was visiting someone. I was on my way back."

"I see. It's nice to have people, isn't it?"

"Wow," I drawl. "You just won't quit."

"Hear me out, Cyra—"

"Tell me your name and I might consider it."

He stops, looking at me. "Still haven't told you that, have I? It's Aladdin."

I exhale through my nose enough to make a noise, acknowledging his admission.

"Hear me out." He tries again. "They said only a lion could win. Lions aren't solo animals. They have a pride. I think that means we need to work together. People are just so caught up with the rules from last year that they aren't seeing that this is an entirely different picture we're looking at.

"Last year, the officials made the rules, so I hear. This year, Issac has a point to prove and an agenda to follow."

His gait is easy as he walks and he makes sure to stay at a pace I can easily keep up with, even though his legs are much longer than mine. The light continues to fade— it will be dark soon—but his leisurely pace suggests he doesn't mind.

"This is our stop, Cyra." He pauses at the end of the town. "I'm going this way. I know a place to stay for the evening. You're welcome to come with me. I think we could help each other out.

"I'm not in it for the airship." He takes a breath. "I just want enough money to move my mother far away from this place and make sure we're both taken care of. You can have the lion's share, as it were."

His logic makes sense. A lion does have his pride, but then, the females do all the work. But he's right—Issac is playing by different rules now.

"I'm going where it's warm."

I perk up at that. That alone might be worth saying yes to his offer. I can shoot him if he tries to get handsy with me.

My eyes drift down to the pistol on his holster, but that's not what I notice.

"What's that?" I ask, nodding to the cog-covered tarnished thing hanging in front of his leg.

"Oh, just an old oil lamp." He shrugs. "I found it in the Cave and thought it might be something I could use to see. Now, are you coming with me, *or...*?"

Oil? From the Cave?

If I look hard enough, I can work out the shape of a lion's face underneath the cogs—a symbol. Most people would miss it.

Issac said no one had brought an oil can out of the Collection Cave. Maybe they didn't know to look for an oil *lamp* instead. I wonder if this is what Issac is looking for.

If I can take it and trade it to Issac, I could probably leverage the information I need to get to the Stourbridge and steal it before anyone else even knows where to look.

If Aladdin is so keen on working with me, it might be easy enough to steal it from him.

"Where are we going?"

"Remember that old lady I told you about? She offered her place. It's in the elite sector—we can probably even get a shower if we want one."

I'm sold. "Lead the way."

# Chapter 11
Aladdin

THE WALK IS STRANGE. THE DWINDLING LIGHT DOESN'T help.

Cyra seems nervous around me. I suppose I would be too in her situation. The promise of a warm place to sleep and a shower certainly changed her mind though—it's so easy to woo girls with the promise of cleanliness.

I had anticipated that it would be harder to get her to trust me, but I'm not going to question it. I found the lion —I'll use her to my advantage. I don't mind working with her until the end and then I'll take the ship for myself.

When Cyra had reached up to brush her hair back under her hood, the lion bracelet jumped out at me—how could it not? The gold gleamed against the dark black leather.

Issac had said the lion was the key to taking the Stourbridge. He must be working with Cyra, or at least her benefactor, to keep the Stourbridge right where he wanted it while he used all of us to find the genie.

We're down the street from Lady de Ghent's address when I realize that if Issac is work with Cyra's benefactor, he might be working with her too. I have to find out if she's a pawn like I was to Kacper or if she's a part of this.

"Hey, did you go to the Cave?" I ask, pretending to make conversation.

"Yes." She's a woman of few words.

"What did you get?"

She eyes me before answering. "A wrench." She reveals it to me—it's oddly shaped. "I'm not sure what it's for yet, but it wasn't worth nearly dying for."

If she had been to the Cave, maybe she didn't know about Issac's quest. Why would he send her there knowing the danger if he had the rest of us already doing his dirty work?

"You nearly died?"

"Surprisingly, you're not the only one who nearly causes my death." Her face doesn't change while she speaks, but her eyes spark as she glances over at me, letting me know it was a joke. "Landslide."

"Right side?" I ask, surprised. She nods. "*You* caused

that? Well done. You made it more difficult for the rest of us."

"Yes, well, I have to keep you on your toes, I suppose." She almost smiles. "How much farther?"

"Around the corner." I nod ahead. I hope Lady de Ghent doesn't mind me taking her up on her offer so quickly.

The house is tall, with rounded angles all around. The silver is nearly a blue color in the glow of the moon. Outside, a garden made of fish tanks and floating flowers glistens as the wind ripples the top of the water in each container. Two poles made of pipe protrude on either side, with a series of off-shoots holding pressure gages and exposed bulbs to light the walk up the staircase.

Issac's car is nowhere to be seen, so if he brought her back, he must be gone now. Walking up to the house will be a risk, but it's now or never and I can't go back on the very first promise I made Cyra that I actually meant to keep. I chose not to fault myself for the promises I made that I intend to break.

I knock on the door once we reach it. After a moment, a small window slides back.

"What?" a voice demands.

"I'm here to see Lady de Ghent," I reply. The window slides shut, and I can hear feet shuffling away.

After a long moment, I knock again. "She invited us," I call.

"Did she?" Cyra whispers accusatorily.

"She did," I hiss back. Just as I'm about to knock again, the door opens, revealing a hallway grander than anything we had in my childhood home. Cyra doesn't look as impressed, though I suppose she wouldn't be having grown up in the Governor's mansion—he's one of the richest people in Horallen.

"I see you made it back safely." I greet Lady de Ghent with a smile.

"I see you didn't get shot." She nods in approval. "Come in."

The foyer is filled with several long, narrow tables covered in globes with metal rings around them. One is clear, the lines drawn on in ink. Another has a series of magnifying glasses attached for closer inspection of the dusty contraption.

Directly opposite of the door is a silver, metal elevator. It's shaped like a normal door, but it's made entirely of intricately designed metal swirls, leaving an opening in the middle and upper third to see out of. Behind it, a collapsible metal grate is attached to the car that moves, keeping occupants in place.

Lady de Ghent opens it and steps inside and closes it over behind us before pushing the button to move it. Upstairs, the room is filled with a golden light from several glowing lamps.

A metal table with a large fishbowl attached greets us,

forcing us to walk around it as we exit the elevator. Beyond it sits a long dining room table with a tall lamp as a centerpiece. It springs up like a table lamp, wide until the top where it sprouts into a chandelier, six arms branching out of it, holding upside down bulbs full of water and plants.

"This is a lovely home," Cyra says, her training kicking in. She wasn't that polite to me. Her posture changes as she strides around the room, examining the artwork and plant life.

"Do you know what else is lovely?" Lady de Ghent asks with a polite smile which she immediately drops along with her hands. "Knowing a person's name."

Cyra freezes in place, then turns slowly. Lady de Ghent marches over to her, looking closer.

"Cyra, ma'am."

"Ah," the Lady huffs her reply. "The Governor's daughter, is it? My husband used to work with Alias before he went to the bone orchard. Should you be out this evening?"

"The Governor doesn't know I'm competing." Her words are soft but urgent. "Please don't tell him."

"If I didn't tell this one's uncle where *he* was, why would I tell Alias where *you* are?" Lady de Ghent motions to me, waving her hand up and down without looking.

Cyra eyes dart to me for a moment and I know I'll

have to answer about my uncle once we're alone. She quickly moves back to conversing with our hostess.

"Aladdin said you wouldn't mind if we stay the night here, Lady de Ghent?"

"I don't mind."

"Lady de Ghent," I interrupt. "What happened after I left?"

She swings around to face me. "Issac was kind enough to bring me home. We left that poor boy, however. Issac sent someone after him, though, I'm sure he'll pay a steep price for attacking me during the competition—and attacking you."

She points to the table and invites us to sit. "I'm sure they'll try to replace his hand soon enough." Her words are casual as if slicing off a man's hand was commonplace in her life.

"What?" Cyra gasps.

"Oh, dear." Lady de Ghent turns to her while pulling her chair out. "A boy attacked me in the streets with his friends and when he tried to shoot Aladdin, I had to do something about it."

"She cut his hand off." I grin, expecting the girl to cringe. Instead, her eyes light up and she smiles at the Lady.

"Bravo, Lady de Ghent."

"Thank you, my girl. Though, I don't think Mr. Von Hinten appreciated my quick wit and valor."

Cyra's face pales. "Mr. Von Hinten?"

"Yes, dear. You know him." She waves a hand at Cyra. "He's running the competition."

"Do you know him well?" Cyra asks. At least I don't have to seem like the nosey one. I'm content to lean back and listen to the conversation.

Behind Cyra, a giant staircase winds at a sweeping angle, curving under the glass skylight. A single tree grows up from the center of the floor, soaking in the light from the moon.

"Not well, dear. We've met enough times in passing to know each other's names. He knew my husband much better, as I'm sure he knows *your* father."

"He's always seemed a bit of a mystery to me."

"I'm afraid I don't have the answers to that particular riddle, my dear. Now, if you'd like to know more about *Aladdin's* father—"

That's my cue.

"Lady de Ghent, would it be possible for us to shower before we sleep. It's been a very *long* few days since the competition started, and I don't know about Cyra, but I didn't exactly sleep in a bed last night."

"Would you mind, Lady de Ghent? You've already been so kind." Cyra turns to her, ready to take advantage of a warm shower.

"Of course not, my dear." She turns. "Detrick? Detrick!"

A small robot clanks into the room, tottering from side to side. The clock built into his chest keeps rhythm with his steps as it makes its way over to the Lady's side.

"Now, Detrick," she begins. "Take Cyra upstairs and show her the guest bath. When she's finished, show her to the red room."

The robot turns on its heels, walking to the staircase. Cyra rises to follow it, her cape trailing behind her.

"Everything you need is in the bath, Cyra. You may browse the closet for something to sleep in and you're welcome to take an outfit tomorrow since people have seen you in *these* clothes and might recognize you once you go back out. Breakfast is at sun up since I suppose you'll be getting an early start."

"Thank you very much, Lady de Ghent." Cyra makes her way to the stairs, leaving us at the table.

"Did your friend make it out, Aladdin? The one you were chasing when you left?" Lady de Ghent asks without looking away from Cyra's retreating form.

"Yes. He's fine." I reply, also watching Cyra walk away. She hesitates on the landing at Lady de Ghent's words but then continues without glancing back.

The older woman turns back to me and I try to look away before she catches me staring at the clock in the back of her head.

"She's quite lovely." The Lady taps her fingers on the armrests of her chair, smirking at me. "Just met, I take it?"

"Yes."

"And why is she here?" She's too smart for her own good.

"She won last year's airship."

"So, you want her to teach you how to steal?" She scoffs. "Somehow I doubt that's what you need her for."

She's perceptive for an old lady.

"Don't give me that look, boy. As long as this heart is ticking—" she pauses to tap the clock on the back of her head "—I'm perfectly capable of seeing what's right in front of me. Now, why do you want her?"

The clock is a pacemaker. Now it makes sense. I wonder if she has to wind it every night.

"I don't know what you mean, Lady de Ghent." I play naïve. "I ran into her after I left you and we worked well together. I think we could make a good team."

"That's not how the game is played…"

"*Are* there rules to this game?" I question. "Aren't we just supposed to steal the airship?"

"Next thing you know, Issac will be asking Horallen to start holding trains hostage," she mutters. She turns her attention back to me. "If you don't have a good motive for keeping her around, cut her lose, boy. She deserves better."

Yes, she does. I don't really care, though.

"If you're just keeping her here because she's pretty,

go give her a rose and then leave her be. There's plenty in the garden in the lobby. Pick one and bring it up."

"I'm not trying to flirt with her." *Yes, I am. I need her to cooperate and that's the easiest way. Girls always swoon when flirted with.*

"The way you've been staring suggests otherwise."

Good. I hope Cyra sees it too.

"I'm being a perfect gentleman," I promise.

"Well, now… I didn't say anything about being a gentleman. There's no fun in that. Just don't *use* the girl."

I laugh. She's an unusual woman.

"You said you knew my grandmother?"

Lady de Ghent leans back in her chair, smiling. She spends the next half hour telling me about my grandmother until she sends me upstairs to get ready to sleep.

Cyra is waiting for me after my shower. Her legs are tucked up under her as she sits on a cushion in the window box in the hallway outside of the room Lady de Ghent's robot showed me to. She's fully dressed as if prepared to bolt if she doesn't like an answer, but she hasn't bothered to accessorize her minimal dress.

I grin at her as I continue to dry my hair with the towel I carried with me from the bathroom.

"To what do I owe the pleasure?" I lean against the

frame that's outlining the recess she's curled up in. She leans away from me.

"You had a friend with you?" Her voice is lower than it was before, though I'm not sure if she's trying to intimidate me or if it's because it's so late and her voice is going.

"I did."

"Then why do you need me around if you already have a partner?" Cyra lifts a knee, propping her leg between us as if it's a barrier. From under the hem of her skirt, I catch sight of a cut on her leg starting to scab over. I shift my weight onto my forearm, allowing it to support me as I toss the towel over my shoulder. She follows the flash of white as it catches the moonlight. To her credit, her eyes stay on my face and not my bare chest.

We'll see how long that lasts.

"Have you seen my friend?" I ask. "Is he anywhere around here?"

"How do I know he won't show up at the last minute? Or worse, hold me back so you can win?"

I hadn't thought of that. Javed *could* keep her back when the time comes. I haven't thought that far ahead yet. Maybe I *should* let her plan some of this.

"Would I have brought you here if I was going to double-cross you?"

I lean into her, tapping her foot so she moves it aside.

I slide onto the cushion next to her and lean in. She shifts begrudgingly.

"I think we'd make a good team. I have street smarts and you're clearly very good at thinking things through, playing out all the possibilities, and coming up with plans of action. What do we have to lose, really?"

"We need to outline our contract."

"Contract?"

A cloud passes over the moon, dropping a dark shadow over Cyra's face. She doesn't flinch as the lighting shifts.

"Okay. A contract," I agree, knowing it won't matter anyway.

"You said you don't want the airship—"

"I can't. I'm under contract to someone else. I just want enough of the profit that I can leave Horallen and get my mother out of here."

"How do you know I don't *also* have a benefactor?" she challenges.

"You're not allowed. Issac made that very clear during the announcement. I doubt your father lets you take outside deals, so that leaves me with one thing: you're a runaway."

"Does it constitute running away when you're eighteen?"

"*Does it?*"

She glares at me. I smirk, this time not just to manipulate her.

"I'm on my own."

"See? You can take the ship, I can take some of the profits. We both win."

"So, you're saying I get the entire Stourbridge and you get *what* percentage of the profits?" She looks like she's trying to calculate something in her head without taking her eyes off of me. "I'll give you twenty percent."

"Ha!" I laugh "Fifty."

"No. I can't afford that."

"The richest girl in Horallen can't afford to give her partner fifty percent of the profits off an airship worth millions?"

"It's not just for me." She drops her voice, suddenly sounding unsure.

"Oh?" Now I'm interested. "Just what is your plan then?"

I consider leaning in closer, but Lady de Ghent's words haunt me.

Then, I do it anyway. I'm here for myself, after all. I don't need to heed anyone's advice, especially with a genie on my side.

"I'm..." She hesitates. Her face plays out her inner struggle as she decides what to tell me. I wait, ready to play off of whatever she says. "I'm turning it into a home for orphans where they can live in safety and work to take care of themselves. I need to bring in enough revenue to pay each of them so that they don't have to grow up to live in the rookeries or on the street."

"Like me?" I lean back against the wall, knocking my head into a cog-based decoration on the wall. *Who puts décor so low?* "Is that why you were in the alley that day?"

"I go there to bring food and money to the children." She bends her head down, not making eye contact. Cyra stares at a pillow next to my hip.

I almost feel bad for tricking her. Almost.

"Why do you care so much about them?" I surprise myself with how genuine I sound. Reaching out, I touch her arm gently.

"I didn't *always* live in a floating mansion." She glances up, looking out under dark lashes. Her hair tips forward over one shoulder, falling down on her chest. Cyra looks away from me, tipping even more hair over her arm, separating us.

I reach up, brushing it back and she gasps.

"I think it's nice what you're doing," I say quietly. "What about thirty percent?"

What do I care? I can settle at whatever I feel like—the Stourbridge will be mine at the end. If Javed says I need it, I'll do whatever it takes to steal it.

Although, maybe I could employ the children like she had planned. I've seen how they struggle every day. There have even been times when I give up my food on my way home if I see a kid who looks like they need it more than my mother and I do.

"I could do thirty, probably," she replies, reaching up to untuck the hair I just secured behind her ear. "Thank you for understanding."

"You're welcome." I pause. "Now, I think you owe me an apology for slapping me earlier."

"No. I don't." She stands to leave.

"Whoa, where are you going?" I stand up too. I nearly reach out to catch her wrist but I'd probably get slapped again.

"To my room. We're done here."

"But shouldn't we get to know each other better? We're going to be partners, after all." I'm not entirely sure if I want to get information out of her to use against her or if I want her to stay because I'd actually like to know more about the woman who won the Empress. Maybe both.

"Are you going to tell me about your friend? The one you left today?"

"I'll introduce you to him sometime," I promise. My father would be so disappointed in me for lying right to her face, but I *do* intend on introducing her to Javed—just in a different way. He needs to handle her for me.

Cyra reaches forward slowly. She takes my hand in both of hers, pulling herself toward me. "Goodnight, Aladdin," she whispers, kissing me on the cheek.

I don't move. I don't even breath.

The girl pulls back, releasing my hand. She turns and walks down the hall toward her room, leaving me standing near the window in shock.

I'm even *more* shocked when I wake up the next morning to discover she's stolen the lamp and run from Lady de Ghent's home.

Chapter 12
Cyra

HE SOUNDED SINCERE WHEN HE AGREED TO TAKE LESS SO I could take care of the children. His story about protecting his mother from whatever they're facing in Horallen appeared to be genuine enough. Lady de Ghent certainly seemed to believe him, and I know she has connections to the Governor.

I just couldn't pass up an opportunity like this.

He had spent the entire time we were together protecting that lamp. He didn't care about any other gadget he was wearing while we were running around Horallen, but his hand always floated toward the lamp, checking to make sure it was still there.

He wouldn't have given it up to Issac, I just know it.

His charming smile might have worked on another

girl, though. He's the type of man women throw themselves at and he knows it. Aladdin tried to use that smile of his to lull me into trusting him, but I played him right back. He never even saw this coming—clearly.

The birds continue chirping as the sun starts to rise. I fled the house an hour ago while Aladdin was still tangled in his sheets, resting inside of Lady de Ghent's house. I wish I hadn't had to betray her hospitality, but I'll thank her once the Stourbridge is mine. I hope she'll understand once she sees what I'm doing with it.

Aladdin runs out of the house, struggling to sling his shoulder guard over his head while also tugging on a boot. When I had crept into his room, I noticed he had picked out an outfit and had laid it over the back of a chair. I'm impressed he managed to get his utility belt and gauntlet on before chasing after me. His scarf is haphazardly thrown around his neck, tucked in his jacket, but somehow it looks perfectly in style—I've always been jealous of men who can just roll out of bed and look perfect.

His hair is tousled, flopping in front of him as he turns to yell an apology to Lady de Ghent before he storms off, calling for me. I wait until he's out of sight to continue working on piling my hair on my head beneath Lady de Ghent's home. There's just enough space for me to sit under it without having to lean forward to avoid bumping my head.

Fastening my hat slightly off center, I ensure the rose-colored feather faces out, the small jewel under it directly over my right eye. The ribbon of gold lace around the hat accentuates the look, allowing me to blend in with the upper crust women of Horallen. If Aladdin is looking for the girl covering her face of yesterday, he won't find her.

When Lady de Ghent bustles out of her house and down her drive, I wait another ten minutes to be sure it's safe before coming out of my hiding place. I risked Aladdin not wasting time to check the grounds before going after me and it paid off. Thankfully, he went in the opposite direction of where I want to go—the Hall.

The luxurious brown skirt with forest green bodice Lady de Ghent lent me is perfect. The white collared top is outlined in brown to match the dress that bunches and flares at the hips, and nearly looks like an intricate clock face. The top of the skirt pulls away to reveal a longer skirt underneath, but it's created in a way that no one knows its separate pieces, leaving me the perfect place to hide my weapons, including the gorgeous set of knives I found in the dresser upstairs that fan out should I need them to.

I tap the photograph tucked away in the pocket under the top of my skirt. I had asked Lady de Ghent if she knew who the woman was while I was waiting for Aladdin to finish showering last night, but she didn't know. I'll have to be careful to sneak it back into Issac's office once I take the Stourbridge so he doesn't find out.

The streets are quiet as I take the main path to the Hall. No one is up this early. I veer off to the left and make my way to the train station, deciding to save myself an hour's walk.

Light streams in from the end of the tunnel as I walk out onto the platform. Golden rays of sun mix with the steam floating about the station, transforming it into the vision of perfection. Loud clanging sounds around me as elevator shafts move workers up and down so they can prepare for the morning commute.

I only have to wait a few minutes for my train to arrive, then I step off the steel platform and into the red-coated car. Each seat is separated from the others, providing a more comfortable ride. I settle into the plush seat and let my fingers trace over the intricate design work of the armrest.

Each window is surrounded by a frame made of liquid running through clear tubes around metal bars. Tiny bubbles offer the riders something to stare at aside from the landscape rushing by. After a moment, we begin to move, slow at first, but then we build steam. Something clanks overhead, but I ignore it, as it sounds like it's outside of the car.

Leaning my head back, I want nothing more than to close my eyes and rest, but I have to stay sharp. Anyone could be on this train—competitors, people who know me and might try to drag me back to the Governor's mansion, even Lady de Ghent or Aladdin.

I focus on a row of clocks at the front of the railcar. Each ticks out a unique time that only the conductor and attendants know how to read. The main clock is larger and grander than the others. Its face is large and pale, with the most gorgeous hands I've ever seen.

My mind drifts as I set my eyes in a specific pattern to check for dangers in the car. As I bounce from location to location, I think about my conversation with Aladdin last night. Admittedly, I wish *I* was that gorgeous in the moonlight. It didn't help my focus that he wasn't wearing anything from the waist up.

"Did you hear Von Hinten changed the rules?" a voice behind me says. There's only a handful of other people on the train, so it's not hard to overhear conversations from a few rows away. "He's offering the Stourbridge to the first person who steals it *or* to the person who locates a specific item that is the key to winning the competition."

"Oh?" a gentleman asks. "And what is this *item?*"

"I'm not sure, the rumors are just starting about it. I caught part of it before I reached the station this morning."

Issac is sending people to look for the lamp—or rather, an oil can. If he's willing to send people back to the Collection Cave to look for it and promising them the Stourbridge if they find it, it must be incredibly valuable to him.

I move the fabric on the left side of my hip, revealing where I hid the lamp. Taking it out, I inspect it, turning it over in my hands to make note of each cog and gear on the lamp. The bottom is flat so that it will stand upright on a table. The handle is wide enough to easily fit my fingers through, but a man might have trouble fitting an entire hand around it.

Simon would be delighted with the contraption. Maybe I should take it to him to help me figure out why Issac wants it so badly. Perhaps I should change my route and go to the Industrial District first.

A small handle rests on the side. It looks like cranking it might actually expand the size of the oil lamp, making it grow larger. I shake my head once with a sigh, wondering what the creator was thinking when they designed this piece.

Turning the lever, I watch as the cogs begin to spin. The train dips a bit on the tracks and I nearly drop the lamp. Fumbling, I catch it before it flies into the seat ahead of me.

"You kept me in there—"

"What?" I jump out of my seat as a man suddenly occupies the chair next to me.

"—all night, Aladdin? You know I've—" His eyes grow

wide as he takes me in, looking just as panicked as I must look.

"*Who?*" I had originally meant it as an inquiry as to who the man was, but my question morphed into a demand for information as soon as I heard Aladdin's name come out of the man's lips.

From the corner of my eye, I see a trail of smoke dissipating from the end of the lamp. The faintest wisps of white float off the man's arms and legs, so light and innocuous that you'd have to be right next to him to see it. I can feel panic rising inside me for just a moment before I shove it down to protect myself and think clearly.

"You're not Aladdin…" His words trail off, though his finger hovers in the air still as he points at me, jaw open. His eyebrows dip down a touch and he looks off to the side as if he's as much surprised at what *he* said as he is with me.

"*Javed?*" I screech, recognizing the man in front of me. It took me a minute to reach back into my childhood to pull his picture from my memory, but everything about him is the same.

His eyes are uncertain, open slightly wider than normal as his gaze shifts from one of my eyes to the other as he tries to figure out what is happening. He's right though, I'm not Aladdin.

"Cyra," I inform him.

Javed squints, leaning in slightly. "Why, yes you are. You've grown." The genie smiles.

Suddenly, his entire body relaxes, and he sinks back into the seat, stretched around to half-face me. He eyes the lamp for a moment before bouncing back up to look at me.

"Miss, are you all right?" A man leans over the back of my seat partner's chair.

"Yes, the jolt just frightened me, that's all. Thank you." The man nods, offering Javed a glare before returning to his seat.

"How did you come into possession of my lamp, Mistress?" Javed asks, still smiling. I've forgotten how easy Javed always made life seem. He wasn't with my family for long, but I assumed he had been taken the day my parents were killed.

"I stole it from Aladdin." My words sound prouder than I mean them to.

"You *are* Mahin's daughter." Javed sways a little, pride written on his face.

"Oh. Javed. You don't know." My eyes tip down. "She died."

"I'm sorry to hear that, Mistress." His voice dips down to a whisper. "If I could cry, I would, but genies cannot produce tears."

I wonder if perhaps he *did* know.

I pat the back of his hand as it sits on the armrest between us. He sighs deeply, lamenting the past.

"Where have you been all this time, Javed? And have you always had this lamp? Mother never let me see it."

"She was protecting you, Mistress." He reaches up and swipes at his nose with the back of his knuckles. "I have not been out of the Cave since your mother hid my lamp there."

Realization slams into me. Javed's oil lamp was inside of the Collection Cave and I stole it from Aladdin so I could take it to Issac to trade for the Stourbridge. *I nearly gave a genie away.*

"They can't hear us, Mistress," Javed says, hands in the air as he tries to soothe me, misinterpreting my reaction. "They won't be able to hear our conversation until we leave the train. My block will hold that long."

"No, Javed, that's not it." I shake my head, though I am grateful no one is taking notice of our conversation. "A man has been searching for you. He's been sending people into the Cave to find you. *I* was taking your lamp to him just now."

Javed's face darkens. "You're working with Issac?" He starts to pull back. His actions wouldn't matter anyway—I'm the Mistress of the lamp now—but it cuts into my soul that he thinks I would try to hurt him.

"No, Javed, I didn't know this was yours. I had no idea

you were connected to any of this. I thought he was just looking for—"

"Issac has been searching for me for the last century." He cuts me off.

"Century?" Issac is a bit younger than the Governor—he's not even close to being a century old.

"Issac is no ordinary man, Mistress, nor is his search for our lamps and bottles any ordinary quest." He takes my hand. "Did your mother ever tell you anything about the genies?"

"Only that we needed to help protect you." I shake my head. I was so young when I lost her. "I know that they weren't actually banned like the officials have been telling us."

"I was not always a genie, Mistress. Our existence has only been for the last century or so, but the stories say we've been around longer—it removes our humanity." He sighs, patting my hand under his. "Issac was the one who bound us to servitude. I was friends with the woman he was supposed to marry, as were all of us that were transformed into genies. He felt we were keeping Leandra from her calling."

Leandra is a name I know. *How?*

"Issac is as old as I am. We only knew each other briefly, but Leandra and I had known each other for many years. One day, he asked for help with an experiment—Issac was an inventor and an alchemist, you see."

"He built the Stourbridge," I add as he nods. "And he built the Empress."

"Empress?"

"The airship I won last year."

"Ah, yes, Leandra would be proud to hear that." He smiles. "But you don't know why yet, do you? We'll get to that."

I pull my hand out from under Javed's as the train dips again on the tracks. Quickly, I secure the lamp under the fabric of my upper skirt and turn back to continue listening.

"It's a long story that I'll tell you sometime, Mistress, but the end is the same: Leandra discovered that Issac had bound us to the whims of those who commanded us and put a stop to it.

"When Issac discovered what he had done—*giving us power over wishes was an accident on his part*—he bound us to keys, which he controlled. Leandra took the keys from him and bound us instead to the lamps and bottles in an effort to conceal us from her fiancé." The genie looks at the back of the chair ahead of me, studying the fabric as he speaks.

I've never heard this version of the genie tales before. Unlike most of Horallen, I knew they existed because I had seen Javed when I was a child, but now I know the truth.

"Leandra hid our lamps and bottles until she could

find a way to free us. Her sisters were the only ones who knew about her plan…that is, until Issac found out. Leandra's only solution was to do the unthinkable—she turned herself into the most powerful genie of us all. Her older sister was to be her Mistress and wish all of us free —it was the only way to break the bond of servitude— but Issac found her, killing her just as the other sister rushed in to help.

"Leandra's younger sister wished the genies to be hidden so that Issac could never find them by himself— they had to be retrieved by someone else who had the lion's heart. The lion was always Leandra's symbol, and a fitting one at that—she wore it on at least one piece of jewelry or part of her wardrobe every day. Leandra's younger sister escaped after wishing Leandra away from Issac, leaving her slain sister behind."

"Why didn't she just wish them all free?"

"That's a good question, Mistress. Your mother would have asked that as well. The genies, you see, must all be in the same place for the wish to work. The first step was to get them out of the hands of Issac, then bring them together."

Javed sighs. This looks painful for him. I hold completely still as he talks.

"While they were going through the wishes, Issac discovered them. They were about to bring us all together, but when Issac murdered the older sister, the younger sister had to move quickly. The only way to save everyone was to ensure Issac couldn't reach them at that moment—if he had gained control of Leandra, it would have been easy to find the rest of us and he would have had complete control." Javed's hand twitches against his leg. He turns slightly to get a better view of me. "Wishing Leandra away was our only chance—I'm sure she didn't want to risk bringing the other genies into Issac's grasp. She separated us, protecting us as best she could, and then she escaped."

I suppose if I had a sister, my first reaction would be to protect her too.

"The younger sister went into hiding, and the lion's heart was passed down through her daughters, all the way to Mahin, and now you.

"*You*, Mistress, are the one who can call forth Leandra —the lion—and end this."

I'm related to Leandra. That's why I knew her name. She's a distant aunt of mine.

"But your lamp—" I protest, thinking of the lion. Surely Javed is the key, not me.

"Has a lion built into it, yes. That was how Leandra knew it was us and not junk when she stumbled upon us. The lions are hard to find in the sculpture of our homes, but not for those meant to find it."

"I'm related to a genie?" My mind is whirling as I try to process Javed's words.

"You are related to the *greatest* genie…and my dearest friend. We must rescue her, Mistress."

"You can use my name, Javed."

"My servitude does not permit that unless it is to hide my identity, and even then, you will rarely hear me say it."

"Do you know where Leandra is?"

"Yes, but I'm not permitted to tell you or take you there. It's a way to protect the other genies as part of our bond of servitude. You must figure it out on your own. I'll guide you as best I can. But, Mistress, there's something else you should know."

"What is that?"

"We must find Aladdin."

The train slows to a stop. The steel squeaks as the brakes slow us down, and steam releases in a rush of air as the car settles on the tracks. People stand up around us, ready to disembark. Noise fills every part of the cabin and the ceiling makes that same, strange noise again.

"Javed?" I reach into my pocket, realizing I might have something of value. My words come out in a whisper. "Is this her?"

Tears form in his eyes as I show him the worn photo. He smiles, holding back his emotions, but his voice catches slightly. "That's your great-great-aunt Leandra. Mistress, we need to save her."

"We're at the Market," I inform him as the people in

the train stand up to leave.

"We cannot stay here and look suspicious," he whispers. "Come."

The genie clears his throat and offers his hand to me. It feels surprisingly human-like. He guides me off of the train and out onto the platform. His long coat billows behind him as he walks.

I try to hand him the photo—he obviously needs it more than I do—but he waves me off. I slip it back into my pocket to protect it.

"So that's what she looks like?" I ask, grateful to have a reference for when I see her.

"Similar to that, anyway," Javed replies. "We still age, but only during our time out of the bottle with our Masters. I'm a few years older now than when I was bound, but it's been a century."

Together, we shift away from the platform and down onto the street. Holding my head high, I pretend I don't have an agenda for being in the market place. The less interested I look, the less noticed I will be, which will be helpful since I'm standing next to a giant.

"We must not be seen," Javed whispers.

"Should you go back in the—"

"No." He cuts me off. "We need to speak. That is only if absolutely necessary and not where anyone can see us."

My priority shifts from getting Issac's help to protecting the genie. Issac can't gain control of a magical being—he'll use it against Horallen until he finds Leandra by whatever means necessary. I believe Javed's story and I'm willing to fight to protect him as my mother was.

"Are you hungry, my friend?" Javed asks, louder—a show for the sake of the people.

"No, I'm fine. Let's continue on." I'd prefer to stop and eat, but I can't risk going up to the merchants and having them recognize me with Javed.

Once we find an abandoned place on the street out of view of the crowd, I turn to the genie.

"Leandra sacrificed everything to save us. The path to her bottle will require sacrifice by all involved, Mistress," Javed speaks before I can. "Those with the lion's heart must sacrifice the most. Are you prepared for that?"

If my entire family history is built on giving ourselves to save Leandra and the genies, I'm willing to take my place in history. Leandra is the only family I have now—which is a lot more than I had yesterday—and I'm willing to fight to get her back, especially since Issac Von Hinten has already taken so much from us.

"If sacrifices must be made to free the genies, I'm willing to take the risks."

"I knew you would help, Mistress. You've got your mother's heart." He smiles at me.

"Now, why exactly do we need Aladdin?"

He quickly explains that genies have the ability to see certain things in the near future. "What I know is that we need Aladdin to help us take the Stourbridge. We need the Stourbridge to get to Leandra to free her. Without Aladdin, all is lost."

"You can't tell me more than that?"

"No, Mistress. We simply need to find him and sway him back to our side. I've seen a glimpse of the airship, and he's there with us—we need him. It's very important."

I feel like he knows more than he's saying, but I also understand that he's bound by certain rules and can't tell me everything. I resign myself not to ask questions I know he won't answer.

"How are we supposed to find Aladdin?"

"I do not know, friend."

"He was your Master." I whisper the last word. "Surely you must have some idea of where he would go."

"He found me in the Collection Cave only two days ago. I spent the evening helping him to escape, and then a day with him before you decided to steal my lamp." His voice is slightly condescending as he reminds me I shouldn't be stealing. Clearly, Javed doesn't live in the world where airships like the Stourbridge exist. He would be appalled at what I did to get the Empress.

"As Mistress of the lamp, you get three wishes, but you must choose wisely." I open my mouth to wish us to Aladdin, but he swipes a hand in the air. "No."

"But—"

"I will help you make these decisions but be very

careful of what you say—you don't want to accidentally waste a wish. You don't want to deplete your wishes on something you can do yourself." He explains how the wishes work and why we need to discuss them before I make them.

"So, if I wished for a way to care for a group of orphans—a home, jobs for them, protection—we could do that?"

Javed's face brightens, looking impressed with my question. I'm sure I'll be asked details once we figure out what to do about finding Aladdin.

"We'd need to examine the potential outcomes first, but yes." His eyes narrow. "But no flying. My powers are guided by the laws of this world."

I definitely wasn't going to ask about flying.

Javed gives me a list of tasks he cannot accomplish as a servant to the lamp. I nod quietly, trying to keep track of what he can and can't do.

"Now," Javed concludes. "We need to find Aladdin. This is only going to work if you two work together—I've seen that much."

"What exactly is it that won't work?" I duck my head, turning away slightly as a trio of men strolls down the street toward work.

"The Stourbridge, Mistress. The Stourbridge," he repeats. His eyes sparkle. "But first, we have to locate him...and then we have another genie to find."

Chapter 13
Aladdin

MY FINGERS CREEP OVER THE EDGE OF THE WALL I'M hiding on, peeking over to look at the girl below me.

"Is that really possible, though?" Cyra asks Javed. "Can a man actually have his brain transplanted into another body?"

Neither she nor Javed look up at my quick movements, reacting to Cyra's question. I *clearly* picked the wrong time to spy.

"Issac is a brilliant man, Mistress. He figured out how to keep living until he can get Leandra back. I'm just glad for everyone's sake that Issac figured out how to get a body that's human-like and didn't resort to putting his brain in a glass case."

"That's horrifying."

What?

Frustrated, I inch back from the side of the wall and walk to the stairs. Rushing down, I pause just around the corner. My hand inches to my utility belt, pulling out the pistol Lady de Ghent gave me. I close my eyes, focusing on what I'm doing—getting my genie back. I can ask questions later.

Javed looks up as I rush around behind Cyra. His eyes focus on me first, then the weapon in my hand. His face falls, but he doesn't have time to warn her.

"The lamp," I demand, growling in a dangerous voice. I rest the pistol on the back of Cyra's head just above her neck so she knows she can't try anything.

"Aladdin," Javed tries to speak, using my name for the first time.

"Don't," I warn.

"Aladdin," Cyra cuts in, raising her hands. With her hair swept up, I can easily see the genie over her shoulder. "We need to talk."

"No, we don't." I'm annoyed now. She stole my lamp, tried to run away, and now she was going to refuse to give it back. The girl must have thought I was an idiot to not wait to see if she was still around—it's exactly what I would have done if the roles had been reversed.

"It's not what you think—" she tries again.

"We don't have time for this, Cyra. Give me back the lamp."

"Aladdin, please," Javed interjects. "Just listen."

"You're supposed to be on my side!" *I can't catch a break.* "I haven't even made my wishes yet, how can you take on a new Master?"

He looks like I slapped him. I shouldn't make it sound like I'm only concerned with my wishes, but it's kind of the truth.

"Whoever has the lamp gets the wishes, Aladdin, but there's something you need to hear. It's about Issac."

"You mean about keeping his brain in a jar?"

"Cyra?" a new voice cuts into the conversation.

"Levi, no!" the girl shouts. She raises a hand toward him as he holds a pistol at me. This is getting messier than I'd like. "Levi, listen to me. Put it down, it's just a misunderstanding."

"He's holding a gun on you." His eyes are wide. He doesn't drop the pistol.

The guy's dreadlocks look like they've seen better days, but it's the dust all over his jacket that draws the most attention...assuming I'm not counting the pistol he's holding at me.

"Get out of here," I command, knowing it won't work. "This is between us."

"No, now it's between you and me," he challenges, taking a step forward.

I grab the back of Cyra's arm, prepared to move her

where I need her to go to get away from the newcomer. He looks like he just walked out of a collapsed building.

"Listen to me, Levi," she tries to speak again. "This isn't about you."

"The Governor will have my head if I don't help you!" he shouts back. "Even if I win, if he finds out I walked away, I'd be done for."

"He's not going to hurt me," she protests.

"Tell that to his trigger finger."

"Perhaps we should all just relax..." Javed tries to redirect us, taking a step between everyone. Cyra and I glare at him at the same time.

"Let go," Cyra whispers, hissing at me over her shoulder. The hat she's wearing swivels with her, the feather flopping in front of my line of sight. "We can work this out. You can have it back, but you need to hear what I've learned first."

"Lamp first," I whisper in return, forcing her to take a step back with me.

"What's going to get you to listen if I give it to you?"

"I wasn't the one who ran off with it this morning."

"How did you find me, anyway?" She sounds entirely unconcerned with her friend as he continues to speak to me. I ignore him.

Javed looks at us curiously, one eyebrow raised at us. Cyra's friend looks far less amused but holds his position.

"I would have done the exact same thing in your position—I would have stayed close. I doubled back and watched you crawl out from under the house. Followed you here."

"On top of the train." She muses.

"Yes."

"Issac is trying to find Javed." Cyra leans farther back to whisper to me. "He's going to use him to find an even greater genie. We can't let him have Javed."

"What do you mean?"

"We're supposed to work together, Aladdin. The genie Issac is looking for is connected to me—I'm the one that has to free her."

"Her?" *I thought all genies were male.*

"Yes, *her.*" Cyra snaps at me, eye narrowing. "We have to find her and free her before Issac can get to her. If he can reach her, he can command *all* the genies, and not just for three wishes each."

This is nonsense.

"Aladdin, this isn't a game. You and I are supposed to work together on this—Javed said so. He'll explain it to you. Go talk to him."

"You really think I'm going to let go of you?" I tug on her arm again.

"Levi!" Cyra suddenly shrieks at her friend. I look up in time to see him lower his pistol at my leg. Quickly, I angle myself behind Cyra, knowing he won't shoot her.

"Back up!" I shout. This is getting out of hand.

"Everything she's saying is true," Javed calls hands up in the air trying to calm everyone. The guy with the gun looks at him warily.

The scent of Cyra's hair floats back to me, making me dizzy for a moment. She turns over her shoulder, moving the pistol slightly in my hand. Spinning slowly, she moves to face me, allowing me to hold her arm. I lower my aim, not liking the idea of aiming it at her face—it's still threatening enough pointed at her stomach.

"Please, Aladdin, just listen." Unlike last night, it doesn't look like she's trying to get anything from me. Her eyes are wide-set and shaped like almonds, lashes long and dark. "I knew Javed when I was a little girl before the Governor took me in. I know he's a genie.

"I knew you were going to double-cross me, and I knew Issac wanted the lamp," she continues. "He asked me to find an oil can for him in the Cave but I said no. Then I realized he was looking for a lamp, not an oil can when I saw you had it—the lion on it gave it away."

What lion?

"I didn't know it was Javed's until I accidentally released him on the train. He explained to me *why* Issac wants it."

"And why is that?" I question, refusing to tell her that I knew Issac was looking for it. I haven't told her about Kacper other than he tried to kill me and I'm not going to.

"You said your uncle sent you into the Cave after Issac told him what to look for," Javed interrupts, walking over to join us. He must have incredible hearing if he heard us from that far away. "You know Issac has been searching for me. He wants me because I'm leverage he can use to find Leandra. *We* need *Cyra* because she's the one who will set Leandra—*and all of us*—free. She needs you to help her get the Stourbridge to get us to Leandra."

"Issac has been searching for the genies for decades, Aladdin," Cyra informs me. "He's far older than he appears—he was here for the creation of the genies. Issac has been shifting his brain around to different hosts over the years to extend his life until he can get Leandra back. She's a distant aunt of mine and she transformed herself into a genie in order to save the men that Issac turned into genies during one of his experiments."

"Nothing about that makes sense. The genies were banned a century ago," I counter, trying to make sense of this new information in connection with what I overheard on top of the wall.

"No, Aladdin." It's strange to hear Javed use my first name, yet somehow feels better this way. "The officials discovered the genies after Issac had started to let people buy our wishes—this was before Leandra took on the mantle. A few of the officials took advantage of it, but Leandra bonded us to our lamps and bottles and hid us away from Issac. Once Leandra was one of us and wished away for her own protection, the officials claimed genies were banned to keep people from looking for us—it would have been mass hysteria if the people found out the genies were hidden somewhere in Horallen."

The competition for the airships is madness enough, but to have an entire country looking for genies? Given what people are willing to do for an airship, I imagine it would have been much worse had they been given wishes.

"Leandra took on the mantle of genie to use her powers to break the bond of servitude, but Issac killed her older sister before she could make the wish to free us. Her younger sister managed to hide Leandra instead so that Issac could never find her. The officials made the announcement of the ban to stop Horallen from searching for us, but we've been here all along and now we must work together to find Leandra and the others and undo what Issac did to us—for us *and* for Horallen. They need to be protected from our power too."

"What is going on?" Cyra's friend yells, interrupting the conversation. He takes a step toward us, pistol still trained on me.

"He's going to find out," Cyra whispers, asking permission to bring him in. Somehow, I doubt she would actually let me say no.

"Why exactly am *I* supposed to be a part of this?" I

ask. "It sounds like *you two* are the ones with connection, not me."

"I saw it." Javed speaks with enough confidence that I question whether I should actually stay. I had no intention of being involved until this moment.

"If Issac is working with your...*uncle*—" Cyra addresses me, but looks to Javed for confirmation of my backstory, "—then what do you think will happen if he gets control of all of the genies and has unlimited wishes? If he's already been letting people buy wishes, what will your uncle do?"

Kill me, of course.

"Think of your mother," Javed says softly, earning a glare. "Do this to save her. Sacrifices must be made to achieve our goals and save our people, Aladdin. Are you willing to save her?"

"*Everything I'm doing is to save her.*" I drop my pistol to my side, knowing there's no way out of an alliance—I need the money Cyra can give me when she gets the ship, especially since I no longer have a genie. Cyra gives me a sympathetic look.

"We have to find Leandra and set her free," Cyra says. "We're going to need help. I'll pay you."

Money is the incentive I need, mixed with Javed's confidence in my involvement—I'm not sure why I trust him so much, but I do. Of course, he slowed a truck down for us, so maybe he has some influence over me as well. In the end, the promise of money wins out.

"What about the airship?" I ask, relenting.

"You're going to need to find it," Javed remarks as the crowd around us begins to grow with people arriving for work. Merchants rush past with their rolling tables and collapsible stands. Officials head toward the Hall. "I'm not permitted to tell you why until we get there."

More secrets. *Just what we need.*

"What are we going to do about your friend?" I ask, nodding past Cyra.

"I think we should bring him in on this," she replies in a tone that implies that I haven't been listening to her. "I think Levi can help us. He is the front runner for the competition, and I trained him."

I nearly insult her training, but I bite my tongue.

"Levi?" Cyra calls over her shoulder. Apparently, we have no choice but to involve him. He launches himself into action, reaching her side in only a few strides. He glares at me. "Levi, something has happened and we need your help."

"The Governor isn't going to like this, is he?"

"We're still looking for the Stourbridge, but something else has been discovered. This is about more than just the airship."

Cyra quickly explains what's transpired as Levi protests the existence of genies. Listening to him argue is as annoying as hearing rats run across the roof of my house at night.

"If we all steal the Stourbridge, what does that mean?" I finally ask, interrupting their discussion.

"The Governor will be fair. You'll still get your share like I promised," Cyra assures me

Everyone leans in at the same time, noting the growing crowd around us. We don't want them over-hearing our conversation. The smell of food drifts over to us and I realize I didn't stop to eat before chasing Cyra out of Lady de Ghent's home this morning.

"The price just went up."

"Excuse me?" Cyra asks, squinting at me.

"You took my genie. You're coercing me into helping you with this insane mission where we'll probably all die, especially if Issac or my uncle discovers us, and you said you *need* me for whatever reason Javed won't tell us about. I'd call that leverage, Cyra. I can walk away and continue with my plan, but *you* can't do this without me...according to the genie." I'm aware he didn't expressly say the mission would fail without me, but I'll take implications and build them up for my own benefit.

The look on her face confirms my suspicions that she needs me more than I seemingly need her. There's room for negotiation.

"No," she protests.

"If you want my help, I need to be compensated for it."

"Aladdin, this is about more than your—"

"Is it?" I cut her off. "This is about me getting my mother away from Horallen and my uncle. This is about self-preservation. If you want me to be involved, make it worth my time, because I'm giving up my own mission to help you with yours."

"So, you're a mercenary," she points out.

"If that's what you want to call it. I think of it as being a strategic businessman." One way or another, I'm going to survive this. If it's alongside of a stubborn but beautiful girl and her genie, so be it. I could do without her friend, though.

"Fine," she whispers harshly. "One thousand coppers."

"*One thousand coppers?*" I balk. "You're getting an airship *worth millions* and your add-on bonus for me risking my life is *one thousand coppers? My percentage* is higher than that."

Cyra's friend starts to say something but she cuts him off with a hand in the air. At least he's not still arguing the existence of genies.

"We can still take care of them, Mistress," Javed offers. "The path to the bottle is paved with sacrifice, and those with the lion's heart must pay the most."

She looks like she wants to argue with the genie, but he doesn't back down. Cyra shakes her head slightly, visibly getting upset as her breathing quickens and she retracts her fingers into a loose fist. Javed only offers her a gentle look and slight nod, encouraging her to move forward.

"Lion's heart, Mistress."

"I know," she mutters, "they will sacrifice the most."

Interesting. I'll be cornering Javed later for more information on this lion's heart.

"What do you want?" Cyra turns to me, clearly annoyed.

"I want one million coppers up front and then we'll be done." I don't need any money trails leading my uncle to me. She can keep the profits from the airship. I just need enough to escape with my mother and keep her comfortable while we're hiding.

"That's it? None of the profits?"

"You said the Empress was worth a million in revenue, right? That means you have at least that much. That will be enough for me to escape and stay hidden. If you start sending me my share of the profits, that could lead my uncle to me, so consider it an upfront payment of a portion of what I would have earned."

"Fine." Her words are harsh, but I can tell she's glad to have it settled.

"I really don't see how finding the airship is going to help at this point. Why don't we just go to Leandra? Why do we need the airship?" Levi asks.

"To reach Leandra, we're going to need the Stourbridge. Or another airship, but the Stourbridge would be more helpful from what I hear," Javed supplies. He runs a hand over his beard.

"We can't just steal the Empress?" I look to Cyra. "Isn't that kind of your ship anyway?"

"The Empress belongs to the Governor. He won't press charges against me, but he will against you. The Stourbridge is the only ship we *can* legally steal. I'm not even sure where he stands on Levi—he might charge him too."

The guy's eyes get wide and he fumes, but he doesn't say anything, clearly believing he deserves more respect from his benefactor.

"Fine." I sigh. "Where is the Stourbridge?"

We follow behind Cyra as she guides us through the Market and out of sight of the onlookers—the last thing we need is for people to be questioning why two men who are obviously competitors are conspiring with a rich girl in the middle of the market alongside a giant. Once out of sight, our de facto leader pauses, summoning Javed back into the lamp as proof. Levi's eyes grow wide.

"Is this true, Cyra?" he whispers, then points at me. "This isn't some ruse? He's not trying to pull anything?"

"I've known Javed since before the Governor took me in. This is real, Levi. There are genies in Horallen. Are you with us?" She places a hand on his arm, stepping closer to him. He watches her closely, mouth drawn thin. "The Governor wouldn't want Issac to have that kind of power, especially if he's been at this for so long. He's fooled us all."

"And getting better at it every year," I add. Both flick their eyes over to me—I shouldn't have interrupted.

"Levi, are you with us?" she asks again. He sighs.

"Can I at least get a wish in before this is all over?" He smiles at her just enough to be noticeable, eyes nearly pinched shut as he shakes his head over giving in. "What's the plan for finding the Stourbridge?"

"We were hoping you knew where it was." Cyra turns the lever on the lamp, calling Javed back out.

"Nothing yet. Issac has been running us all over Horallen. I've been told he wants something from the Collection Cave and if we bring it to him, he'll tell us where to find it. I was hoping to intercept the person bringing it to him."

Sounds like he was being lazy to me, but Cyra praises his wisdom for not wasting his energy. Thankfully, his decision worked to our benefit.

"Javed, any insight on where the Stourbridge might be?" she asks.

"I'm afraid not. We'll need to find it on our own."

"I think we should threaten Issac," I comment. "He knows where it is. Let's just force him to tell us."

"That would get us disqualified," Levi protests angrily. He shifts to stand closer to Cyra.

"I'm sponsored; I can't win anyway. I can go get the

information and pass it to you." I shrug. Issac will likely come after me for threatening him, but if I'm leaving Horallen anyway, it won't matter.

"But if he realizes what's happening—and clearly he will—Issac will just move the Stourbridge," Cyra replies. "We need to handle this with a little more finesse. Come with me."

She spins on her heels, walking down the abandoned alley toward the Market. We rush after her, hurrying to keep up with her brisk pace. Her skirt shifts in the wind as she walks, attempting to billow out behind her but unable to due to the way it was sewn.

"Where exactly are we going?" Levi asks as we follow her.

"We're taking the train to the Industrial District."

"Why are we leaving? We need to be here to intercept Issac," I point out, running my hand through my unruly hair. "We can't be running around Horallen when our target is right here."

"First, Issac isn't even here every day," Cyra counters. "Second, *I'm* the one who is going to talk to Issac. He wanted a lamp, so I'm going to give him a lamp."

Javed glances at her from the corner of his eye. Cyra turns, taking us onto the main street toward the train station.

"I made a friend last year during the competition who can help us. He's going to make something similar enough that it's believable, but not close enough that Issac will figure out it's a lamp and not an oil can that he's looking for just in case this doesn't work out."

Her shoes click against the metal steps as we reach the station. A train pulls away, releasing a loud hiss as it takes off. At the top of the platform, she waves us over to a large column made out of silver steel that supports the building.

Lowering her voice, she adds, "I'm going to trade for the location. By the time he figures out it's not an enchanted oil can, we will have a head start to the airship."

"And your friend can make something that will convince him to play with it for a while before coming after us?"

"I'm sure he can." She nods, backing up her own words. "But if not, we can always use a wish to make it look enchanted, right, Javed?"

"Perhaps."

We stand huddled under the support beam for a few minutes, trying not to talk much as a small crowd gathers around us. Every minute or so, we step closer, bumping into each other. I'm close enough that I could take the lamp from Cyra, but at this point, why bother? My hand drifts toward it, though, even though I don't mean it to.

Cyra rests against the column, biding her time until the train arrives to takes us to the Industrial District. Levi leans away, taking stock of the platform as more people climb up to join us. The majority of the men are dressed in long coats and some form of hat, with goggles resting around their collarbones like Levi, or on their head, like me. We blend in perfectly.

Javed shifts as more people step up with us, bumping into me enough that I sway forward, catching myself on the beam with my forearm. I hover over Cyra and she glances up in a panic, wide-set eyes sparkling. She blinks a few times and I grin as I apologize for intruding on her space. She doesn't push me away.

"Apologies." Javed turns to make amends to a woman that bumped into him.

Levi looks offended when he turns back to face us, so I lower my arm, but instead of righting myself, I lean against the column with my shoulder. Annoying him is likely going to be my new favorite pastime.

Without drawing attention to myself, I quietly tap my utility belt, analyzing everything I brought with me from Lady de Ghent's house. She was kind enough to lend me much more than I needed, even going as far as to stock my utility belt and the pocketed strap on my shoulder guard.

My arm shifts next to Cyra as I reach down to tap the holster strapped to my upper leg and she leans closer to me, appraising my outfit. "Lady de Ghent did well."

"I picked out my own wardrobe, thank you," I respond, smirking.

When I turn back, her eyes spark to life, a smoldering deep brown with copper flecks. "But she had a nice selection to choose from. I see she did well for you, too."

"It might not be my first choice for stealing an airship, but I've been known to wear this kind of thing on an everyday level," she replies. "You can ask Levi if you like since he lives with me."

She's quick on the fly.

"And here I thought you could do better than him." If she wants to play, I'll play.

"What, like some dipper?" she challenges. "*Hardly.*"

"Are you accusing me of griddling? I hardly ever pickpocket, *madam.*"

"But you *do*," Cyra replies, reaching up to brush back a strand of her hair. "You just said you did."

"Isn't that precisely what *he's* also doing?"

"He's doing this because I trained him to do this. He doesn't steal from people outside of the competition." She crosses her arms, rolling her shoulder to lean closer to me. From the corner of my eye, I see Javed pretending not to notice.

"How was he selected for sponsorship, Cyra? He had to have a background somewhere." Her face falls as I make my point, calling her out. "I'm not as glocky as you think, Cyra."

"We'll see." She spins away from me, deciding instead to talk to Levi. Javed shakes his head at me, sighing.

Cyra engages Javed in the conversation with Levi. I hover on the edge of the conversation, but keep part of my focus on the platform, trying to memorize the people coming on and off the stairs.

A woman brushes by me and I slip two fingers into her jacket pocket, pulling out an ear cuff with a drop-down clock hand. Shifting it into my other fingers, I wait for Cyra to drop her hand after speaking and tuck it into her palm. She jerks slightly under my unexpected touch, but her fingers curl around my gift to her and she waits a moment before turning to look at me.

I grin and her nose wrinkles in disgust as she realizes I stole it for her. I blow her a kiss, further infuriating her, but she slams the metal jewelry into her pocket, not knowing how to return it.

Small victories.

Levi is so engrossed in the conversation he's having with Javed that he doesn't even notice the exchange, and if the genie has caught on, he doesn't show it. When the train pulls up, the two walk toward it, leaving us to trail behind them. I guess Levi is over his disbelief of genies.

"Did you really steal that?" Cyra hisses.

"*You* stole for the game." I shove my hands in my pockets.

I allow her to step into the train first. Cyra wanders to

the seat behind Levi and Javed, still caught in their discussion.

"No." She grumbles as I try to sit next to her. "Go over there."

"Oh, come now. I gave you somewhere warm to sleep last night. The least you can do is let me sit next to you."

"Why, so you can steal that back?"

"Consider it a gift."

"Trust me when I say you are no gift, Aladdin."

"Wow." I lean back against the fabric of the seat, grateful to be inside the car instead of on top of it. Unlike the last train, the aesthetic of this railcar is a deep mahogany. The wood is accented by deep brown cushions. Though, the same set of clocks is up front, just like they are on every car. "You wound me. And you stole from me. Remind me why I'm working with you again?"

"You were going to steal from me, too." She crosses her arms, sliding in the seat to face me.

"You can't prove that," I counter. "I have *evidence* that *you* stole though."

"Are you *always* going to hold that against me?" The train starts moving forward, gradually picking up the pace as she speaks.

"I could hold *other* things against you if you like." I tease mercilessly.

"Threatening to shoot me again?" Before I can answer,

she changes her tone. "So, your uncle is trying to hurt your mother?"

She doesn't like flirting. *Shame*, flirting is so easy. I'd prefer not to talk about personal things though, so I try to redirect. "You were forced to train your replacement?"

"Yes, but we're not talking about me. We're talking about you. What happened?"

When I hesitate, she adds, "*You* can tell me or Javed can tell me."

"Fine, but then you're explaining your connection to this Leandra."

"Hush," she hisses at me. "Don't say her name where people can overhear."

"Fine." I hold my hands up. "Tell me about your connection."

She rolls her eyes, sighing dramatically as I force her to reveal her secrets first. "Javed told you how she became...you know. We mentioned that she's a distant aunt of mine, and her sister that died saving her was also an aunt, but my great-great grandmother was the one who was supposed to help find her and restore her and the others. My mother found Javed at some point, which is why I knew him as a child, but he was lost when she died."

"I'm sorry about your mother." The memory of my father's death hits me as if it was last week instead of last year.

"Thank you. What about *your* mother?"

"My father died last year. Ever since Kacper has been trying to cause problems between my mother and me. He sent me into the Collection Cave with two other men he sponsored."

"You're *Kacper's* nephew?" Her eyes grow wide. We need to stop constantly surprising each other; it's not good for our faces.

"He sent one of those men to kill me." I choose not to continue talking about Kacper.

"Why?" She leans in, waiting for more information on the conspiracy. "Is he in love with your mother?"

"I suppose. I'm not sure. There was a switch in him when Father died…" I drift off, unsure of what the motivation had been behind what had transpired the last year of my life. "Kacper thinks I'm dead—I would have been if Javed hadn't known how to escape the Cave. Did you know there was a back entrance?"

"*What?*"

Clearly not.

"So, you know my uncle?" I change the subject, shifting to look at her better.

"I've met him once or twice. Apparently, I was right to not care for him." She leans back against the seat to get more comfortable as we talk. I need to stop staring at her hand on the armrest…I don't get to hold it.

"Well, at least you made *one* good decision," I tease.

"Sounds like he didn't make the worst decision either," she replies, commenting on her distaste for me. She leans in to whisper. "Lady de Ghent had some charming little knives in the wardrobe. They spread out like a fan, so when I hold it, there's a lot I can do with it. *You should remember that.*"

She darts forward, lips moving quickly toward mine.

Chapter 14
Cyra

"*THAT,*" I SAY, PULLING BACK WITHOUT TOUCHING HIS LIPS, not bothering to hide the satisfied smirk on my face as I beam in my victory, "was for earlier."

He looks shocked, bottom lip moving up and down slightly as if he can't remember how to use his vocal cords. Aladdin closes his lips and swallows, bobbing his throat up and down. Seeming to break out of his trance, he blinks a few times and sits back.

"I wasn't expecting that," he finally says, pulling back with a grin. "Nice work."

I smugly settle back into my seat. Two can play at this game.

Admittedly, he is handsome. If he wasn't such a liar, I could see myself paying attention to him. My mind flashes back to last night in Lady de Ghent's house. Sitting across the table from him in the tungsten light could have been nice. The moonlight conversation would have been even nicer.

"Remembering me without my shirt on?"

"When didn't you have your shirt on?" I ask innocently, despite having been caught.

"You're turning out to be more interesting than I thought." He muses.

"You didn't find me interesting when I slapped you yesterday?" I bat my eyelashes at him. "If it takes this much to amuse you, I have a feeling you're going to enjoy meeting Simon."

"Is he going to try to flirt with me, too?" Aladdin tips his head to the side, knocking his hair over his eye.

"No, but he's probably going to flirt with *me—try not to get jealous.*"

"Do you really think he can make a replacement lamp?"

"Simon is the best at what he does. He might be a little eccentric, even for Horallen's standards, but he's the only one I'd trust for the job."

"Do you think Issac is going to fall for your act?"

"He specifically tried to get me to go back to the Cave to find it. He's a desperate man—if I come to him with oil can in hand, he's going to believe me."

We spend the rest of the short ride to the Industrial

District discussing how the oil can replacement should look. We finally settle on a design as the train slows to a stop.

"You're really okay with all this?" I ask as we stand up to disembark.

"Just make sure you pay me what I'm owed, and yes, I'm fine with this." He walks away, not bothering to wait. I find it amazing that he's more interested in the money than in saving the genies.

I lead the men to Simon's factory. Aladdin trails quietly behind me as Levi blatantly ignores him to talk to Javed. Occasionally, he grumbles about our companion to Javed or me, but Aladdin doesn't respond.

I can see Simon's outline standing against the front of the factory from down the street. I tell the men to wait for me, knowing Simon can't sneak us all inside the factory at once.

"Well, well, who do we have here?" Simon croons, catching sight of me. "And so lovely as well."

"You get more visitors in a week than I get all year," Taren mumbles beside him. He puts his pipe away and turns, shouldering the door open.

"That's because you don't have friends other than me, Taren," Simon calls after him, lifting up onto one foot to lean toward the door. He spins back to me. "I've never seen you in a dress before, love. *It suits you.*"

"You should have come to the competition announcement," I point out. "I believe everyone was supposed to be there."

"Men like me have other priorities." He tips his hat. "Now, why are you here?"

"I need you to build something for me, and while you do, I have a story you're going to be very interested in."

"I take it you need some assistance with your... friends?" He uses his eyes to point toward where I left the genie, my trainee, and Aladdin. I nod. "You know the way in, my love."

Simon pulls away from me, sauntering over to the group of men I left behind. I turn, slinking back against the factory wall until I reach the back exit. Once inside, I make my way to the boiler room where I assume Simon will meet me with the others.

Ten minutes goes by and no one joins me. Twenty minutes passes and I start to worry. Finally, the door crashes open, scaring me.

"Well, my love, your men seem to be doing quite nicely at their stations."

"Their *what?*"

"Stations, love. I put them to work." He walks over to pull his teapot out from behind the boiler. "Couldn't very well have them standing around all day while I work, now could I?"

"Simon, you didn't!"

"No." He laughs. "I hid them in different rooms. I have

to bring them in one at a time, but the boys are watching."

The light reflects off his goggles, bouncing across the room. Putting the kettle near the boiler, he turns back around to me.

"That's an interesting group you have, love. Care to explain?"

"I'd rather explain what I need you to do for me." I lean forward, resting my forearms on the back of the chair I pulled from the side of the room.

I quickly explain the situation down to the replacement oil can we need. Simon whistles.

"Well, now, that's going to take some time. Which one is the genie? Tell me it's the blue-eyed one. I'd love to make him jump through a few hoops."

"Not a fan of Aladdin, huh?"

"Not a fan of anyone trying to take my beautiful Cyra away from me." He winks, grinning. "Should I bring him in here first and give you a little *alone* time?"

"Only if you want me to use a wish to make you work in this factory for the rest of your life," I retort, threatening him for his humor.

"Don't do that, love, or I'll have to destroy your decoy." Simon slinks toward the door. "Have yourself some tea and I'll be back with your companions in a bit. Work on the oil can will have to wait a bit—I need to at least *pretend* I'm working, but Taren can cover for me a little later."

He tips his hat, leaving me to my tea.

When the door opens again, Aladdin slides in and Simon is nowhere to be found. Annoyance radiates through my body, but I snatch the teapot and offer it to Aladdin.

"I've been told he's leaving us alone for a few minutes," Aladdin informs me. "*Why* is that exactly?"

"I should be asking *you*. What did you say to him when he snuck you in?"

"He looked us over and brought Levi in first, then took Javed in, then he came back for me. Had me in a room down the hall this whole time." He flips his head up to move the hair from over his right eye. Thank goodness, it was driving me crazy. He sits in the chair in front of me, reaching up to massage his neck. "He didn't really say anything, just kind of…judged me."

"Simon is good at that."

"Is he?"

"He's very good about knowing who to trust and when." I hand him a teacup and pour it for him. "You okay there?"

"Yeah, I just pulled something, I think."

I stretch my neck out, forcing the muscles from side to side. I hadn't realized how tense I had become over the last two days.

"You too?" He glances up at me. Dragging another seat over, I join him, putting the chairs close enough to talk without shouting over the machinery. "Are you going to be okay for confronting Issac tomorrow?"

"Tomorrow?"

"Your friend said he isn't going to be able to build the decoy lamp until this evening. That pretty much means we're here until tomorrow...unless Issac is sticking around until midnight."

"I just want this to be over with." I lean onto the armrest and sip my tea. "But, yes, I'll be fine. I imagine he will be thrilled."

"Settling in?" Simon asks, rejoining us with Javed in tow. He sets a box of metal on the floor. "Here, pick through these and pick the best ones. We need cogs and gears that match the lamp as closely as possible. Organize them into piles for me. Tall One, you can help my love organize. Pretty One, you count how many of each color are on the lamp. I'll be back with your third friend."

Tipping his hat, he turns to exit the boiler room again.

"I'm the *pretty one*?" Aladdin asks, scoffing. I choose not to reply.

"You're the one who is going to help Javed organize the box of metal," I say instead. "I'll count the colors on the lamp."

"Don't trust me?"

"You're a mercenary, Aladdin. I definitely don't

believe you won't walk off with the lamp if given a chance. It stays with me."

"Fair enough." He turns to join Javed as he turns the chair into a table and begins organizing the box of scrap parts. I'm shocked he didn't fight me on it or even protest against my accusation.

I start counting cogs, speaking aloud to keep track of the count for each color. It gives me the opportunity to see how much detail really went into creating the lamp. If Leandra did this somehow, I'm convinced she's magical.

After a few minutes, Levi saunters into the room, followed by Simon. Levi surveys the boiler room, shooting me a look after his inspection. Simon pulls me aside.

"Will you be fine here with your friends for a few hours? I'm going to go work out a form for the oil can while pretending to work." He winks at me. "Then, I'll be back to assemble the cogs on it. I have an idea for making it move a little once your fellow cranks the lever so it seems like something is happening, but it will take most of the afternoon to pull it all together."

"I'll be fine, Simon. Is there anything I can do to help with your work while you're ignoring it for us?"

"You know there's nothing more that I love than throwing a wrench in someone's plan. It's why I was so anxious to help you last year. I can put your two competitors to work though if you don't need them."

"I don't mind parting with them."

"I'll be back, in that case."

True to his word, Simon returns half an hour later with work for Aladdin and Levi to do while I help Javed with the decoy oil can. Once he slips back to his job, he doesn't return for several hours.

"It's been far too long, my love," Simon greets me, kissing the back of my hand. "The men are all out on their lunch break—I forced them to leave—which means we have a unique opportunity."

He swings around to face the men in the room who have gathered in a semi-circle behind Simon. Grinning, he holds both arms out like he's about to bow. After a tiny dip, he continues.

"The building is clear for a very brief time. Two of you are going out to collect what you're going to need for this mission—but don't take anything they'll notice is gone. The other two will remain here to help me. If we can work quickly, we might be able to get you out of here before dark."

Simon turns back to me. "Taren might have come on the project with me, but he doesn't know why, just that I needed help and it involved a pretty lady.

"I'll keep the tall one and the snooty one," Simon

informs me. "Take your pretty thief—*I saw him swipe a screwdriver when I brought him in so* clearly *he's the man for the job*—and go collect what you need."

He hands a backpack to me, tossing one to Aladdin. "Be careful and be quick."

Levi's jaw clamps down as Aladdin and I start for the door. Simon tosses a pair of gloves to him and motions Javed to join them as he begins to set up a station to solder the metal pieces together.

The factory is illuminated by natural light streaming in the windows. It's similar to how it looked last year when Simon escorted me through dressed as a worker, but there are new machines here that hadn't been in the building last year.

Most of the mechanical levers and pulleys are quiet now with their operators out of the building, but a few still move, creating enough noise that we could potentially miss the sound of someone returning from their break.

"Anything in particular you think we'll need?" Aladdin asks.

"Tools, probably," I answer. "Last year, the hardest part wasn't finding the Empress; it was breaking in. Look for anything that has multiple functions."

"Think we'll need rope or wire?"

"Probably. See what you can find."

He nods. "I'll take this way. Meet in the middle in ten

minutes?" It's going to be the fastest sweep of the main factory room ever.

I breeze by the stations, looking under and behind them instead of *on* them. If we have to cover our tracks, it will be less likely that the workers notice something missing from under a table or behind a curtain than something they use daily for their jobs.

"All of the tools are in use." Aladdin comes up behind me, frightening me.

"Just keep looking; we're on a schedule."

"What about…" His words fade into the hum of a machine's chugging as we step closer to it to search.

"*What?*" I raise my voice, knowing if I can't hear him, he can't hear me.

He tries again, but I shake my head. It's amazing how loud the machines are right next to them. Aladdin leans in, putting his hand on the small of my back as he buries his nose in my hair next to my ear. "What about a vambrace? I'm sure they won't realize it's gone until the end of the day. We could go through their coats to see if they have any…or maybe anything in their pockets."

"You want us to pickpocket the workers?" I turn, nose catching the tip of his.

"How is that any different than this?" he shouts back over the noise. "They won't notice until we're gone."

"You don't think that will get Simon in trouble?" I always worry my actions might come back on him.

"Not if we topple the racks holding their jackets. I'm surprised none of them took the coats with them, but I supposed the weather is nice enough. We'll just make it look like everything fell while they were gone…they'll think whatever we steal just tumbled out of their pockets and they'll spend a few days trying to find it." Admittedly, it's not a bad idea. I shrug, not consenting, but also not saying no. "I'll handle unscrewing the rack, you check the pockets. Hurry before they come back."

He grabs my hand and pulls me across the room to the row of jackets mounted to the wall. Shoulder guards and utility belts rest on top of—and under—some of the jackets. I shove my hands into each one, quickly sorting through the pockets

"This side is ready," Aladdin calls as I come up with a handful of coppers and a magnifying glass.

"Just hold it," I reply, glancing at him. "If we leave the other side intact, it will look like the screws came loose over there. We'll just knock a few off on this end."

He nods, eyes darting between me and the door to watch for anyone returning. I finish the row of coats, finding enough items to make the bag slightly heavy as it hangs off of my arm.

"Finished?" Aladdin asks. I nod and he slowly lowers the rack to the ground, letting the coats crumble beneath it. "Did you grab those vambraces?"

"I did. What did you get?" I knock a few coats at the

far end onto the ground, ensuring some of the contents of the pockets spill out and roll across the floor.

"Wire mostly—" The door flies open at the far and of the factory floor. Aladdin turns to me, motioning me to his side. I hurry, trying not to trip over the jackets strewn across the floor. *"Hurry."*

As soon as I reach him, he takes my hand, making sure I stay upright. The men walking into the room don't notice us so far away and we duck down under the first counter we reach.

On our knees, we crawl toward the curtain that separates the factory floor from the other rooms and hallways. Aladdin checks over his shoulder for me and I resort to tapping his ankle every few feet to let him know I'm still there.

I cling to the backpack, tucking it against my chest— at least Aladdin had the foresight to swing his over his shoulder before dropping down. I hadn't had time to maneuver mine around.

Looking back, he notices me struggling and reaches for the pack. I hand it up to him and he situates it under him, tucking one of the straps first around his neck, then after a few feet, slipping it under one arm to hold it in place, freeing his hand to crawl more easily.

"Almost there, princess," he whispers, eyes flashing in amusement.

The curtain sways as he dives under it. Aladdin had

tried to scoot under on his hip, but it had knocked the curtain anyway. I sit up against the wall next to the exit, trying to see if anyone had noticed. I can't tell what they're looking at from here—it could be at me, but it could also be at anything along the back wall.

"Are you coming?" Aladdin whispers from behind the other wall.

"We can't risk the curtain moving again," I inform him. "They're looking in this direction."

"It's plastic and fabric; it moves." He says it like it doesn't matter. It definitely matters.

"Not like that, it doesn't. I'm going to try to roll part of it up. If you hold it, I'll slip partway under and then I can hold it while you slide me the rest of the way through —I don't think I can do it myself in this skirt."

I begin bunching up the fabric overlaid with plastic, checking over my shoulder as I work. When it's high enough that I can fit under it and not hit it with my chest, I show him where to hold it.

Laying down, I use my feet to push myself under the curtain toward Aladdin and the darkened room he's hiding in. With hands braced on either side of the door, I push. Once my face is through, I realize how tiny the small box-of-a-room is that connects the factory floor to the back rooms and halls. Without a light source of its own, it's a bit hard to see in.

"Okay, hand it to me." I take the curtain from him. "Now, take my hand and—"

"Hold still," he commands, placing both of his hands under my shoulders like he's going to lift me. His fingers come up under my arms. He pulls hard enough to slide me several inches, lifting me into a sitting position. "Now, drag yourself backward."

Aladdin holds the curtain until I can scoot far enough back that I can lift my knees, pulling my skirt toward my body. He slowly releases the curtain and offers me a hand. "Somehow I feel like you prefer wearing pants for these missions, but you spend the rest of your year in things like *that*."

"You'd be right on both counts." On the other side of the curtain, the machines start back up. "Time to go."

The hall attached to the small room off the factory floor is lined with shelves and recesses behind curtains. We quickly check to see if there's anything we can use there, but our search only lasts a second before the factory floor curtain is flung open.

Aladdin's arm darts out, sweeping me behind him. I'm slammed into a wall, curtain pulled closed as he separates me from the walkway.

"What are you doing back here?" a deep voice asks.

"Just grabbing this," Aladdin answers, reaching back. His hand runs over my leg, searching for something. I hand him the first thing I can find.

"You need a dowel?" the man asks skeptically when he pulls it out.

"Yeah, one of the guys dropped a piece behind his machine; I was going to help him fish it out but needed something to reach it with."

"And you just magically knew it was back here?"

"I saw it when I was getting parts last week and assumed it was still here."

"Get back to work," the man grumbles, pushing past Aladdin and stomping toward the hallway where we were going.

When the curtain opens, I start to step out, but Aladdin steps in, forcing me back. "He'll be back through and I can't go back to the main floor. We wait here."

The recess behind the curtain is dark. There's enough room that we could fit a third person in with us if we really needed too, but the thick fabric traps the heat in, making it seem warmer than it should be and far less comfortable.

His breathing sounds loud next to me, but so does the sound of my own breath. In the silence, my heart starts pumping in rhythm with the machines outside and I can hear the blood rushing in my ears as if I was submerged under water. I close my eyes, unable to see anyway.

Minutes tick by and Aladdin shifts next to me, bumping the back of his hand into mine. "Sorry," he whispers. After another minute, he leans forward, separating the curtain enough to peek out.

A sliver of light leaks through above his head and gives me a better look at the small closet recess we're in. Shelves line either side, stocked with small baskets of things, mostly medical supplies. I hadn't had time to see them before the man interrupted us.

I lean forward, grasping Aladdin's shoulder for support as I draw near to his ear. He glances at me from the corner of his eye, the glassy part catching the light from the still-open curtain. "There are medical supplies in here. I'm going to pull some. Warn me if I need to stop moving."

"Okay." He slings his pack off his shoulder and hands it to me.

Pulling away, I reach for the shelves, but Aladdin's arm wraps around the front of my stomach until his hand reaches my far hip. He taps my hip to let me know that's how he will communicate with me when the man comes back through. It's a strange feeling having him hold me like this, but it's better than being caught. He might accidentally miss me if he wasn't attached to me and tried to tap me to get my attention. I don't want to think about what he might accidentally topple over if his hand didn't connect with me.

My back is tucked against his hip as he watches out of the curtain. I fiddle with the boxes on the shelves, searching while trying not to think about how close I am to him.

I pull down bandages and cotton balls, a few disinfectants and wraps, and collect them in the bag hanging off my arm. I make it through most of the top two shelves, pulling a little from each basket before Aladdin's grip tightens on my hip. I freeze, waiting.

The curtain closes, cutting off the light. Aladdin leans back, pulling me closer to him. He must have noticed I was too close to the curtain or my skirt was pushing it out, because he wraps his far arm around my other hip and drags me to his chest as he leans back against the wall. I hold my breath, waiting to be caught as the man stomps into the hallway and pauses.

My lungs expand and contract against Aladdin's chest, his doing the same in different rhythms so that our breathing is offbeat. He lowers his face to mine as if he wants to say something but doesn't want to risk even a whisper being overheard. His grip on me tightens as the man outside the curtain takes a step toward us.

If he opens the curtain, I'm going to kiss Aladdin. It's the only logical explanation—a worker gets caught with his girlfriend. I'm sure it's happened in here before. They might end up firing Aladdin from a job he doesn't actually hold, but that's the worst that could happen if they believe he's just an employee caught in a compromising situation on work hours. If they figure out he doesn't work here, though…

I lean toward him, hovering inches away. He shifts slightly, wrapping his arms around me more, catching on to my plan. His body is warm, and even being in the suffocating heat the curtains are trapping inside, I don't mind absorbing the heat coming off him. I can barely see him in the darkness, but his arms move each time he turns to glance at the curtain and then look back at me.

After an agonizing minute, the man rips open the curtain closest to the exit—at least I assume it's the one closest to the exit since it sounds farther away—takes something off the shelf, and stomps away.

"Think he's stealing from the workplace?" Aladdin asks, grip loosening around me. I rock back on my heels.

"That was far too close."

"Let's just get back to the boiler room," Aladdin responds. I wait for him to lean around and check. When he opens the curtain, light floods the space again, and I turn to exit.

Chapter 15
Aladdin

SHE NEARLY KISSED ME.

I nearly kissed her.

Closets are *not* a safe place for two people to hide, especially when *one of us* is focused on a rescue operation and *the other* is trying to free a genie.

It's far too easy to become distracted.

The boiler room seems as warm as the closet did when we dart back inside. Cyra drops her bag on the ground, pulling out the medical supplies and the wire I found to organize it. I kneel down next to her, pushing my luck.

"You okay?" I finally ask.

"Fine. You?" She's being cold again. Distance will

likely be our friend in this case—we'll be going our separate ways as soon as we steal the Stourbridge anyway.

She reaches across me, picking up one of the gadgets she pilfered from the workers. "What do you think this is?"

"Find anything useful, my love?" Simon asks, joining us at just the wrong moment.

"Any idea what this is?" Cyra holds it up and the two discuss it for a moment before Simon announces he has to handle something out on the factory floor. He promises to return shortly.

"Go see what we've done in the meantime." He waves his hand toward Javed and Levi. "I've worked a bit of magic of my own."

Once the door closes, Cyra walks away without a word. Putting a hand on my knee, I push myself up off the floor. The oil can is aged and dented but certainly looks like it could have come from inside the Collection Cave.

"He just needs to finish the inside part," Levi informs us, demonstrating where it will go. "Then, he'll put on the last few pieces and add the lever."

"It's quite a clever plan, really." Javed sounds impressed.

He passes the oil can to me to inspect. The cogs will all move similarly to Javed's lamp once Simon is done. I'm impressed with the skill level of his work. I have yet to figure out what he does in this factory, but whatever it is has trained him well.

The main boiler hisses, letting off a whining trail of steam. Javed glances over, not having adapted to his new surroundings as quickly as the rest of us.

"Javed, what did you do before Issac turned you into a genie?" I ask, realizing I don't know much about him.

"I was an inventor, friend. Not like Issac though. I didn't do alchemy, but Leandra focused heavily on it for a time before she had planned to join us on our project, which is what upset Issac to begin with. His experiment on us was to stop our work…it just functioned differently than he had planned.

"I was working on an airship in those days—it seems Issac stole my work after I was gone."

"*You* created those?" Cyra asks.

"I created some new technology for those," Javed corrects. "I haven't seen the new airships personally, but it sounds as though Issac made some developments of his own along the way."

"That might help us when we try to break into the Stourbridge," I add.

"Would it help to see the schematics from the Empress?" Levi asks. He reaches into the inside pocket on his dusty jacket and pulls out a paper. Unfolding it, he reveals the plans for the Empress. In the top right corner there is a drawing of the airship, complete with a crown emblazoned on the side—*how fitting for the princess.* "The Governor sent them with me in case it would help with the Stourbridge."

The airship would be a nice place to live should one choose to spend all of their lives on it. By the time Javed and I have committed the plans to memory, Simon has returned.

While he's busy soldering the rest of the oil can decoy, the boys and I divide up what Cyra and I collected and conceal it in our pockets, utility belts, and under Javed's top hat. I feel a bit weighed down, but nothing that will slow me too much.

"Do you think we can make it before the work hours end?" Cyra asks.

"You plan on retrieving the airship in the middle of the night, do you?" Simon tilts his head at her. "Fortunately, that wouldn't be your worst plan."

She pats the back of his shoulder, smiling as she turns away from him. It's clear the two understand each other in a way the rest of us don't. He reaches a gloved hand out to catch hers and pulls her back to him, leaning in to say something. I turn away to give them space.

After all, the man completed a task he said would take all day in time to have us to the Hall before closing—he gets as much space as he wants.

After a moment, the two of them laugh and Cyra joins us.

"I'm going to the Hall as soon as Simon is done. You can come with me as far as the Market, but they can't see that we're together. If anything should happen, you three might need to escape. Whatever you do, free Leandra."

I think she's forgetting the part where the lion's heart has to be the one to set Leandra free. Unless, of course, the wish didn't mean in a literal sense. Given Cyra's ancestors knew Issac was trying to kill her, maybe it's not as literal as Javed is taking it.

"Here it is," Simon announces, walking over to hand the oil can to Cyra. She examines it before passing it to Javed.

"Is this close enough?"

"I haven't seen the other bottles and lamps, aside from Leandra's, but yes, it seems to fit." The genie hands it back to her. "What about *my* lamp?"

"I'll be leaving it with Simon."

"Here?" Levi and I ask at the same time.

"Simon has decided to come with us for this particular part of the plan. He won't be joining us to steal the Stourbridge, but he's going to try to delay Issac for us when he figures out what we've done. He will give it back to me once I'm out of Issac's office."

She'll trust *him* with the lamp, but not the rest of us. I have to keep reminding myself that I'm just here for the money. The closet was just a distraction.

The walk to the Market is tense. The group is quiet as we make our way through the Industrial District, following the metal cogs in the road, guiding us back to the center of Horallen.

Once there, we agree to wait at different points in the Market and garden island in case Cyra needs help. Simon takes a spot near a merchant, hovering over his goods mixed amongst the shrubbery. Levi waits across from the platform in front of the Hall, keeping in contact with me as I hover near the stairs. Should my uncle appear, it will be easier for me to hide around the corner of the building than to blend in where Levi is standing. Javed is tucked away inside the lamp on Simon's belt to ensure Issac doesn't see him.

"Are you sure about this?" I ask Cyra as I walk with her to the staircase. She starts to climb as we part.

"It has to be done. I'll be fine. I stole an airship; I'm pretty sure I can handle the Proprietor—"

Her words cut off as I jerk down on her wrist.

There, at the top of the platform, is Kacper staring down at me with Byron by his side.

My uncle's face twists into shock, then morphs into a look of horror—he's seeing a ghost. If I were alone, I could pretend to be haunting him in hopes he would be gullible enough to fall for it, but ghosts don't travel with other people.

"*How?*" Kacper growls.

I pull Cyra back. She trips down into my arms and I pull her away from the stairs as Byron crashes down after us, his legs clanking against the steps with a metallic ping. From the corner of my eye, I see Levi start to run, but I hold a hand to the side, stopping him.

Wait.

We're going to need help, and if Levi and Simon move now, they'll give themselves away. They need to come after. Levi jerks to a halt, turning at an angle so they don't notice him, but I doubt Kacper and Byron have noticed anything other than the dead nephew come back to life.

I wrap an arm around Cyra's back, ensuring that she stays with me as we dart away. It would be far too easy to lose her as we run, and I can't afford for Kacper to get his hands on her. The girl holds up her skirt, keeping pace with me as I guide her through the outskirts of the market place.

Looking back, Byron is right behind us, but Kacper hasn't bothered to follow. He's still by the steps, calling for his vehicle to pick him up so he can cut us off.

The streets turn into a blur as we move. The feather on Cyra's hat flattens straight back as she runs. "Your uncle?" she asks, already knowing it was him from the few times they had met.

"Run faster," I shout back, pushing us forward.

"What do we do?" Cyra calls, fighting to speak around gasping. "Go up?"

"He'll follow us," I reply, shaking my head.

"Can he jump though?"

"I don't know," I reply. I've never seen Byron jump and I'm not sure if all that metal will weigh him down or give him an edge. "Maybe."

"Should we try?" she asks. "Or should we split up?"

Splitting up might be her best shot. Kacper isn't going to hesitate to kill me if Byron catches me, especially since everyone already thinks I'm dead, and he'd have to have Cyra killed too to keep her quiet.

"It might be your only chance," I call back, preparing to release her. "Just keep going and don't look back. If I can get away, I'll join you. Go handle the Stourbridge."

"And leave you to handle this on your own? I don't think so."

I pull Cyra down another alley, twisting my way through the city to try to lose Byron. We gain a slight lead, but my uncle's minion stays close. I don't have time to think about where Kacper's car might be looking for us.

"You have a mission, Cyra. You *have* to see it through. If he catches us, my uncle will have us both killed and then no one can do...that thing." I worry about saying it out loud. Byron is far enough back that I don't think he can hear us, but I'm not going to risk it.

"You didn't survive the Cave just to die before reaching the Stourbridge, Aladdin. Figure something else out."

"Fine, let's split up." If I can draw Byron far enough away, at least I'll give Cyra a chance. With enough of a lead, she won't be able to do anything to get involved and she'll know it's foolish to insert herself after a certain point.; she'll still have time to turn around and escape.

I pull to the side before she can argue, leaving her no choice but to split away. She runs up a small set of steps up to a door and leaps over the railing, crashing down on the other side. Following her lead, I spring up, catching hold of a pole hanging off of a building. Swinging up, I catch a second poll and drop down on the other side of a small fence.

Byron glares at me once before deciding to follow Cyra, even though I intentionally gave her the lead. Veering to the right, I swing into Byron's line of sight, but he ignores me, opting to go after the girl.

No matter how close I get or how easy it would be for Byron to swing around and gain the lead on me, he doesn't. His sights are set on my companion. Cyra looks over her shoulder, realizing what's happening and tries to gain the lead. When it doesn't work, she climbs.

Byron follows her up the fire escape. I don't have time

to run across the street and catch him. My only choice is to pray I catch up if I follow him or to beat him to the top of the buildings on this side of the street and get ahead of him there.

I take the closest fire escape, slamming face first into a set of chimes made out of old pipes and a few cogs. The loud clanking is sure to get Byron's attention and probably some of the neighbors. The metal doesn't cut me, but there will be a bruise at some point.

I'm out of breath by the time I reach the roof. I get there just in time to see Cyra leap from one roof to another. Byron hesitates, judging the distance. From where I stand, the first jump will be the easiest for him.

Knowing I need to keep up, I run, leaping to the building next to mine. I drop onto the roof, pushing off to give myself enough momentum to keep going.

I make it to the next roof before daring to look back. Byron made it to the first roof but stops before the second. He quickly picks up a board, preparing to use it as a walkway between the buildings.

Cyra pauses, noticing me hesitate. I point back and down, indicating Byron's descent, then motion that we should keep going. She has an extra building to jump than I do, meaning I can get to the ground before she can. I hope it's enough to stop Byron.

I take the last two buildings, out of breath by the time I dive onto the fire escape. Byron catches up to her as I reach the last landing. Cyra mounts the fire escape, looking for a way to dodge Byron as he approaches the steps.

It's higher than I'd like to jump from, but I need to move faster than I am. I jump over the side of the railing, crashing a story down, landing on a small yard made of dirt. I tuck and roll, bouncing up to my feet. Reaching out, I push up on a garden box as I lose my balance and topple over.

Byron reaches the first landing by the time I join them on Cyra's side of the street. She glances over the edge of the fire escape from the second landing, eyes latching on to mine. Byron is half a flight away from her and moving fast.

"Go," she mouths to me.

Down the street, I see movement—Simon and Levi run toward us, but they aren't close enough to help.

"Jump," I mouth back to Cyra, holding my arms out to indicate that I'll catch her. Her eyes widen, but she instantly launches herself up onto the railing.

Swinging her legs around, she drops down, dangling from the second story landing. Inching down, she moves until she's at the bottom of the posts and wraps her hand around the main support beam. Releasing the hand supporting her, she crashes down, only slowing herself with the arm wrapped around the round, metal column.

Cyra's entire body jars to a stop as she crashes into

the railing on the first floor. She cries out in pain. Byron's eyes are wide as he turns in furry and chases her down.

"Jump!" I command her. Cyra barely looks over her shoulder before dropping off the railing toward the ground.

Levi and Simon shout from a few paces away. Cyra's boots slam into the ground in front of me, but I hold her upright. She cringes into me in obvious pain.

Before I can react, Levi slams into me, scooping Cyra over his shoulder and runs. I turn back to fight off Byron, but just as he reaches the mid-point on the final set of stairs, Simon pulls something from his pocket and throws them at the steps.

Byron pitches forward, slipping on the ball bearings. Simon turns to me, pushing me away, offering me a chance at escape. "Go, go!"

We run after Levi who is already slowing under the weight of carrying another person. Cyra struggles to pull something out from her utility belt under the fancy part of her skirt, but she's unable to achieve her goal while bent over Levi's shoulder.

"Put me down," she hisses at her friend. Levi acts like he doesn't hear her.

"Put her down!" I growl, catching up to him. I hover over Levi until he stops to let her off his shoulder.

"Can you run?" I ask the second she's on her own two feet.

"Yes." She nods, turning. Levi and I position ourselves on either side of her in case she needs us.

As we run, she pulls out her fan that folds out into several knives. Opening it, she waves it slightly so that it catches the late-afternoon light impressively.

She gasps a few times as we run, pain snapping somewhere on her body, but to her credit, she doesn't slow. Levi and I loop an arm through each of hers, helping to support her until her body cooperates again.

A gun goes off behind us. The bullet slams into a post next to me.

Byron.

I jerk us to the right, taking a new street.

"Who is that?" Simon demands to know, catching up to us.

"My uncle has been trying to kill me—he just found out I'm still alive."

"That's your uncle?" Simon gasps, looking over his shoulder to where the blond man is just rounding the corner.

"That's the uncle's minion," Cyra answers for me. She turns as if she wants to throw the knives, but we're too far away.

"Anyone have any idea where we are?" Levi interrupts.

Looking around, I realize we've strayed so far from

the Market that we're in the rookery. Another few streets and I might run into my mother.

We navigate around another corner and Cyra gasps. "I know where we are, come on." She pulls us down another street, tugging on my vambrace-covered arm. Releasing my arm from hers, she straightens her necklace. Whistling, she acts like she's summoning someone and holds the necklace away from her chest.

"Where are we going?" Levi asks as Cyra slows us to a near-stop.

She spins on her heels facing a small shack-like tent. A small hand pulls back the fabric revealing a hole in the wall. The child hides behind the curtain, waiting for us. Cyra drops to her knees and climbs through.

"Hurry," I instruct, letting Levi and Simon crawl through first. I scramble past the curtain and turn just in time to see it drop.

Cyra tugs on my arm as I crawl backward, away from the hole in the wall, refusing to take my eyes off it once I'm through. "It's okay. We're safe."

Her murmur in my ear makes me shiver. I cover as I stand, acting like it was from the movement. Cyra reaches down and puts her hand against the fabric curtain.

"I'm here."

We wait, surrounding her as she kneels next to the child on the other side of the curtain. Byron crashes into the alley, one foot clanking heavily as if something on his metal leg came lose during the chase. He searches for us. The child gasps as he flings the curtain back to check the shack. Cyra throws her head back, eyes closed as she waits to determine if she needs to pull the child through the hole and run.

He leaves as quickly as he came, storming out of the alley. Once he's gone, I look around and realize we're in an abandoned building. The walls are crumbling to the point where it looks unsafe. I shouldn't be surprised given that I've lived here for the last year of my life—I know the conditions of the rookery, I just don't spend much time here other than to sleep.

After a moment, the child pulls back the curtain.

"You're Cyra?" he asks.

"Yes."

"Amany told me about you."

"Amany has told a lot of people about me. I'm glad you recognized the necklace. Do you know where she is?"

"A few streets over. Want me to go get her?"

"Can you be safe about it?"

"Yeah." He looks at her in disgust. I smirk. I've given her that look before. "Just stay here."

Cyra stands, turning to me. "That was you as a child, wasn't it?"

"I'm wounded." I tap my heart. "But seriously, I'm

pretty sure we *will* be wounded if we stay here. This place is falling down."

"Agreed," Levi volunteers.

"You fit the aesthetic perfectly, though, Levi." Cyra smirks.

"We should check you out." Simon turns to Cyra. "Where does it hurt, my love?"

"I'm fine, I just pulled something. I just need a few minutes."

Simon gives her a look, silencing her. She points to her ankle.

By the time the young boy has returned, Simon has officially cleared Cyra to walk again…and built her an ankle brace out of some of the metal pieces and vambraces we brought with us and a few of the medical supplies. I saunter back over from where I had been examining the crumbling walls and watching out of the windows that are far too high to been seen in from the outside.

We're only a few streets over from my mother's house. I ponder over how to get her a message while Cyra reunites with her little friend. She bends down, hugging the girl.

"This is Amany," she introduces the child. I've seen her around the streets. I might have given her some food once or twice. "Amany, these are my friends."

She points to us, giving the children our names. The

kids quietly watch, though the boy sizes us up. Cyra leans close. "Do you know where that man is?"

Amany shakes her head. "Did you see him?" she asks the little boy.

"No, I came straight to get you."

"It's okay, we'll figure out what to do. You two should go."

"I'm not leaving you if someone is after you," the girl says stubbornly.

"We're going to have to stay the night, Amany. We're not going anywhere until morning, and that man will be gone by then. I just need you to promise to stay away from him—no spying, understood?"

"I'll stay here with you," she protests again.

"You can't. If he comes back, we need to be able to escape, and if we have to stop to make sure he doesn't hurt you, we probably won't be able to escape. Do you understand?"

"Besides," I say, kneeling down next to them. "I have another mission for you. Think you're up for it?"

She brightens, countering Cyra's darkening face.

"Relax, princess," I mutter. "I want her to take a message to my mother to let her know I'm not dead."

"Princess?" Amany asks, swinging to face her friend.

"You're dead?" the little boy asks. He looks a little too pleased at the idea.

"What message?" Cyra looks like she's trying to decide

if she should be gentle with me since I'm trying to help my mother in her grief or if she should lecture me for sending a child anywhere near where my uncle may find her. She's a child from the streets, though. I don't think Kacper would think anything of it.

I dip two fingers into my front pocket as if I were going to steal from myself and pull them out with my pocket watch in hand. "My mother will recognize this." I hand it to Amany. "Just tell her that her son wanted this returned to her. She'll understand."

I *hope* she'll understand.

Cyra finally nods and allows me to tell Amany how to find my mother. "Don't say anything else," I instruct. "Just go to the door, hand it to her, tell her that her son wanted this returned to her, and leave. Don't come back here and don't ever go back to that house again."

"Amany," Cyra says sharply. "Do *not* come back here. They might follow you. Once you deliver the watch, go straight back to the orphanage and stay there for a few days, okay?"

"Fine." Amany takes the watch from me. She hugs Cyra before slipping out of the hole in the wall and disappearing. The boy goes after her, pocketing a coin Cyra handed him to take to the headmistress.

"Spending the night?" Simon says incredulously. "In this dump?"

"Will it even be standing in the morning?" Levi asks.

He tosses his head, sending his braids flying over his shoulder.

Cyra and I look at each other and roll our eyes. We've both been exposed to these kinds of conditions before, though I imagine she's seen worse than I have given that she was an orphan for a while.

"Should we bring Javed out?" I ask.

"I suppose we can," Cyra replies. She holds her hand out to Simon who gives her the lamp and she cranks the lever. Steam starts to puff out of the spout.

Javed doesn't speak, just raises his eyebrows in silent judgment as he accuses us for jostling his lamp around.

"I *feel* everything, you know."

"Sorry, friend," Cyra says softly, reaching out to touch his arm. "We had a bit of a run in with Aladdin's uncle."

"The murderer?" Javed whips around to face me like it's the most interesting story he's heard in a century. "How did he find you?"

"We were getting into position for Cyra to walk into the Hall to confront Issac when Kacper and his henchman, Byron, walked out and nearly collided with us.

"So, you didn't make it in to see Issac, I take it." He turns to face Cyra whose hand is still on the genie's arm. Javed faces me again. "Is the henchman still around or are we safe?"

"We're not sure where he is, but we're spending the night. We'll confront Issac tomorrow."

"Couldn't be easy, could it?"

Settling down on the ground, we huddle next to each other to keep warm. Simon and Levi take posts next to Cyra, leaving Javed and me on the end next to Simon.

Cyra leans against the wall as the others settle into sleep. Gazing over at me, she barely whispers, "Are you okay?"

"Fine. You? How is your ankle doing?"

She squints, struggling to hear me as I whisper. Pulling herself up, she moves around Simon and Javed and takes a seat next to me. Propping a leg up, Cyra wraps an arm around it.

The dust in the air glitters in the moonlight seeping in through the windows and opening in the roof of the building that *must* have a condemned sign hanging outside. Cyra turns to me and asks me to repeat my question.

"It's okay. The brace is working well." She tugs up her skirt, revealing a coppery brace, complete with cogs and gears. Cyra flicks her skirt to cover it again.

"Just remember you're wearing that thing the next time we get into a fight," I joke.

"I'll remember to be careful of it." She rolls her eyes.

"I *meant* so you could use it as a weapon," I reply, making her snort. "That thing might be more dangerous than your knives, princess. Sorry you didn't get a chance to try them out—I would have loved to have seen what they could have done to Byron's face."

"You're so helpful," she jokes.

"We'll have to be careful tomorrow. Kacper has seen you now. If he tells Issac you're working with me, we could be in trouble."

"He'd have to admit he tried to kill you to do that," she reminds me.

"We don't know that he doesn't already know. Maybe that was a part of it, though it certainly doesn't seem like Kacper would give away a genie knowingly."

"I guess we'll find out tomorrow." She pauses, tucking her hair back up. She'll have to restyle it before tomorrow, but in the moonlight, it looks incredibly alluring. "We'll just have to be exceptionally careful."

I pull my elbow out from under me where I had propped myself up. Laying down, I watch the stars through an opening in the ceiling. Suddenly, the world feels overwhelmingly heavy and I just want to sleep.

"Aladdin?" she asks as I yawn. The strain I've put myself through the last three days is taking its toll on me. I fight to stay awake, but sleep is dragging me under.

"Hmm?" I mumble, eyes flickering open and shut. I fight to stay awake to talk to her.

"You have bruises on your face."

My face scrunches, trying to figure out her words. *What bruises?*

"What?" My mind searches, but exhaustion is cutting off my ability to think.

"On your face," she murmurs, reaching out to point. "What did you do? Was this when Byron was after us?"

"Oh." I chuckle. "Yeah, I ran into something when I was trying to get to you."

She sighs. "I'm sorry." Cyra's fingers brush my hair back from over my eye. "It doesn't look *terrible.* Want me to take a look at it?"

"Sure," I mumble, eyes drifting closed again. When I open them, she's hovering over me so close I can feel her breath against my cheek.

It's hard to see her clearly this close. The light is muted, and her face is in the shadows, but she leans even closer to examine my minor injuries.

I blink again, trying to stay awake for the conversation, but it's a losing battle. She moves, attempting to see the other side of my face, pulling back quickly as I forget myself, giving in to everything I've been trying not to feel since last night, and brush my lips against hers.

Chapter 16

Cyra

I PULL BACK, STARTLED.

Aladdin's eyes are closed, but he doesn't move. His breathing is slow and steady, chest rising and falling. I hold myself up on both hands, leaning my weight on my hip from where I had been checking his bruises, my breath far faster than his.

His lips were soft against mine, barely touching me when he kissed me. They're slightly parted now as he sleeps.

How does a man kiss you and then promptly fall asleep?

I blink. It's all I can think to do.

I can't believe he just kissed me like that. No warning. No burying his hands in my hair and pulling me to his chest.

My imagination runs away with me as I picture what could have been. I promptly banish the thoughts from my head, refusing to think of our several other near-kisses.

Does he think this is some kind of a game?

"Aladdin?" I whisper, but he doesn't move.

I poke his arm, but he still doesn't react. I try his name a few more times, but it only elicits soft breathing from him. When I slide my fingers along his jaw and onto his cheek, I expect *something*, and yet he truly has fallen asleep, lost to the intensity of the day. Not even my touch makes him open his eyes.

I sit back, leaning against the wall again. No one can see my reaction—they're all asleep—so what does it matter? Running my hands through my hair, I try to figure out what it means.

I doubt he'll even remember it in the morning. I can't decide if I'm glad he won't remember it or furious. I'm not even sure how *I* feel about it.

After a few moments of watching him sleep peacefully and the annoyance growing in my chest that he could just so passively kiss me and then move on with life, I decide to go back to my spot between Levi and Simon and try to sleep.

I check each man as I walk by them, making sure they really are asleep. Finally assured that no one witnessed the humiliation of putting a man to sleep with my kiss, I lay back down. Tears form in my eyes, but I blink all but one away. It slowly drips across the bridge of my nose and around the outline of my other eye as lay on my side. As if the tear wants to draw out my pain, it takes the slowest path possible to drop off of my face and onto my shoulder.

I stare at the feather on the hat lying next to me until I fall asleep, too.

It's irrational to be angry when I wake up. Aladdin was exhausted and didn't know what he was doing last night. I shouldn't be so hurt as he strides around the broken-down building, preparing to leave.

He offers me a smile and nod when I catch his eye, but that only makes it worse. Watching him joke around with Javed and warm up to Simon while avoiding talking to me only annoys me.

I try to catch his eye, but he only offers a weak smile and nod each time. Turning away, I brush out my hair with my fingers, attempting to style it into something that might work to stay aligned with the dress I'm wearing. Each piece snarls around my fingers, but I eventually work out the knots.

"I'm headed out," Levi walks up to me, tugging on his gloves. "You'll be okay?"

"I'll be fine."

"See you at the Hall." He nods, heading toward the hole in the wall acting as our exit. Levi waits until Javed nods from the window where he's watching the street and then disappears back into the alley.

"Are you okay, my love. You look distressed." Simon's gentle hand on my shoulder makes me turn. "Are you going to tell me what this is about?"

I sigh. Keeping anything from Simon is impossible.

"Is it because he kissed you?" My stomach drops. Sucking in a deep breath involuntarily gives me away and Simon smiles sadly. "He mentioned it to Javed this morning."

"What did he say?"

"I didn't hear much…"

"Simon." As much as I can't hide things from him, he can't hide things from me.

"He was commenting on how stupid he was for kissing you and trying to figure out what to do."

That hurts worse than being left alone last night, but it explains his strange reaction to me this morning. I glance over at Aladdin for a moment before looking back to my friend.

"I'm just upset that he did that. There was no reason for that and now it has put us in this weird position and we still have to work together…but it's fine. I'll deal with it since he obviously isn't going to fix this."

"Why don't you go next, love? I'll follow."

"No, we stick to the plan," I say, resigning myself to being alone with Aladdin. I'll confront him and get it over with before we run off to handle Issac. At least I'll have some physical distance between us after we talk to think things through before we have to interact again.

"If you're sure—"

"I am." He nods at my words. After a moment of staring at me, he pulls back and calls carelessly to Javed, covering for our serious conversation.

I watch as Simon and the genie speak for a moment. Aladdin wanders over before Javed looks outside once more. Simon adjusts his goggles over his eyes, tipping his hat toward me before he ducks out.

"I'll give you two a minute," Javed says quickly as soon as Simon is gone. "See you at the Stourbridge."

I wait for the lamp against my leg to vibrate as Javed returns to his home, but then I remember that I have the fake one and Simon has control of the real one so there's no chance that Issac can find it. I tuck the decoy further back on my hip, ensuring it's tucked under my skirt.

Aladdin watches me from where he's leaning against the wall near the window. His finger is looped through his utility belt, other hand holding onto the strap that secures his shoulder guard across his chest. I ignore him, working on my hair again as I try to twist it up and secure it.

He pushes off the wall and saunters toward me,

expression unreadable. Aladdin makes it across the empty room in record time.

"What?" I grumble, still working my hair into order. I barely glance up from where my eyes are focused on the ground as I work. I sway back on my heels, putting a little extra distance between us without actually stepping back.

"I know that you're a little upset that I kissed you last night, so I wanted to come clear things up."

Oh great, Simon told him to come talk to me.

He doesn't slow his pace. I step back in surprise, but he doesn't seem to mind my reaction. He steps with me until I'm flat against the wall and he's hovering in front of me.

Aladdin's lips are more forceful this time. He kisses me slowly and deliberately, moving my lips with his in clearly defined kisses that leave no room for my imagination to come up with reasoning. His hands migrate to my hair and I drop the strands I was working with to wrap my fingers in his hair.

"Yes, I meant to kiss you." His hand moves to my neck, thumb tracing my collar bone. He makes a noise in his throat as he kisses me.

My fingers quickly work their way through his hair. He isn't playing fair as he moves closer and I shudder against him.

"Yes, I'd do it again," he says in that same, sultry voice. He pulls back just enough to tip his face to the other side and runs his hand out onto my shoulder and down my arm. My mind can't keep track of both his lips and his hands, so I melt into him and let him guide our kiss.

"Yes, I held back this entire time because I didn't think it could work." His lips move faster, and he uses his movements to tip my chin up to him as we kiss. Aladdin's hands find their way to my back and waist, and he draws me closer to him.

Two can play at this game.

Leaving my right hand to roam through his hair, I drag my left down his chest. I hit the strap of his shoulder guard, but I don't let it stop me. My fingers push against the fabric of his jacket and vest and he sighs against me.

I pull his face closer to mine as I lean back against the wall and reach up with my hand to tug on the scarf around his neck, pulling it out from under the neck of his jacket.

Aladdin leans back, laughing for just a second as he grins. Closing his eyes, he leans forward and kisses me, tugging on my bottom lip with his lips.

"I'm sorry about last night," he murmurs as he pulls away, lingering. "I got carried away and I messed up. But I like you, Cyra, and I'd really like to kiss you again if that's all right with you. I hope this makes up for messing up last night."

He reaches up with his free hand and brushes his

thumb against my jaw, tipping my chin up with his other fingers as he looks into my eyes.

"It's been very hard to read you, Aladdin," I inform him, trying not to lean into his touch.

"It's been hard to read you too, princess." He smirks. I roll my eyes, making him chuckle.

Leaning forward, I surprise him with a kiss, but he gladly obliges, rolling his lips over mine furiously for another moment.

"I wish I could kiss you more often," he says.

"I *wish* you would put your hand back in my hair," I whisper back. There's no genie to grant our wishes, so it's safe to say the word.

"I *wish* you would hold me." He kisses me as I wrap both arms around the small of his back and pull him toward me.

"I *wish* you would stop talking…"

He laughs but doesn't pull away, letting his lips brush against mine as he speaks. "Has Javed let you use *any* of your wishes yet?"

"I've been able to do everything on my own so far."

"Think he's trying to prove a point?"

"That we don't need wishes?" I consider his words. It would make sense. Most people go through life with having to make their own wishes come true. Maybe we don't need Javed's magic to set Leandra free. "Maybe we need to make our own magic."

"I'd say this is pretty great magic." He smirks, leaning forward to kiss me again.

Reaching over his shoulder, I wrap my arm around his neck and take control of the kiss, making him purr under my touch. This is definitely better than the kiss last night.

"We don't have to go," he says, voice husky after another minute.

"We do," I whisper back, nodding. Aladdin lingers close, never taking his eyes off of me as we engage in a battle of head shaking and nodding, insisting we should move, but never doing it.

Finally, he pulls back, peeling away from the wall. When the air hits the front of my body, it feels cold where he had been leaning against me. I move forward with him, reaching for his hand as he steps backward.

I let him lead me a few steps before looking away. He takes that as his signal to turn around and get back to the mission.

"I'll be right behind you, but don't stop for anything. Just get to the Hall and trade with Issac for the information."

"As long as we don't run into your uncle's man, we'll be fine."

"And as long as he hasn't told Issac, we're fine." He holds the curtain back for me, motioning that I should climb through.

Dropping down to my knees, I crawl through the exit, lifting my head on the other side.

"We're okay now?" I ask.

"If that was just *okay* for you, I can't wait to see what your *incredible* turns out to be," he jokes.

I can work with this new side of him.

"Hey, princess," he calls to me as I start to slip out of the tent into the alley. "*You* have to tell your friends about this. If *I* do, they'll murder me."

"Guess you won't have to worry about your uncle then, will you?" I tease.

"And here I thought you wanted to kiss me again."

"Maybe I do and maybe I don't. Guess you'll have to wait and see what I wish for."

"Any chance showing off will help my case because I can do that." He pulls back from the opening of the exit in the wall and motions to his abs, clearly reminding me of what I've already seen. An electric shock runs through me.

"Is that supposed to mean something?" I call over my shoulder, slipping away. He protests in the background as I take off down the street.

Everything seems quiet in the early morning sunlight. Aladdin's touch still lingers on my skin, warming the places his fingers glanced over moments ago.

I force the replay out of my mind, focusing on my surroundings as I hurry toward the Market. Simon and

Levi hover near the edge of the market place just out of sight as the merchants set up for the morning. The Market is a different place without the officials there.

Aladdin's hand on the center of my back is searing when he sidles up next to me. "I see you made it," he whispers, wrapping his fingers around mine.

"You aren't supposed to be here." I turn to look over my shoulder.

"Just letting you know I arrived, princess. I'm leaving."

I almost tell him to stay, but we can't be seen together like we were yesterday. He slips away quietly, tugging my hand once.

Levi makes his way out into the Market, taking up the same place he did yesterday. Eventually, Simon wanders out too. I wait, watching for Issac to enter the Hall before I leave the safety of the alleyway shadows.

When the Governor steps up onto the platform in front of the Hall, I duck. I'm too far away for him to notice me, but I can't miss him in his black attire that I've become so accustomed to. Peeking out, I see Levi has noticed him and has made an effort to stand behind a group of people, trying not to be seen.

More officials make their way up the stairs and across the platform. Finally, Issac appears, still wearing those ridiculous stilts.

Aladdin comes out from hiding—he's picked a hat up somewhere along the way—and takes his place hovering near the stairs. He doesn't appear to be looking for me, but the moment I get close, his eyes latch onto mine.

"Careful," he murmurs, passing me. He keeps his head down, using the brim of the hat to obscure part of his face.

Once inside, I make my way to Issac's office, breezing past the tiny robot made of nuts and bolts. Careful to avoid the Governor's office, I slip silently through the halls until I reach the Proprietor's door, knocking before I can get in my head and overthink the situation.

"Who is it?" he calls from the other side.

"Cyra. I have something for you, sir." I hear movement on the other side of the door and then it opens, swinging inside.

"This is unexpected," Issac croons, looking down at me. "If you're here for help with the Stourbridge, the next clue doesn't come out until this afternoon."

"I'm not here for a clue," I reply, looking up. He appraises my outfit. "I'm here for a trade."

"You don't have anything I want." He smiles at me like I'm a young child, eyebrow raised.

"Don't I?" I challenge, trying to be coy. "I didn't even have to go to the Cave to get it."

"Then you *certainly* don't have what I'm looking for."

"Oh, but I do. You see, a boy brought it out of the Cave. I stole it from him." Smiling, I try to draw it out to make him want the decoy even more. "It wasn't that hard —he was naïve."

"And where might I ask, is the oil can, Cyra?" His tone dips down into disbelief as he motions me in.

"I want to make a deal with you, Mr. Von Hinten. The oil can for the location of the Stourbridge and a guarantee that it will be mine."

"Show me the oil can first." He tips his head up to look down his nose at me.

"I need a sign of good faith. Tell me how to break in first, then I'll give you the oil can, and you tell me where to find the airship."

"Fair." He nods. "You'll need tools to break in—"

I pull the wrench out of a pocket in my skirt. He nods and lists a few other things. Issac explains specifically how to break into the airship using a panel and what to do once I get inside to get it to move.

"The oil can, Cyra," he reminds me, motioning with his hand. "The location will be yours. I think you'll be quite pleased."

Balancing on the edge of his desk, he waits for me to reveal the fake oil can. I turn, moving the top decorative part of my skirt to reveal it. As I unhook it from my utility belt, I ask, "Why is this so important, anyway?"

"It belonged to someone I cared very deeply for. It's all I have left of her," Issac lies.

"What happened to it?" I play along as I move my skirt

to pull it away from my body. It catches the lights from the office and his eyes widen. He looks like he's going to pounce at me to take it.

"Someone very bad stole it from me," he informs me, waiting for me to step forward to hand it to him. I linger, pretending to wipe it off with part of my skirt as if I'm shinning it for him. "My men tracked her down as she was leaving the Cave where she hid from me, but it was too late, and the officials had prohibited any of us from entering the Cave for any reason, so it was lost until now."

I'm acutely aware that it was Issac specifically that the officials banned from the Collection Cave, but I don't call him on it.

"What happened to the person who stole it?"

"She's dead. She was trespassing—they had no choice." His lips snarl up into a grin that he tries to hide, confirming his lie. "She paid the price for helping that miserable—"

He cuts himself off as I hand the oil can to him. "She and her husband both died, taking the location of the oil can with them. They say she was warning her husband not to give away the oil can's location, but she only got a few words out before she was shot. Bled out right in the street. Serves her right."

As I let go of the cog-covered oil can, I realize he's talking about my mother and father. They must have hidden Javed's lamp it in the Collection Cave so that Issac couldn't find it. Her dying words—assuming Issac's story is true—were to help protect the genie.

I hold my breath, wondering if he's seeing bits of my mother in my face as he studies me. It's as if this moment was meant to be—me arriving to avenge my parents' death. Issac watches me, still holding the oil can as my fingers slide off it.

He looks down, tearing his gaze from mine as he inspects it. His fingers brush over the cogs and gears Simon soldered onto the bent container.

"Is that it?" I ask. I wonder if he can spot the vague lion Simon worked into the design, or if he even knows about it.

"I believe it is." He looks up, clutching it to his chest. "The Stourbridge is nearby. In fact, we're standing on top of it. I've hidden it under the structure of the Hall. All you have to do is go down and retrieve it. It's waiting for you."

He grins as if he's won everything he was seeking.

"When you're done, Cyra, come see me," he continues. "Perhaps we can reach a new arrangement. After all, if you've won both the Empress and the Stourbridge, I think it would be wise to keep you close. You and I might be able to accomplish great things together, and I'm sure the Governor wouldn't mind sharing you."

"Under the Hall?" I question, staying on task.

"Yes. Below the lower platforms, there's another level. Take it and you'll have full access to the airship. Just do me a favor and try not to die down there—it's easy to fall."

"I'll be careful."

"I left a rope down there. Use it. Tell my men I said *oil can win* and they'll know to let you have it."

I nod, backing toward the door. He folds an arm around the fake oil can, cradling it. Issac watches me, chin high in the air as I retreat—he's celebrating his victory. We won't have long before he realizes we duped him.

As soon as the door is closed in front of me, I turn, running down the hallway. If the airship is below us, we'll have even less time to escape—Issac has an entire team of guards at his fingertips here at the Hall. He won't have to explain himself, just say we were trying to damage the Hall. He can have us arrested, or even executed, and then move the airship without anyone knowing our true motives.

As soon as I make it out the door, I rush across the platform. From the corner of my eye, I see the boys moving.

"It's below the Hall," I shout, flinging myself toward Aladdin at the bottom of the stairs. "It's been down there the whole time."

"And to think I told those guys it was under the

waterfall!" Aladdin gasps next to me. I'll have to ask him later what guys he's talking about.

"We need tools," I inform him instead, tugging him down the flight of steps. "We have to hurry."

"What tools?" He hurries with me, brushing against my skirt. I rattle off a list. "I have the screwdriver from the factory, but where do we get the rest from?"

"I'll send Levi for them!" I don't take the time to explain. "We're going to need that wire you found, he said something about using a rope he left down here and that I had to be careful not to fall."

Once on the lower platform, Aladdin and I look around. There has to be a door or a hidden entrance...*something* that's different. Aladdin branches off from me, searching for anything that might lead us to the airship.

After a moment, there's crashing behind us as Levi and Simon join us. I run over to explain.

"Levi!" I crash into his chest, nearly spinning both of us. He wraps his arms around me to keep us upright. "The Stourbridge is beneath us. Issac said we'd need tools. I had a woman dump a ton of them into the water-fall two days ago—I'm sure she hasn't fished them out. I need you to go get them."

"In the water?" he asks skeptically.

"Yes, hurry!"

"Why did she dump them into the falls?"

"I paid her to," I reply, annoyed. I pull the pliers I purchased from her out of my pocket and snap them open and shut while talking. "She was selling a bunch of fakes mixed among the good tools, so I preemptively made sure the other competitors didn't get them."

Levi grins. "Now *that's* the Cyra I know." He shoves a strangely-shaped tool into my hand.

"Hey!" Aladdin shouts before I can turn Levi back to the exit. A gust of wind comes rushing through the platform area. When I turn, I find Aladdin's silhouette outlined by an open door. "We're going to need those tools!"

Chapter 17
Aladdin

The wind pushes at me from under the platform. The top of the Stourbridge hovers where the ground should be. Cyra rushes over to me, followed by Simon and Levi.

A single rope is attached to the wall near the door providing a way down to the platform beneath where a competitor could try to work their way out to the airship to break in. Off to the side, two men stand, looking up at us. They must be Issac's men that are meant to force competitors who did not enter the Cave to wait before leaving with the Stourbridge.

"You're going to need this," Simon announces, pulling a mechanical gauntlet out of his jacket. "It will help you get down there. And this." He shoves the lamp and glove at Cyra.

"Levi, go get the tools—we're going to need them to break in." Cyra fastens the lamp onto her utility belt. She glances at the men below us. They do nothing but stare, hands clasped behind their backs.

Simon shoves another gauntlet at me, pushing it into my chest. "You too," he murmurs.

As Cyra continues to give directions, explaining what each of us has to do, I bend down to retrieve the wire from my bag. Simon helps me locate an area we can attach it to, enabling both Cyra and me to drop down to the lower level to break into the airship. Once we're on board, Levi can join us while Simon holds off Issac. With any luck, he can trip him off the platform and let him fall into the sky below us. It's so expansive down there that I can't see an end to it from up on the deck.

"It's like Horallen was built on the clouds," Cyra murmurs.

"*Oh*, there's ground beneath us," I reply. "There's just *sky*, too."

I hand her a wire and she wraps it around her gauntlet. The glove comes to life—and invention of Simon's, so it seems—and clamps itself around the wire to guide her descent.

"Are you ready?" I ask, taking hold of my wire.

"I'll send Levi down with the tools as soon as he gets back," Simon assures us. "For now, I'll keep watch. Stay safe, love."

Simon reaches forward, kissing Cyra's cheek before turning to run back to the entrance. I shouldn't be jealous, *I know*, but I am.

Cyra doesn't seem to notice as she swings herself off the platform and drops down the wire much faster than I'd like her to. Following, I kick my feet out and plummet down to the lower deck.

When I come to a stop, Cyra is there waiting for me. Still holding the wire with one hand, she leans forward to place her other on my chest and presses her lips against mine. I sway into her movements, but she only lingers against me for a brief moment before turning to the airship, all business.

Cyra hurries over and says something to the men. They nod and she races back to me before ignoring the men completely. She quickly starts tinkering with the outside panel, trying to break into it so she can force the main doors open similarly to what she said she did the previous year. I step up beside her, waiting for instructions.

The gap between the platform and the airship is enough to make anyone with a fear of heights nauseous. This end of the ship is close enough that we don't have to lean far enough that it's dangerous but I still don't like it.

Cyra leans forward quickly, testing to see if the airship will move if she leans her weight against it. My arm lashes out, darting in front of her, prepared to pull her back if needed.

"What are you doing?" She turns to me, clearly surprised.

"Making sure you don't fall." I would hope that would be obvious. She glances down, looking at my arm wrapped around her upper abdomen, then back to me. Her eyes scream at me to release her. I lean in seductively and whisper my words from yesterday in her ear, "You really think I'm going to let go of you?"

She smirks at me. "What, no pistol this time?"

Cyra directs me on what she wants me to do and we work together to open the panel. It's much harder than it looks.

"Issac killed my mother for hiding Javed in the Cave," she murmurs after a few moments, checking to make sure the men aren't close enough to hear us. I work the screwdriver into a screw on the panel, hoping to pop the section open. "He killed my father too—that's how he knew it was an oil can. Or, assumed it was an oil can. It's what my mother was saying when they shot her."

"What?" The news ripples through me as if I touched an electrical wire. I stop helping her to turn and look at her. "You didn't know how they died?"

"No. I didn't know they were at the Cave hiding Javed's lamp." She sniffs. Using the back of her hand, she wipes the corner of her eye. "I just assumed it was from being on the streets. A neighbor told me about it, I think. All I remember was being turned out onto the streets."

"Did he *say* he killed your parents?"

"He didn't know it was me," she promises. "At least he didn't let on if he knew. He was being vague about it when I asked why he lost the oil can. I'm not even sure he was the one who killed them—he probably had someone else do it. But I know my mother had Javed with her the last time she left, and Issac said the woman who hid the oil can and her husband died that night. I made the connection."

I put a hand on her shoulder to comfort her. I have nothing to say.

She ignores it, though I can tell she appreciates it by the way she leans into my hand as she focuses on the panel she's trying to break into. It snaps, clicking open.

"There!"

Running her hands over it, she looks for the wires she needs to open the main door. We try a series of connections, but none swing the door open.

Cyra reaches under her top skirt and pulls out a monocle. Flipping it over her hair, she settles it over one eye, then moves a series of levers to adjust the magnification as she leans in.

"I'm going to look at the door; keep trying," I instruct.

Rushing to the end of the platform, I wrap the wire around myself so that it can support me as I lean off the deck. I space my feet apart to stabilize myself, then tip forward.

Using the screwdriver I picked up, I pry it between the door and the ship, hoping to break it open. Nothing pops, but I don't give up.

"Anything?" she calls after a minute. No one has found the lower deck where the Stourbridge is being kept yet, but the threat of Issac's retribution looms over us like an airship that passes over the rookery at the wrong time of day.

"Not yet. You?"

She gasps as something clanks against the side of the metal airship. My heart drops in my chest.

"Well, that wasn't good." I look over to find her staring down into the clouds below us.

"What did you drop?" I call over, relieved it wasn't her falling. Suddenly, something pops in the door. I jerk my head back to look.

"Did you get it?"

I move the screwdriver again, popping something else. Cyra hurries over to me and I direct her to wrap the wire around herself like I did, still bracing myself against the side of the ship. The airship is angled enough that this end sits farther from the deck than the control panel.

Together, we pry the door open only to be faced with another panel.

"Issac wasn't playing around this year," Cyra whispers. "Would have been nice if he had told me that the panel I was supposed to be breaking into was *behind the door.*"

"And saved you some time? Where's the fun in that?"

"I don't know, where's the fun in escaping his wrath?" She glances at me, concern on her face. "He has to know by now."

"Coming down!" Levi yells, repelling off the platform above us, tools in hand. "I'm with them."

He shakes his head as his feet touch the platform, spraying us with water. The men look to Cyra for confirmation. She nods and they let Levi pass.

"Next time, the *new guy* takes the dive job." He points at me.

"Bad news," he continues. "A couple of the competitors saw me. They're definitely following me, but Simon is going to try to redirect them. I lost them, but I left a trail of water behind me, so I'm sure I can't be *that* hard to find."

Cyra turns back to the control panel and starts demanding tools from Levi. I attempt to help her, following her lead, but I overthink things and misread her cues. We bump into each other more than we help the other.

"Help her," I say quietly, motioning for Levi to take my place. The two of them have worked together long enough that they have a rhythm. He'll strengthen her approach where I'll only hold her back.

The two work quickly, using shortened words to communicate, proving they're the team for this mission. I don't like watching, but I'm resigned to look over their shoulders.

"We need Javed," Cyra finally snaps.

"On it," Levi says, rushing toward the guards to distract them. I turn my back to them, blocking for Cyra as she reaches down to crank the lever on the lamp under her top skirt once Levi is in place. Steam bubbles out of it immediately and Javed appears next to me. "Javed, what do we do?"

"You found it." He pauses and steps back, examining the control panel, oblivious to the guards. "There."

The genie points out what Cyra should do. Issac stayed fairly true to Javed's original designs, but it was easy enough for Javed to figure out what he altered in order to help Cyra.

She pulls the wrench she got from the Cave out and unfastens part of the paneling, revealing a hidden compartment. While she struggles inside it with a strangely-shaped tool, Javed turns to me. We ignore Levi when he returns.

"My friend, do you remember when I said I could see certain things around corners and a few moments ahead in time?" Javed steps back to speak to me privately. If the others weren't so preoccupied with opening the airship, they easily could have overheard us.

"Yes," I reply skeptically. "Do you see something?"

"I got it!" Cyra shouts. The door pops out and slides open, revealing an entrance.

The interior glows a soft yellow color. Warmth flows out of it, stretching across the gap between the airship and the windy deck. A key hangs on a ribbon inside the airship, beckoning us to enter.

"Okay, I'm going over." She turns to nod to us. I take a deep breath and nod back. She doesn't bother looking for Levi's permission or approval.

"And you did it without using a single wish," Javed points out to her, not sounding nearly as excited as he should as he confirms our theory about not using the wishes. "You changed destiny without my help at all. Everything you've accomplished is because you decided to make it so. You didn't have to rely on anyone but yourself."

Cyra smiles and quickly unties the wire from around her waist, handing it to me to hold. Turning, she leaps off the deck and my heart jumps in my throat, sinking back down once she lands inside the Stourbridge.

Pulling the key down, she unfolds the note. Cyra reads it silently as I turn my attention back to Javed.

"It says we need a second key." Cyra looks up in dismay, eyes wide.

"We can rig the wires," Levi suggests, trying to calm her.

"No!" I shout, suddenly remembering the key I took from the Cave. I dig it out of my pocket and shrug. "I took the back exit, they didn't search me."

Cyra grins as I hold it up for her—it's similar to the one she pulled down in the entrance.

"Come on!" She turns before I can speak and disappears deeper into the airship, looking for the bridge of the Stourbridge to take control of it.

"Go." I nod to Levi, handing him the key with the brass colored cog. Once he's made the jump, I turn to Javed, but Simon's call distracts all three of us, turning us toward the platform door before Levi can disappear to follow Cyra.

"Guys!" Simon's voice echoes through the lower deck.

"*What did you see?*" I hiss at Javed, knowing whatever Simon is warning us about is something Javed has knowledge of and waited to tell me.

"*Saw*, my friend. I *saw*." He answers slowly, hanging his head. "I'm deeply sorry, my friend. There was no other way."

Javed reaches out as if he wants to touch my arm but

he holds back stiffly. My mind is throwing around so many possibilities that I almost become lightheaded.

"What do you mean?" Something is wrong—*off*—about his behavior. His hand closes and opens at his side until he finally looks up at me. "A sacrifice must be made, Aladdin. Not just Leandra's."

It takes a moment to wrap my head around his meaning. My first instinct is to bolt—*to protect myself*—but I can't. If I leave, that means the others will pay the price.

The dead guy can stay dead, or the others can join him, my mind argues with me.

"The lion's heart..." Javed's words drag. "It's not just Cyra. It's *you*. I knew it was you the moment we met—I saw it in your heart as I pulled you out from the landslide. It was always meant to be you. I hadn't anticipated Cyra's role though."

Simon—or something—slams into the platform door, nearly jarring it open from the other side. Simon is clearly struggling out there.

"I'm sorry, Aladdin. There's nothing I can do about it," Javed murmurs.

"Levi, get to Cyra!" I demand, whipping around to face him. "Don't let her back out here."

Levi makes eye contact with me, nostrils flaring. Finally, he looks to Javed. "You'll pay for this, genie, I'm sure." Slamming the airship door closed, I hear him race away after Cyra.

The guards have taken notice of our behavior and step forward. Cyra is inside the ship and to them, it might look like she left us behind and they might need to stop us since Cyra has clearly taken control of the ship.

"Go," I instruct Javed. He hesitates, staring at me. *"Get inside, Javed. You're the only one that can take them to her."*

I no longer have patience for his hesitation.

The door flies open above, but it's not Simon—it's Issac.

Taking the rope, he immediately jumps down. Behind him, several of his men rip the wire from my hands, also tugging on mine. Spinning, I uncoil myself as they attempt to drag me away from the airship.

As they rapidly approach, more faces appear at the door above us. Something glints, catching my eye, and I look up just in time to see a flash of a metal mask—the pistol boys are back with their lion masks, their red-headed leader nowhere in sight. They catch sight of me and push to get to the edge to join us on the platform.

"Javed!" Issac's words are shocked, rising high in pitch as he springs toward us on his stilts. I snap my attention back to him. *"Finally."*

"Go," I command the genie again. Issac jerks his attention toward me and his eyes rake over me, assessing what type of threat I pose to him.

"Give me the oil can, boy." Issac holds his hand out. "I'll let you take the airship. You just have to give me *him.*"

I take a step back, keenly aware of where the edge of the platform is. The masked boys make their way over to us, but the two guards posted to watch over the Stourbridge stop them, holding them back for Issac and to give Cyra the time she needs to steal the airship under Issac's previous command.

"Why, so you can destroy him? Bond him to you forever?" I challenge. "I know what you did to those men and to Leandra."

"Don't you speak her name, *boy.*" Issac scrunches his eyes, glaring at me as he tries to take a menacing step toward me on his leg extensions. He looks like a lion ready to pounce—perhaps Leandra should have given her symbol over to her former fiancé.

"Don't anger him, Aladdin," Javed says quietly, trying not to move his lips.

"I told you to go, *genie,*" I snarl. If Javed hadn't kept this to himself, we could have been prepared for this—we might have even escaped. Instead, he held onto the bit about sacrificing one of us to get back his friend. I may have been in this competition for myself, but even I would have given a person a chance out if I knew it would end like this for them.

I turn back to Issac. "I don't have it." His eyes narrow

even further as he realizes the girl on the airship is in control of the genie.

More men slide down the wire, prepared to back Issac up. The boys in the masks struggle to get around the guards, but the older men don't budge. In the doorway, more people fill the space, staring down at us.

The Proprietor doesn't even seem nervous about being on the platform with me, mere feet away from the edge where either of us could plunge to our deaths. He takes another step toward me.

Then, something pops loudly behind me. Ordinarily, it would worry me, but there are so many other things that could kill me before the popping sound does. Issac glances to the side, worry flashing on his face as his ears pull back. He steps back. The men surrounding him look nervously at the sound. Maybe I *should* be worried.

Turning, I find the Stourbridge pulling back away from the platform. It had been tethered there by several chains that are now ripping out of their holds, taking part of the platform with it.

"I guess Cyra played us both." The creator of the airship's voice is dark.

Issac pulls the decoy oil can out from his utility belt under his extra-long jacket. Throwing it at me, he tries to topple me off the platform, but Javed takes the blow, stopping it before it can hit me. He glares at Issac.

"You won't win this, Issac."

"I already have, Javed, and as soon as I have your sad little home, you can lead me to Leandra. You can't win; you can only make it easier on yourself." He changes his voice, sounding like he's speaking to the boy who hid us in the alleyway of the rookery. "Why fight if it's only going to work against you in the long run?"

"You're a chiseler, Issac." We need to work on Javed's insults when this is all over. Or, rather, Cyra does, since I'm about to be sacrificed for the cause.

I trust Cyra to hold up to her end of the deal, but I whisper to Javed anyway. "Once you find Leandra, you get my mother out of here. Swear it."

Another snap sounds, dropping another chunk of the platform down as the airship pulls further away.

"What is this?" a man shouts from the upper level.

"None of your concern, Alias." Issac doesn't take his eyes off me as he yells up.

"I should have known you had the oil can," a new voice calls—*Kacper.* "Do what you need, Issac?"

They're working together. I can't tell if Kacper knows about the genie or not, but he's more than willing to put the blame on me and let Issac do his dirty work.

"*What* is this?" Governor Alias demands, words pointed.

"Cyra has control of the Stourbridge!" I call, hoping the Governor can at least give her and Levi a chance.

"Aladdin!" Simon shouts, forcing his way in front of

the officials standing on the landing above, struggling against someone trying to hold him back.

"Give me the genie, boy!" Issac yells so loudly the men on the platform react, pulling back.

The group of men at the top of the landing all pull back at the word *genie*. They turn and mutter to each other as Simon fights against a guard.

Kacper doesn't flinch. I lock eyes with my uncle and he narrows his gaze. He quietly raises his left hand where it's hidden between his body and the door frame and waves at me by bending the tops of his fingers, pretending to be sad. His lip pouts for a moment before curling up into a sneer.

Issac rushes forward, pulling my attention away from my uncle. He grabs my jacket lapels before I can escape—those stilts are incredibly fast.

"Give it to me!"

"Aladdin!" Cyra suddenly screams behind me as Issac steps us toward the edge of the platform, intending on pushing me over, or at least threatening to. Cyra's voice makes me twist to see her, despite the impending fall. She tries to threaten the man from her place on the deck of the Stourbridge. "Let him go, Issac!"

"You used to be so polite, Cyra," Issac calls back. He smiles. "No."

He pushes me forward again, eliciting a scream from

both Cyra and Simon. Their voices are like a strange echo of each other from opposite ends of the space.

"Issac, please!" Cyra begs. "I have Leandra."

Issac whips his head to her. Cyra defiantly holds up a piece of paper.

"I took her, Issac, and you can't have her back."

"The photograph," Issac whispers so quietly that I can barely hear him. Then he switches to a roar, forcing me to turn at an angle and run down the platform backward toward Cyra. "Give it to me!"

When Issac finally stops us, I turn to see the Stourbridge pulling away even more, Cyra standing in the door waving the photograph.

"Come get it," Cyra taunts him.

"I'll kill him."

"You touch him and I'll rip this to shreds. You'll never see her again!"

In the background, the Governor yells, trying to control the situation and protect Cyra. Issac's men draw closer, waiting for their orders.

The platform snaps again and the boys in the lion masks take that as their cue to leave. They scramble up the wires, attempting to push past the officials as they watch in horror, trying to piece together information about Issac and the genies—I wonder how much they knew about Issac from before because they look shocked that this could possibly be the same man who created the genies. I would be too given Issac's actual age.

"If you want him, come get him," Issac calls back to Cyra. He swings me around to the edge of the platform again, but this time, I'm ready. Forcing my body forward, I attempt to knock him over.

Issac stumbles back but doesn't fall. I pull my leg out from under his stilt and jerk the leg extensions out from under him. Losing his balance, he falls but immediately kicks at me, forcing me to the edge of the platform. I tumble off but catch the edge, wishing I still had Simon's gauntlet on to hold me up—if only I hadn't needed my hands to break into the airship earlier.

"Aladdin!" Cyra and Javed scream in terror as they watch me dangle.

Javed turns to confront Issac, blocking him from me while I work my leg up and over the edge of the platform. It cracks again under our weight, lurching down a foot before stopping. Issac's men scramble back, no longer as brave as they had been moments ago.

I'm nearly on the platform again when I catch Kacper's gaze. He smiles.

That's when I notice Byron sliding down one of the wires. The other men scramble up, leaving Issac to his own devices. Byron stalks over to me, ready to kick me off the platform for good. Cyra calls to me but I block her out, focusing on the task at hand.

I pull myself up and run at Issac—I have one chance at ending this, and even if I have to fall *with* him, I *will* throw him off this platform. Rushing past Javed, I tackle Issac, but he's ready for me, swinging us with my momentum.

Javed throws his hands to the side, metal arm whirring, and a pulse erupts from him, shaking the entire platform. Issac dips with me, his stilts taking the impact of the jolt. I grab his hands around my lapels out of terror, holding myself up.

"You won't win," I promise him through gritted teeth.

Byron rips me away from Issac, throwing me to the ground. He kicks and I curl around his foot as I take the impact of his boot. I can't breathe. I can't think.

Black spots appear in front of my eyes and dizziness floods me over as I sit up. Kacper's henchman lifts me up by my jacket collar. Somewhere in my vision, I see Cyra shout to someone on the platform, but I'm too out of sorts to hear her words. She looks back at me and locks eyes.

"I'll find you," she mouths, and I finally catch what she's saying. I nod. She looks miserable, but she holds her tears back, ripping her hand through her hair as she rises up on her toes to watch the further the airship pulls away.

The platform dips again and Byron begrudgingly drags me over to the wires as the officials shout that I am not to be hurt. Kacper has to keep up appearances, so his minion can't hurt me publicly.

"He helped the girl steal from Issac," Kacper announces loudly as we approach.

"Cyra didn't steal from Issac. She won the competition fairly," the Governor protests loudly. Everyone starts to argue as the Stourbridge pulls away, completely clearing the space Issac used as a hanger.

I pull away from Byron in an insane attempt to reach Cyra and help her escape, despite the airship being out of jumping distance. I suppose when death is inevitable, a dying man is willing to do just about anything.

Issac grabs my collar and pulls me back, tripping me as I fall.

"I'm sorry," Javed says, disappearing. Smoke fills the space, more than I've ever seen the genie or lamp produce before. Cyra or Levi has called him back to his lamp, keeping him safe from the Proprietor.

The officials behind us gasp, realizing what evil they were dealing with. I'm sure they have to know the truth behind the genies being banned all those years ago. Simon shouts next to them, explaining how this Issac is the same man from a century ago, insisting he's tricked the other officials.

All I can see is Cyra's face as the door slides shut on the airship. Levi pilots it away, leaving a giant open area where it had been. The platform creeks and Byron pulls me away in one fist, Issac in the other—I'm sure Kacper has a plan for helping him since he clearly has knowledge of what is happening.

I let him carry me back.

Javed sacrificed me to save Leandra and the others. He sacrificed me to save Cyra.

I sacrificed myself to save her.

Suddenly, I regret letting my mother know that I survived—I doubt I'll be alive for long.

The lion has control of the genie and the Stourbridge, though, and I have faith that she'll set things right with the magic Issac brought into this world. When she's done, she'll fix my world, whether I'm still in it or not. I know she won't stop until she rescues my mother from Kacper and she'll force Leandra and Javed to help her. In the end, I'll get what I was after—safety for my mother. I breathe deeply, resigning myself to my fate.

When we reach the top, Issac's men have the officials surrounded. It's over. Issac has won and all he has to do now is catch Cyra. Her only hope is finding Leandra first. I'm sure both Kacper and Issac have a plan for finding her.

For now, though, Cyra has stolen the Stourbridge. She's in control of the airship, and with the help of Levi and Javed, they can free the most powerful genie Horallen has ever seen.

Whatever it takes, I'm going to see that she has every advantage.

Turning, I strike, attempting to attack Issac and his men, leaving Simon, the Governor, and the officials yelling, and Cyra flying away on a steam-powered ship worth millions. The lion-shaped cogs and gears all turn together, making the image move as they sail away.

My voice turns into a roar as I claw at the man trying to destroy us all.

If Javed wants a lion's heart, I'll give him one, *but he's not going to like how this ends if I escape.*

Acknowledgements

My hometown is known for many things, one of which is that we were the site of the first train in the United States. In this story, I've buried many references to the town and the first successful train run in the States.

From names to symbols, the original Stourbridge Lion and Honesdale, PA are painted into the storyline of the Stealing Steam Series. If you'd like to learn more, check out the Stealing Steam world portal on my website.

The *distant* past now brings me to the *near* past…

Once upon a time, I was on a live broadcast answering fan questions when the topic of me writing a steampunk someday came up. As we were talking, the idea of steampunk Aladdin came up…Jess, I know you had to wait nearly two years, but I hope it was everything you wanted it to be.

Thank you, fabulous fans, for coming on this journey with me into the world of Steampunk Aladdin (as I've been calling this series for the last two years) I hope you enjoyed Aladdin and Cyra's journey…or at least the beginning.

If you haven't checked out the original Aladdin story,

you might be shocked to discover some very big differences from the movie version we all grew up loving. While I focused on the Arabian Nights version in my retelling, the very first version of Aladdin's tale actually came from China. If you take a look at the original, you'll see quite a few parallels to my version of Aladdin's story and the upcoming books in the series.

Special thanks to Jess and Elle for all of their help with this series.

Shout out to my fabulous street team and Elites—you're all amazing, as always!

Be sure to check out the world portal for Aladdin and Cyra's story on the website, friends, and stay tuned for the sequel…it only gets more dangerous from here!

Keep reading for a first look at the sequel, Pistons and Prisoners, as well as find out how to get bonus scenes, play an interactive game to see if *you* can find something inside the Collection Cave that will help steal the Stourbridge, and more!

Stay inspired!

-K.M. Robinson

PISTONS AND PRISONERS: BOOK TWO OF THE STEALING STEAM SERIES

All wishes offer opportunity...but are you willing to endure the repercussions?

As Aladdin fights for his life, Cyra is faced with a terrible choice: save him or save Leandra and the genies. Aboard the Stourbridge with Javed and Levi by her side, she's forced to leave Aladdin and Simon behind in order to hunt down the most powerful genie of them all—her great-great-aunt.

With Kacper and Issac in charge of Horallen's people, Aladdin has no hope of survival as they search for the remaining genies in the country's darkest depths, but his sacrifice will give Cyra her best chance at freeing them before the monstrous men holding him can leverage the power of the ultimate genie.

All wishes offer opportunity, but they might not be able to survive the repercussions of stealing the bottle.

Coming May 2019

pistonsandprisonersinfo.kmrobinsonbooks.com

FIRST LOOK: PISTONS AND PRISONERS

Chapter 1: Aladdin

The cracking sound behind us barely makes Byron flinch as he drags me across the lower deck. Metal tears against other metal as the platform below us gives way. It drops another foot, rendering itself unusable.

Issac glares at me, following quickly behind us as Byron and one of Issac's men drag me backward away from the Proprietor. He reaches up, wiping away blood from his lip where I managed to get a punch in before Byron held me back.

"Hold your tongue, *boy.*" Kacper hisses, taking a place

next to his henchman. My uncle seethes as he examines me—I doubt he'll bother to pretend to care this time.

"Enough!" Issac shouts, getting everyone's attention. "That is enough. Here's what's going to happen: my men will take you all back to the Hall. The guards you've employed to watch over your offices all work for me and will be ensuring that you stay in place for the next few days."

I wrestle around trying to find Simon in the crowd, but Byron's metal arm pierces into the flesh between my neck and shoulder, prohibiting me from moving too far.

The officials cower as the guards hover over them— Issac had planned this perfectly. The Governor glares at me like it's my fault Cyra got mixed up in stealing the Stourbridge, but I doubt I'll be given the chance to tell him about her plan to help Javed save Leandra from her bottle.

"What is this, Issac?" Governor Alias finally demands, turning on the Proprietor. Issac turns to him, still balancing on the curved leg extensions he uses like stilts. Miraculously, he managed to hang on to his walking stick even as I attempted to beat him.

"He's trying to steal the genies—" My words are cut off by a sharp smack to the face. My head jerks to the side as my Uncle Kacper pulls his hand back. From under the brim of his pilot's cap, his eyes shine with excitement.

"My nephew lost his father last year," Kacper turns to

the officials. Given that he's not cowering with them, I wonder if they've figured out he's working with Issac yet. "The poor boy hasn't been right since.

"I know it wasn't my place to spare him from the decision of the officials all this time, but he's been stealing and causing problems in Horallen for the last year," he admits, pretending to be sorry. If he's good enough to fool my mother, I can only imagine how he's been leading the other officials on all this time.

"I suppose if I hadn't protected him, we might not be in this predicament. I apologize deeply and humbly ask for your grace and mercy, my colleagues." He bows, the coat draped over his shoulders flaring out strangely with the movement. "I vowed to protect my brother's son, but I see that my ways were misguided—I was blinded by my love for my nephew."

Ordinarily, I'm skilled at controlling my facial expressions, but there's no holding back at Kacper's words. My lips pull back, baring my teeth as my eyes narrow at the man who sent a man to kill me just three days ago.

"It's true!" Simon shouts from his place behind the officials, interrupting Kacper's monoologue. "Issac is the man who created the genies—"

His words are cut off as someone punches him—I can see his top hat over the crowd and it pitches forward as if he's doubling over on himself with the strike.

"Issac has been trying to locate the most powerful

genie so he can control their power!" I yell, continuing where Simon left off. Byron pushes down so hard on my shoulder that I'm forced to my knees with a loud smack. "Cyra is trying to save them!"

My only hope is that the Governor can do something to stop Issac and give Cyra enough time to get the Stourbridge to wherever Leandra's bottle is hidden. His eyes bore into me as I speak, but Kacper's hand comes down again, snapping my head back.

"*Kacper*!" The Governor admonishes him.

Pushing up, I attempt to get around Byron's machine-like grip on me. Now that I'm in Kacper's grasp, I won't be making it out alive—fighting back isn't going to add any more danger than I'm already in. It gives the freedom to resist.

I throw myself toward my uncle, pulling out a knife I hid inside my boot from Lady de Ghent's house—the only weapon they didn't find on me already. Kacper reaches up to block me as I propel him backward, but Byron is fast enough to rip the blade from my hand.

Kacper topples over, taking me down with him. His jacket sprawls under us. My fists find their way to his collar and I nearly lift up his head and smash it into the concrete below us, but I know better than to kill him. Instead, I release a hand and pull back, preparing to drive my fist into his face—he deserves at least that much.

Somewhere off to the side, Simon is yelling my name, trying to get my attention. *Now is not the time.*

"Get him up." Issac's voice cuts through the noise, clear as day. He looms over us on his slits as two of his men pull me back. Byron stands to the side, pinned under Issac's glare. "I've had enough of this. Take the boys to my office and escort the officials back to their offices."

He turns to address the officials again. "The Hall is now under my command. The competition will continue with one minor change—they'll be helping me look for my genies. Cooperate now and I'll bring you in on this, gentlemen, but if you work against me, you won't like the new world you find yourselves living in a few days from now."

"You're really him?" one of the officials asks loudly. I can see him trying to figure out how Issac could still be alive after a century. Issac just stares at him. "How is that possible?"

"It doesn't matter, now does it?" Issac replies. "You have a choice to make. I'll have a word with each of you later today. For now, you will spend the rest of the afternoon in your offices and we'll reconvene later today.

"I suggest you walk of your own accord, gentlemen, because if you don't, we'll have to make it look like you're traitors, and that wouldn't do very well, now would it?" He offers them a tight smile and nods to them. "You don't want to be associated with the boy here."

Issac turns and walks toward the stairs leading to the garden island level where merchants are still attempting to sell their wares. I wonder if he has a plan for the officials who are still inside the Hall and didn't see the Stourbridge being taken.

"What are you going to do to the boy?" The Governor calls as the guards force me to follow behind Issac.

He turns slowly. "Kill him."

"You can't just kill him," Kacper says with fake concern in his voice. My uncle puts on a good show, I'll give him that.

"He's been stealing from Horallen for a year, you said so yourself, Kacper." Issac glances back at Kacper. The two clearly have a plan. "We'll put him on trial and be done with it, but either way, he's a traitor. He dies today. So does his friend."

I can't let them hurt Simon, Cyra will never forgive me for letting something happen to her friend. Not that it will matter if I'm dead, too, but Simon has done nothing to deserve this, other than helping Cyra when it was illegal, making a fake lamp to trick Issac, and holding off other competitors and officials to keep them from stopping us from stealing the airship.

Maybe Issac does *have enough to use against us during a trial.*

The light is incredibly bright when we reach the top of the stairs. I have to squint to see as I fight back, trying to dig my heels in to stop them from pushing me up the second flight of stairs. Once they get us through the doors to the Hall, we won't be coming back out. This is our only chance of escape.

"Run!" Simon shouts once we're in public, struggling against his captors a few feet away from me.

I elbow the man on my right, catching him off guard. The man on my left compensates, dragging me around in a circle to prevent me from striking again. A sharp, piercing pain radiates from my right hip as the man punches me. I lurch forward but stay upright as the second man holds me in place.

Turning, I attempt to kick his knee out, but his hand finds its way to my shoulder, and he manages to angle me so I can't force his leg out from under him. Simon throws his head back, crashing into one of his guards. His top hat tumbles on the ground…he looks different without it.

A crowd gathers, watching the brawl. The officials quietly file past us to the stairs where they step out onto the deck to watch—they're playing their part beautifully as Issac's men watch over them, weapons tucked away just out of sight under their jackets.

"Let go!" I demand, wrenching my arm away from the man who managed to keep his grip on me until now.

The crowd starts shouting, filled with merchants, housewives, and a few competitors. The school kids wander over, leaving the stands where they were buying their lunches. The girls look on warily, but the boys hurry over, eager to watch the fight.

One of the men kicks me, forcing me to stumble back. In an effort to keep myself from falling, I spin, running forward a few steps to fix my balance. The guards clamp down on my arms again, holding them straight out to my sides while they force me to my knees.

In the second row of the crowd, I catch a familiar face. He locks eyes with me but doesn't recognize me. That's when I realize it's the boy from the Market a few days ago; the one obsessing over some girl and the competition.

He was obsessing over *Cyra.*

"Hey!" I shout to him. "Cyra's in trouble, you have to help her!"

He lifts up on his toes, eyes wide. Clearly a young man in love, he pushes the boy in front of him aside to get closer.

"What about Cyra?" he demands.

"She took the Stourbridge—" The guard tries to stop me from speaking by kicking my hip. My entire mid-section lurches forward, but the men still hold my arms, preventing me from falling. Agony pierces through every part of my body, quickly blooming into more than it should. "Issac is trying to hurt her—you have to help her!"

My world goes black.

· · ·

***

"Good morning, Pretty One."

I blink, trying to get my bearings. Simon is tied to a chair in the dark room with me, his goggles resting around his collarbone. One side is smashed, the glass left broken in the frame.

"What happened?" I ask, trying to remember what occured after I was knocked unconscious.

"Cyra took the Stour—"

"I know that." I bite harshly. "After they hit me."

"Which time?" Simon's voice drops, revealing that the voice he had been using all along was really an act. He waits a moment before answering. Something about seeing him without his hat and goggles, using his real voice makes me realize what a bad situation we're in. "We're inside Issac's office—I'm assuming it's his anyway."

I glance around. It's not my uncle's so I would be inclined to agree.

"They beat you up pretty badly after you were out. Are you okay, Aladdin?"

I try to move my arms and legs to see if anything is broken, but I'm bound to the chair's arms land legs by leather straps. Glancing over, I note that while Simon is tied to a chair, they clearly think I'm the bigger threat and have used extra binds on me.

"I'm fine. Simon, do what you have to do to survive," I say, knowing this won't end well for either of us. "My uncle is going to kill me, but you don't have to die like this. Play whatever cards you need to—sell me out if you have to—just don't be all noble and take the fall, okay?"

"And risk losing the affection of my love, Cyra? Never." Simon adopts his eccentric voice again. It makes the situation seem less dire even though it clearly isn't. He drops his smile. "The boy you yelled to seemed quite taken back. What did you say to him?"

"I saw him in the Market before the competition started. He was talking to his friends about some girl and the competition, which I now know was Cyra. I told him she was in trouble. I don't know if it will do any good, but..."

"Hmm." He smirks at me. "Perhaps he will be the knight in shining armor that *you* were not..."

I give him a dirty look, but it only fuels him more.

Before he can say anything else, the door slams open and two men walk in. Stomping over to Simon, they bend and lift the entire chair into the air, Simon still strapped in. His eyes are wide as he looks at me, jaw clenched.

"Where are you taking him?" I demand. Everything inside of me says Simon is about to die. I scream at them, *"Where are you taking him?"*

I attempt to stand while still in the chair but it's like

the heavy metal piece has been bolted to the floor. I struggle, calling after them.

As soon as Simon is in the hall, Kacper strolls in, closing the door behind him.

"Well, if it isn't my wayward nephew."

"What do you want?" I hiss back. If I couldn't get out of the chair to save Simon, I can't get out to claw at Kacper, but that doesn't stop me from trying.

"Sit down, Aladdin, you're not going anywhere." He props himself on the edge of Issac's desk and places his pilot's cap on the table next to it. "I want to know what happened in the Collection Cave."

"You tried to kill me," I retort. Heat creeps up my chest, to my neck, and into my face as I glare at him.

"Yes, I was hoping for more details on that."

"Didn't your man tell you how he buried me alive?"

"He did. What he failed to mention was that you weren't actually dead."

Kacper's eyes bore into me, livid that I still breathe. His fingers curl around the edge of the desk as he leans forward toward me. The last time we did this, he was bandaging me in his study after I fought with a peg-legged man in the Market.

"What happened, Aladdin?" He takes a deep breath, but it still looks like he needs more oxygen so his face will stop turning red.

"Ren started a landslide, *Uncle*. He left me for dead."

The door opens again, revealing the blond guy who tried to murder me. His nervous energy fills the room as he's pushed inside. "There was no way he could have survived," he points out. "The entire room collapsed. I could barely see through the entrance, there was so much debris everywhere! This couldn't have happened!"

"But it did, Ren." Kacper's voice holds no mercy.

"Please!" Ren shouts, shaking.

"No!" I yell, trying to get out of the chair again as Kacper's man raises a pistol to the back of Ren's head and pulls the trigger. The boy drops.

My mouth hangs open, each exhale coming out in a loud huff as I take in the sight. Ren failed to kill me. He paid with his life.

I stare for what seems like an hour just watching the blood drain from his body. I can't tell if I'm overwhelmingly hot or if there is ice running through me.

"Clean it up," Kacper instructs. The guard steps out, allowing Bryon to step in and take a position against the wall on the far side of the door.

"Have you lost your mind?" I rage, whipping around to face Kacper again.

"No," he sneers at me before I can go on. "Apparently I've *found* a mind."

My body temporarily shuts down as Kacper indicates he knows everything about Issac's past and what he's done to reach this point.

Kacper leans back on the desk, releasing his white-knuckled grip on it. He grins.

"Did you know Issac didn't always look like that?" He blinks at me while talking. "Turns out, the old chap was the one who created the genie you found in the Cave. *Clever boy* keeping it away from him—too bad you failed.

"I was livid when I found out he had me retrieving a genie for him, but then Issac made me an offer that healed the wound. Once we collect all of the genies and Issac puts their bondage to good use, I'm going to be his second in command, and as such, I get control over one of the broken-count genies."

That must be what Issac's calling them once there's no longer a wish limit. I'd think he could get more creative.

"Now, tell me how you survived the Cave, boy."

"The landslide didn't kill me. The genie got me out."

"So, you used a wish?"

"I didn't say that." I tip my head, pursing my lips. He's going to kill me one way or another, so I might as well enjoy taunting him a bit.

Kacper pulls a knife out of his pocket and flips it open. He lets it gleam in the muted light from overhead as he watches it spin under his finger.

Standing, he takes the one step that separates us and makes eye contact with me before leaning down. My arm is bound tightly to the armrest and I can't shift under the leather straps. Byron joins him, pushing down hard on my hand to hold it in place as Kacper releases the binds.

If he plans on sawing off my hand with that little knife, it's going to take a while. *He probably planned that.*

Kacper nods and Byron flips my arm over roughly. The knife starts at the top of my arm, lightly dragging over the fabric of my shirt sleeve until he reaches uncovered skin. My uncle skips over it, cutting roughly into the vambrace I'm still wearing. The leather jerks as he tears through it, but it eventually falls open on either side of my arm.

The knife is cold against my skin as Kacper opens it up. Blood silently bubbles up, forming small pools of red that grow until my uncle calls my attention away.

Watching me, he slashes at me again, creating a painful, off-center line somewhere on my arm. His nostrils flare and he grits his teeth, but Kacper restrains himself from plunging the knife all the way to the bone, leaving only superficial wounds.

"Don't worry. I'm not going to kill you...yet," he announces. "I think you still have a future, *boy*. At least for a few more days."

Kacper tips his head to the side, examining me. Retracting the knife, he wipes it on the knee of my pants, and my leg involuntarily spasms under it, making me flinch. He grins.

"You have one final mission, Aladdin." He moves back

to the desk and Byron releases my arm. I don't move it, allowing the blood to clot. "You're going to help me find the genies."

"No."

"Oh, yes, you will, Aladdin. You will help me find those genies because you're the only one that can stop us from killing the girl when I find her."

He wants to trade Cyra for the genies.

"You don't have *her* or *them*. What kind of a deal is that?" I challenge him. He won't catch Cyra.

"There's no one to prevent me from finding her, nephew. Issac is about to enlist everyone in Horallen with the promise of more riches than they've ever seen. They won't even know that they're looking for genies. Nothing is going to stop us."

Byron huffs next to me. When I look at him, he's smiling conspiratorially at Kacper as if I'm the only one not in on the joke.

"I saw the way you fought for her downstairs, Aladdin. You have a crush on the girl. You can't be with her, of course, given the circumstances, but perhaps you can keep her alive for the Governor's sake.

"Help me find the genies, and Issac and I will agree to let her live her days out under the care of the Governor—assuming *he* follows the plan."

"Is he in on this, too?" I growl. If Cyra's father was a part of this...

"Not yet, but I'm sure he will be once we threaten the girl. It's only a matter of time, Aladdin."

"She's smart enough to have stolen *two* airships. What makes you think you'll *ever* be able to find her?"

"Did you notice how Issac wasn't overly distraught when the Stourbridge pulled away?" He pauses, waiting for me to catch on. "It's Issac's airship, Aladdin. He knows *exactly* where it is."

How did we not consider that Issac would have a way to track the Stourbridge?

"But even if he didn't," Kacper continues, "We have people to leverage against her, too."

I take a sudden, deep breath and force myself not to bite my lip. It's me—I'm the leverage.

"Don't be so conceited, boy." Kacper scowls at me, trying not to grin. "This isn't about you—she barely *knows* you. But she knows the Governor, and I'm sure he can talk her into cooperating.

"*But*…if you think you have influence over the mindless girl, I'm willing to allow you to use that to our advantage." He leans in to whisper, "Do you think you can save her."

I lean forward, pulling against the restraints around my bound arm. I claw at him, just barely missing him. Kacper laughs in response, enjoying my limitations.

"You're a hopeless romantic, just like your father. In the end, you'll pay the same cost he did." He sobers. "I take it that means you've reached a decision to work with us and spare the girl the same fate as you. Wise."

Kacper stands, stepping around me. Byron doesn't move as he towers over me.

"Good news, Aladdin. When we're all done, Issac wants to spend a little time with you. It seems he has some *experiment* he wants to discuss with you."

Kacper's lips curl up as he looks over his shoulder at me, cap in hand.

The threat of being under Issac's control is more terrifying than death itself.

Once the door is closed behind Kacper, Byron steps forward.

Coming May 2019
pistonsandprisonersinfo.kmrobinsonbooks.com

BONUS SCENES

Want to read bonus scenes from the Stealing Steam Series? We're giving out exclusive bonus scenes over on the K.M. Robinson Facebook page where you can read scenes from some of the other characters' perspectives.

Get them by sending the page a direct message
at
www.facebook.com/kmrobinsonbooks

We're constantly giving out additional bonus scenes for preorder swag, giveaways, and more, so watch the social media pages carefully for the next scene giveaway.

K.M. Robinson also has bonus scenes and extras from all of her books on

newsletter.kmrobinsonbooks.com

Sign up now for weekly emails with special bonuses, extras, live broadcasts replays and upcoming dates, events, coloring pages, games, introductions to new authors+live broadcasts with them, and more.

WORLD PORTALS

Ready to learn exclusive facts about the Stealing Steam Series and other K.M. Robinson Series?

World Portals are now available on www. kmrobinsonbooks.com

Learn behind the scenes facts, watch videos, play games, check out our book filters, find out where to get bonus scenes, view fan art, and get access to other secrets we've hidden away inside the World Portals on the website.

The World Portals are constantly changing and information is being taken away and added all the time, so check back frequently for new content!

SURVIVE THE CAVE INTERACTIVE GAME

THINK YOU HAVE WHAT IT TAKES TO ENTER THE Collection Cave and find an item that will help to steal the Stourbridge? Now you can find out if you'll survive!

Those who survive will be rewarded.

This interactive, choose-your-own-adventure game is played through Facebook messenger so you never miss a mission.

PLAY THE GAME

at

survivethecave.kmrobinsonbooks.com

ABOUT THE AUTHOR

K.M. Robinson is a storyteller who creates new worlds both in her writing and in her fine arts conceptual photography. She is a marketing, branding and social media strategy educator who is recognized at first sight by her very long hair. She is a creative who focuses on photography, videography, couture dress making, and writing to express the stories she needs to tell. She almost always has a camera within reach.

Visit her at her website: www.kmrobinsonbooks.com

CONNECT ON SOCIAL MEDIA

facebook.com/kmrobinsonbooks

instagram.com/kmrobinsonbooks

twitter.com/kmrobinsonbooks

Get free excerpts and full novels from K.M. Robinson at
excerpt.kmrobinsonbooks.com

ALSO BY K.M. ROBINSON

The Golden Trilogy

Book One: Golden

Forged: A Golden Novella

Book Two: Locked

Book Three: Edge

The Complete Series Boxset/Omnibus with Tempered: an exclusive bonus novella

The Jaded Duology

Book One: Jaded

Book Two: Risen

The Complete Series Boxset/Omnibus with exclusive epilogue

The Siren Wars Saga

Book One: The Siren Wars

Book Two: Darker Depths

Book Three: Beyond The Shores

Origins of the Siren Wars: Prequel Novella

Book Four: Forbidden Waters (coming soon)

The Legends Chronicles

Along Came A Spider: A Prequel Novelette

And They'll Come Home: A Prequel Novelette

The Archives of Jack Frost Series

The Revolution of Jack Frost

The Redemption of Jack Frost (coming soon)

Stealing Steam Series

Book One: Lions and Lamps

Book Two: Pistons and Prisoners

Book Three: Railcars and Rulers

Top Hats and Telegraphs: A Prequel Novella

The Complete Series Boxset/Omnibus with Vambraces and Victories: an exclusive bonus novella

Virtually Sleeping Beauty: A Novella Retelling

The Goose Girl and The Artificial: A Novella Retelling

The Sinking: A Little Mermaid Novella Retelling

Cindrill: A Cinderella Assassin Novella Retelling

Sugarcoated: A Hansel and Gretel's Witch Novella Retelling

Blood Is Silent: A Red Riding Hood Circus Retelling

JADED: BOOK ONE OF THE JADED DUOLOGY

If the only way to stay alive was to convince your new husband not to murder you and make it look like an accident, could you do it?

At eighteen, Jade shouldn't have to be forced to marry the son of her father's enemy as part of a revenge plot for a failed rebellion. When she's thrown into the life of being the wife of the Commander's son and heir, her only hope for survival is convincing Roan Diamond to actually fall in love with her so that he doesn't kill her on his father's wishes.

While a dutiful son, Roan shouldn't have to trick his new wife into believing his family accepts her, but as the only one in a position to make the country believe Jade is part of their family, he will do what he has to before his family murders his young bride and makes it look like an accident to get back at Jade's father.

With half the country trying to protect Jade and the other half oblivious to the atrocities committed at the Commander's hand, it's a race to see who will win at a deadly game of cat and mouse.

One chooses life. One chooses death. In the midst of chaos, only one will succeed.

Now available!
Learn more about The Jaded Duology at
jadedinfo.kmrobinsonbooks.com

GOLDEN: BOOK ONE OF THE GOLDEN TRILOGY

Goldilocks wasn't naive. She was sent on a mission and Dov Baer is her new target.

When Auluria tricks the Baers into letting her into their home, they have no idea she's actually been sent by the enemy to destroy them. Intent on gathering information for her cousin to hand over to the Society seeking to destroy all of the rebel factions—including her own—she's willing to sacrifice Dov Baer to save her people... until she realizes her cousin lied to her.

Now that she's seen who Dov truly is, she has to decide between staying loyal to her only remaining family or protecting the man she's falling for. If her allegiances are discovered, either side could destroy her—assuming the Society doesn't get her first

Available now!
Learn more about The Golden Trilogy at goldeninfo.
kmrobinsonbooks.com

**THE SIREN WARS: BOOK ONE OF THE
SIREN WARS SAGA**

War has hovered around the kingdom of Scylla for generations ever since the original sirens left the mer collection generations ago after nearly drowning the human prince. Over the years, select mermaids from the royal bloodline have been trained as spies to work for the reigning kings and queens, keeping the collection safe from sirens and humans.

Celena and her partner, Merrick, work covertly for the royals—not even her twin brother knows. When they discover the sirens have broken through the barriers the mer set up to keep the sirens out, Celena and her friends must race to the old kingdom of Metten to stop them from starting a war within their borders.

When she's dragged to the surface, Celena realizes that the war above the waters is as deadly as the one below the waves—and sacrificing herself may be the only way to protect her family.

The Siren Wars have only just begun.

Available now!
Learn more about The Siren Wars Saga at sirenwarsinfo.
kmrobinsonbooks.com

deadlier, and he knows he can't trust the girl who snuck into the competition this year...but Cyra might not survive his ruthlessness either in a game where only the lion's heart can win.

All wishes require sacrifice, and someone is going to pay the price for the Stourbridge.

Available now!
Learn more about The Stealing Steam Series at
lionsandlampsinfo.kmrobinsonbooks.com

ALONG CAME A SPIDER: THE FIRST PREQUEL NOVELETTE TO THE LEGENDS CHRONICLES

Little Hacker Muffet
sat on her tuffet
destroying her cords and Way.
Along came a hacker named Spider,
who sat down beside her
and frightened his opponent away.

WHEN FET, ONE OF THE MOST SKILLED HACKERS IN THE Legends, discovers her best friend and leader of her group has been abducted and held for ransom, she must escape unnoticed and find Peep before it's too late.

When Spider, a new recruit training to join her hacker ring, slips out with her and claims to have a plan to save her friend, Fet is forced to bring him along. As she discovers he's not who he claims to be, she faces grave danger and learns just how deadly a spider bite can be.

Now available!
Learn more about The Legends Chronicles at
acasinfo.kmrobinsonbooks.com

VIRTUALLY SLEEPING BEAUTY

To wake her up, he has to enter the game and help her beat it...

Surely the class president wouldn't illegally over-juice to stay in the virtual reality game citizens are allowed to play for four hours a day, but when Royce's aunt calls in a panic because her goddaughter hasn't left the game yet, his only option is to go inside the game and drag the girl out.

The golden knight quickly discovers the princess' absence in the real world isn't of her own doing—*she's trapped inside the game by unknown forces*—and if she can't escape soon, she could die for real outside of the game. He's even more shocked to discover that Rora outranks him inside of the game, which means she'll have to fight to *protect herself* from the evils locking her inside a dangerous world.

Can Rora and Royce work together to outsmart a vicious queen and evil magician, and defeat digital dragons, or will Rora slowly fade away until there's nothing left but an empty shell and the game ranking she will leave behind?

Now available!

Learn more about Virtually Sleeping Beauty at vsbinfo.kmrobinsonbooks.com

THE REVOLUTION OF JACK FROST

No one inside the snow globe knows that Morozoko Industries is controlling their weather, testing them to form a stronger race that can survive the fall out from the bombs being dropped in the outside world—all they know is that they must survive the harsh Winter that lasts a month and use the few days of Spring, Summer, and Fall to gather enough supplies to survive.

When the seasons start shifting, Genesis and Jack know something is going on. As their team begins to find technology that they don't have access to inside their snow globe of a world, it begins to look more and more like one of their own is working against them.

. . .

Genesis soon discovers Morozoko Industries, but when a foreign enemy tries to destroy their weather program to make sure their destructive life-altering bombs succeed in destroying the outside world, only one person can shut down the machine that is spinning out of control and save the lives of everyone inside the bunker—Jack.

Now available!
Learn more about The Revolution of Jack Frost at
jackfrostinfo.kmrobinsonbooks.com

THE GOOSE GIRL AND THE ARTIFICIAL

WHAT WOULD YOU DO IF YOUR ARTIFICIALLY INTELLIGENT handmaiden stole your identity?

Threatened by her Artificial, Arta, Princess Goselyn is forced to switch places and pretend she isn't human when she reaches Prince Corinth to negotiate a treaty they both need to be able to take their respective crowns one day. If she doesn't comply, her Artificial, controlled by her evil cousin, will not only kill Goselyn's mother, but Prince Corinth and his father as well.

Can the quiet princess outsmart a machine created to be more intelligent than she is, all while surviving the other

Artificials and robots working against her in the foreign palace, or will Corinth and his father find out and destroy her chance to save them all?

360

Learn more about The Goose Girl and The Artificial at goosegirlinfo.kmrobinsonbooks.com

THE SINKING

The sea witch wants to silence her, but not for the reason you think.

WHEN A QUIRKY OLDER WOMAN PAWNS A FANCY SEASHELL necklace at her mother's antique shop on the pier, Cara doesn't think much about the story the woman spins about the wearer turning into a mermaid.

On her way home, she accidentally drops the necklace into the ocean and is swept out to sea where she meets—a merman who volunteers to take her to his mother, the sea queen, to help her get her legs back.

.   .   .

Cara soon learns that it's Quay's eighteen birthday—a day that has been a curse for his family—and is meant to be one for her too. Now she must fight to survive the sea with Quay at her side.

Fans of The Little Mermaid will love this twisted take on the beloved story.

Now available!
Learn more about The Sinking at
thesinkinginfo.kmrobinsonbooks.com

CINDRILL

CINDERELLA IS AN ASSASSIN OUT TO MURDER THE PRINCE... *but he's hunting her too.*

The nanobots Cindrill's master gives her to use as a mask allow her to slip into the ball wearing a face that isn't hers, but when the assassination attempt goes sideways, Prince Davin doesn't understand why her face changes when he injures her, slicing her foot open around a unique pair of shoes as she runs away.

When Cindrill runs into the prince the next day without her nanobot mask on, he doesn't recognize her, but immediately decides her skills will be useful on his hunt for the would-be-assassin woman who nearly killed his father and his fiancée the night before.

Both are tasked with the job of murdering the other, but things don't quite go as they had planned when Cindrill's master and Davian's fiancée interfere as the two try to decide whether or not to kill the other.

It's hard to recognize a woman when she uses technology to change her appearance, but Cindrill is going to use that to her full advantage as she destroys the prince. ***Will either survive?***

Now available!

Learn more about Cindrill at
cindrillinfo.kmrobinsonbooks.com

SUGARCOATED

Hansel and Gretel's witch was actually on their side...

ANNIKA'S JOB IS TO CREATE A CAKE TO MATCH THE CANDY-colored rooftops, nightly firework shows, and daily parades ending in unexpected executions for the mad king's ball, but her true mission is to sneak a thirteen-year-old assassin into the palace using her gift of illusions.

Hansel's job is to protect his little sister, Gretel, once she assassinates King Levin and ends the destruction in Candestrachen, using his power over light to rescue the young girl from the chaos her influence over life and death will create.

. . .

When the entire forest reconstructs itself under Gretel's command while trying to save herself from a king's guard, Hansel and Annika must put their feelings aside and ensure their plan holds true—even if it means one of them has to sacrifice themselves to protect the mission.

Her illusions were meant to save her....but not everyone will survive the assassination attempt.

Learn more about Sugarcoated at
sugarcoatedinfo.kmrobinsonbooks.com

BLOOD IS SILENT

RED **R**IDING **H**OOD *IS A CIRCUS AERIALIST AND THE WOLF IS ready to cage her.*

Sienna has grown up working for the circus, dangling off her signature red silks every night. Her grandmother has been known to wander off to train new acts for their boss, but when Sienna tries to find her to bring her back to the show, she doesn't expect the dashing and dangerous Elijah to join her.

When they finally find Grandma Ida has been transformed deep in the heart of the woods, Sienna will stop at nothing to save her—but the wolf has her right where he wants her, and she won't be able to escape his claws.

She was told not to go into the woods alone.

Now available!

Learn more about Blood Is Silent at
bloodissilentinfo.kmrobinsonbooks.com